PRAISE FOR *THE NEW NEIGHBOR*

"One of the protagonists of Leah Stewart's new novel, *The New Neighbor*, reads mystery novels, and only mystery novels, but she is a snob about them: she wants to read only the best. Well, she would love, love, love *The New Neighbor*, which is as tense and as tough-minded and as ingeniously structured as our best mystery novels and our best literary novels, too. A major new work by one of our most psychologically astute writers."

—Brock Clarke, author of *The Happiest People in the World*

"Intellectual intrigue. . . . Stewart also offers the thrill of sharp realism that has characterized her previous novels. She's skilled at creating characters who are all too recognizable in their foibles and desires; she dissects the way ordinary, flawed people think of one another and their social spheres—the silent preferences and judgments that accompany any interaction."

—*Knoxville News Sentinel*

"Readers who like an unhurried pace, an element of mystery, and plenty of symbolism will be satisfied as Stewart brings her tale to a surprising conclusion."

—*Library Journal*

"Stewart's prose is remarkable for its well-shaped sentences and non-showy but sharp observations. Quietly incisive."

—*Kirkus Reviews*

"Keenly engrossing and multilayered, this mystery and literary-fiction hybrid will elicit rich book-group discussions."

—*Booklist*

"A promising exploration of the secrets we all carry and our refusal to forgive ourselves."

—*Publishers Weekly*

"A truly fine absorbing novel; the finest new novel this reader has discovered so far this season. Highly, highly recommended."

—*Hudson Valley News*

PRAISE FOR *THE HISTORY OF US*

"Leah Stewart possesses magic. It is awe-inspiring to see how clearly and sensitively she presents the numerous ways her characters are broken and then finds a way to offer some hope of healing. With the family at the heart of *The History of Us*, Stewart shows that she is unafraid of difficult characters and that she is equally unafraid of making sure they matter to us."

—Kevin Wilson, author of *The Family Fang*

"A sprawling novel with some of the off-kilter charm of Anne Tyler's work, *The History of Us* glows with affection for its wounded, familiar characters."

—*Boston Globe*

"Touching drama. . . . Faced with urgent choices, Eloise and the grown kids react with varying degrees of wisdom and pigheadedness, but as Stewart tenderly demonstrates, they remain—for better or worse—a family."

—*People*

"Stewart's novel reminds us how family ties trump all else."

—*Parenting Magazine*

"Stewart is a wonderful observer of family relationships, and she adroitly weaves the stories of Eloise and the children she's raised—their work, their loves, their disappointments and dreams—while focusing on what ties families together, and what ultimately keeps those ties from breaking."

—*BookPage*

"With a playwright's precise, sometimes excoriating dialogue and an insightful novelist's judicious use of interior monologue, Stewart crafts a tearful yet unsentimental family coming-of-age story."

—*Kirkus Reviews* (starred review)

"Stewart portrays the yearning and conflict of very recognizable people. . . . [She] makes the reader care about these good people—and applaud as each finally dares to break out of familial inertia, to act instead of yearn. . . . Like her mentors Eliot and Austen, Stewart explores the delicate dilemmas of family life: balancing loyalty and self-interest, giving and receiving joy and sorrow, achieving togetherness and separateness."

—*Washington Independent*

PRAISE FOR LEAH STEWART

"A deeply human book: funny, tender, smart, self-aware."

—Elin Hilderbrand

"This narrative voice is so alive. . . . I cherish this wry, funny, aching, intelligent character and this book!"

—Marisa de los Santos

"Deftly exposes the passionate and particular bonds of female friendship, from adolescence to adulthood. Poignant, fierce, and compelling, this is a story all women will recognize, and one all too rarely told."

—Claire Messud

"Leah Stewart captures, as few other writers do, the passions and pains and pleasures of friendship. Anyone who has ever lost or found a friend will respond to this beautifully written and suspenseful novel."

—Margot Livesey

"Full of genuine feeling—and gripping, too—this book about a friendship between two women announces that Leah Stewart is a marvelous writer."

—Ann Packer

THE
NEW
NEIGHBOR

LEAH STEWART

TOUCHSTONE

New York   London   Toronto   Sydney   New Delhi

Touchstone
An Imprint of Simon & Schuster, Inc.
1230 Avenue of the Americas
New York, NY 10020

First Touchstone trade paperback edition June 2016

TOUCHSTONE and colophon are registered trademarks of Simon & Schuster, Inc.

For information about special discounts for bulk purchases, please contact Simon &
Schuster Special Sales at 1-866-506-1949 or business@simonandschuster.com.

The Simon & Schuster Speakers Bureau can bring authors to your live event.
For more information or to book an event contact the Simon & Schuster Speakers
Bureau at 1-866-248-3049 or visit our website at www.simonspeakers.com.

Manufactured in the United States of America

10 9 8 7 6 5 4 3 2 1

The Library of Congress has cataloged the hardcover edition as follows:

Stewart, Leah, 1973–
    The new neighbor / Leah Stewart.—First Touchstone hardcover edition.
      pages ; cm
    "A Touchstone Book."
    I. Title.
    PS3569.T465258N49 2015
    813'.54—dc23
                                                                    2014041617

ISBN 978-1-5011-0351-3
ISBN 978-1-5011-0352-0 (pbk)
ISBN 978-1-5011-0353-7 (ebook)

For
Dr. Florence "Flossie" Ridley

And in memory of
Col. Ellis Cameron "Cam" Stewart and Mildred "Sissy" Stewart
Dr. Nina J. Markus and Capt. Felix "Mac" McAndrews

THE
NEW
NEIGHBOR

The whole world thinks she did it. She knows that. Even in her house with the doors locked and the blinds down, she can feel the weight of it. All that certainty.

Jennifer

Every story is a history . . . and when there is no comprehensible story, there is no history.

—CHARLES BAXTER, *BURNING DOWN THE HOUSE*

Signs of Life

Where before there was no one, suddenly I, Margaret Riley, have a neighbor. I went out on the back deck this morning like every morning, and there she was. Across the pond, sitting on her own back deck. I was startled. That house has been empty a long time. My first impulse was to go back inside, as if I'd come upon something shameful, or embarrassed myself. As if I were out there naked, which of course I wasn't, and even if I had been she was too far away to see. But I am braver than that. I put my coffee cup on the table, as usual, and then I went back inside for my book, which is by P. D. James, a remarkable woman, as ancient as I am and still creating mysteries. I have to make two trips because I need one hand for the cane. Sometimes I try to manage cane and book and coffee all at once, and the result is always coffee stains, or burns, or at the very least a wet book and a diminished cup of coffee. Every morning I'm frustrated anew by the need to make two trips. Impatience and age are not compatible.

She was still there when I came back out. I lowered myself into my chair. I felt self-conscious that she might be watching this slow maneuvering, like I am when someone watches me trying to park my car. The position of my chair ensured that if I looked up from my book I looked directly at her. I knew I wouldn't move my chair—

because it would be rude, and because it's heavy—but I thought about doing so anyway. I drank my coffee slowly, pretending to gaze out over the pond, which is what I do every morning, though usually without the presence of someone who might be watching me.

Strange that she didn't wave. Wasn't it? But I hadn't waved either. I couldn't make out her face, of course—the pond is an acre across—but I could see the yellowish smudge of her long hair, and so I knew she was young, or at least much younger than I. Was it the job of the younger person to be the first to wave? Certainly it cost her less to move. She was wearing something purple. I think it was a purple bathrobe. I like purple myself, but that poem about the old ladies and the red hats has made it impossible for me to wear it.

The coffee cup was empty. I set it down, careful to push it back from the edge of the table, and reached for my book. Before I opened it I looked right at her. There was no way to know for sure but she seemed to be looking right back at me. I lifted my hand off my lap and extended my arm. What I mean is, I waved. I left my arm suspended a moment. She didn't move. My arm fell back into my lap, a heavy thing. I was about to look down at my book like nothing had happened, like a cat casually licking its whiskers, pretending it didn't just smack into the wall. Then she moved. I swear—I know she was far away and even with my glasses I have an old lady's eyesight—but I swear, she jerked first, like she'd started to wave back and been restrained. Then she raised her arm and returned my greeting.

"Hello," I said aloud, though she couldn't hear me of course.

A few minutes went by, both of us sitting there enjoying the morning. A large bird of prey flew high above the pond and I tracked it with my eyes as it headed back into the trees. Probably a turkey vulture, but I liked to pretend it was a hawk. I glanced at my neighbor and saw her head turned up, too, watching until the bird vanished. She looked back at me—of course I couldn't see her eyes but I know she looked—and I nodded. We had watched the bird together. We had seen it disappear, and maybe felt together a needless longing for its return. We were almost companionable. Then she got up and went inside her house.

I was surprised, when she was gone, by a twinge of loneliness. How silly. I am always alone. Sometimes days go by in which the only other people I see are on TV. This house is in the woods between two small towns—villages, really—on a mountain in Tennessee. I live here by myself. It's been years since I lived with another person. I don't ever want to live with another person again. I'm nearly ninety-one now, unimaginable as that sounds, and I will be alone until I die. Before they put me in a nursing home, in forced companionship with the sick and the dying, I will fling myself into the pond. I'll weight my pockets with rocks, like Virginia Woolf, whose books I did my best to understand. All her words float away when I think of her. I see her crouched at the edge of the water, searching for just the right stones.

The Miraculous Now

Milo is still asleep. It shouldn't be a surprise to Jennifer that he's sleeping in, given how lax she's become about bedtime. Last night she resolved on a return to earlier, stricter routines, but when he reappeared at eight fifteen, twenty minutes after she'd said good night, wearing penguin pajamas and a sweet but calculating expression, her scolding held no conviction. "Why are you up?" she asked, and he said, "I want to snuggle with you." Fear and worry have worn her down: she couldn't resist. She let him curl up against her on the couch while she watched *Back to the Future*. Movies from her childhood are the only ones that interest her now. Milo, completely awake, watched the movie, too, and asked question after question for which she had no answers: "Why does he love her?" "Why does she love him?" "Can we go back in time?"

Now Milo is curled on his side with his face pressed against the railing on his toddler bed, one little hand dangling through the space between railing and mattress. She stands there watching him, holding her cooling coffee mug. His room is a mess, strewn with the tiny pieces of his complicated toys, while the colorful bins she bought to contain them go empty, pulled from the shelves and turned on their sides. In her old life she used to make him pick up, but now she doesn't. In her old life she would have picked up some of the mess herself, but now she doesn't do that either. All the urgency has fallen out of her days, leaving only a fluttering, purposeless anxiety. There is nothing she needs to do while he's sleeping, except wait for him to wake up.

Thank God Milo is only four. She thinks with a shudder, for the thousandth time, of how much worse this all would've been if he were older. What she's done to protect him would not have been possible. No matter how much of their old life she jettisoned, what could she have done about his memories? As it is she's often surprised by how much has vanished. He exists in the miraculous now of early childhood. Already he's forgotten that he used to have a different last name.

She doesn't worry about someone recognizing her face. Or, if she does worry, watching the woman who opened her new bank account closely for signs of recognition, she knows the worry isn't rational. Only the local press covered her story, and they're far from home now, in this place she chose for its isolation. On the Internet she found a guide to disappearing, and she followed its steps as best she could. Not even her parents know where they are. She regrets the necessity of that precaution. But Zoe can't know where they are, and what if Zoe asked, and Jennifer's mother couldn't bring herself to lie?

Milo sleeps on. Jennifer catches herself looking with calculation at one of his motorized trucks, lying on its back near her foot. When nudged, it springs to life with a violent beeping and whirring and spinning of wheels, as agitated as an overturned beetle. When Milo is awake it's easier not to think.

Milo's eyes pop open. She feels instantly guilty, even though she did nothing to wake him, she swears. "Mommy," he says with satisfaction. He rolls onto his back and stretches.

She sets her mug on his dresser and kneels beside his bed to put a hand in his hair. "Hi, bubby," she says.

"Scratch my back," he commands, and she flips him onto his stomach and complies. He orders her to move her hand up and down and left and right. He's got an impressive grasp on left and right. "Mommy," he says, after a few minutes, "I need to tell you something."

"You do?" she says.

"I want to wear my Iron Man shirt today, and then tomorrow I'll wear my Spider-Man shirt, okay? I want to wear my Iron Man shirt to the playground."

"That sounds like a good plan," she says. She spreads her palm flat against his sleep-warmed back.

She tries to talk him into the playground in the state park in Monteagle, which is as far as she can tell a ghost playground, only ever populated by the two of them. But he wants to go to the one at the far end of Sewanee, by the community center, because it has a fireman pole, and she acquiesces because she finds it difficult, these days, to deny him much. He careens around the house while she tries to get them both ready, popping out of his seat at the kitchen table between bites of Cheerios. This behavior annoys her less than it used to do, in her other life, when she had reasons for rules and hurry. In fact it hardly annoys her at all. What does it matter? What does anything matter, except that she love him as much as she can? "Sit down and eat, Milo," she says, and repeats. They have, as is often the case, two different conversations. "We can't go until you've had breakfast," she says, and he answers, "The fireman pole is really cool, right, Mom?" Yes, she says. Yes, it is.

At the playground, he leaps from the car as soon as she unbuckles him from his car seat and runs toward the jungle gym, chortling with eagerness and excitement. She follows slowly. To her relief they have the place to themselves. Sometimes she can almost believe they are the only people who live on this mountain, alone among empty houses and empty woods and empty stores.

She reaches Milo, who has stopped by the jungle gym and stands there frozen. "Are you going to climb?" she asks. Then she sees how unhappy he looks.

"There's no one to play with," he says. He sits down hard on the steps. His eyes well with tears that slowly spill over. This is the worst kind of crying, the truly stricken kind. He can lie on the floor and scream all day and Jennifer can remain immovable. But this solemn, big-eyed sorrow, this trembling-lipped heartbreak—this she cannot withstand.

"Oh, honey," she says, sitting beside him and tucking him close. "I didn't know that's what you were hoping."

The tears fall and fall. "I'm all by myself," he says.

"You're not by yourself," she says, hopelessly. "You're with me."

He doesn't respond to this, and why should he? It was a fatuous remark. She knows exactly what he means. He has no friends. He hasn't been to a birthday party in more than a year—so long she's amazed he can still remember their pleasures. The cake, the bag of favors, the manic joy. Though his fifth birthday is still six months away, he asks frequently if there's any place on the Mountain like the warehouse-sized palace of bouncy houses where his friend Sam rang in his third birthday. She hates that place, and all others like it—those windowless hells of whirring air pumps and screaming children. And yet she'd gladly take him to such a place, if there were one nearby, and let him bounce until the cows came home. She's been wondering who would bounce along with him, but she hadn't realized he'd been wondering that, too.

"I'm sorry, baby," she says.

"I want someone to play with me," he says.

She says, "I play with you," but this doesn't stop the tears.

"I want to go to school," he says, giving the last word an angry emphasis.

"School?" she repeats, as if she's never heard of it. School, like birthday parties, is a relic of his past. He went to preschool at three and stayed six months. She'd assumed that, like so many other things, he'd forgotten it.

"It's not *fair*," he says. "I want to go to *school*."

"What's not fair?" she asks, but for this he doesn't have an answer.

Snoop

This morning there was no sign of my neighbor, though I sat out on the deck reading longer than usual, hoping to glimpse her again. Her house used to belong to a woman named Barbara. I wouldn't go so far as to say we were friends, but we waved to each other from our back decks and sometimes we made conversation at the Piggly Wiggly or the post office. She was about my age, and she'd had a professional life, like me, though I can't recall what it was she did. I know she wasn't a nurse, because if she had been we would've talked shop. At any rate she was funny and I liked her and then I noticed I never saw her anymore, and it turned out she'd died. This was some time ago—a year? Two?—and the house stood empty from that time to this, no one arriving to take the place of my friend until suddenly there she was.

But she—the new one—didn't appear today. After I gave up waiting, I put down my book and prepared myself to venture out. Though once upon a time I was a sociable person, I find now that I have to steel myself for interaction. I grow impatient with chitchat. I've read that as we age we lose our internal censors, which perhaps explains why I find it so difficult now to be polite. Last week a woman in front of me in line showed me a picture of herself on her phone—why she showed me I have no idea, as I gave no indication of interest—and said, "It's a terrible picture, isn't it?" I said, "Well, we're not always as beautiful as we think we are." She registered the affront, but then she laughed, because I'm a harmlessly cantankerous old lady, I suppose. I would rather she had cursed me. I don't want to be harmless. Who in the world would want to be that?

My gravel country road takes me to a paved country highway that takes me to town—or town as we understand it here, which is to say one gas station, one bank, one liquor store. I go right for Monteagle, left for Sewanee. Bumping down the road today, I took special note of the mailbox belonging to the house that once belonged to Barbara. It's just a plain old mailbox. It said 936, just as it always has. I was driving at a crawl already; it wasn't hard to stop. I sat in the car debating whether the effort of getting out would be worth the result, but in the end curiosity won. It seems I have become a snoop.

I won't bother to describe how long it took me to inch my way round the car to the mailbox over the treacherous gravel. Of course I'm old and my footing isn't always steady, but my problem is not my legs and feet, which work as well as can be expected, so much as it is my balance. On occasion I turn too quickly and am suddenly swimming in vertigo. No one can tell me why. So I try not to turn too quickly, and of course I try not to slip. I kept a hand on the car all the way around it, feeling those treacherous pebbles under the soles of my white sneakers. It was a journey, believe me. It was a mighty quest. My reward was a utility bill bearing her name: Jennifer Young.

I drove the rest of the way to the Piggly Wiggly saying *Jennifer Young* aloud to myself, trying to determine if I'd ever heard the name. Was she a relative of Barbara, someone I'd met many ages ago? Had some gossipy acquaintance seen me at the post office and told me she was moving in? I couldn't recall. I know so many, many things— the tragic tale of Vivien Leigh, the capitals of all the states, how to find a vein—and yet I can access such an infinitely small portion of what I know. Someday they'll download our brains into computers, and nothing will be lost. It won't matter anymore what you've managed to remember and what you've managed to forget. None of it will matter to me, of course, because I'll be dead. For me my death is the end of time.

When I got to the grocery store I couldn't remember what I'd come for, so I poked my way down each aisle and put whatever struck my fancy into my cart. Thanks to the assorted populations of this place, you can avail yourself of pickled pig's feet or organic preserves in jars with fancy labels. I stick to the middle. Bacon and Smucker's strawberry jam.

It's my general policy not to talk to the cashiers. Some of them call me *honey*, you see, despite being many decades my junior, and the youngest ones chew gum. But today I risked conversation to ask if they—the cashier and the bagger and another cashier one aisle over, who was bored and listening in eager hope of something to interrupt her boredom—knew anything about my neighbor. "Jennifer Young," one repeated, and the others thoughtfully echoed her, their accents dragging out the vowel. It took them a long time to confess that the name was unfamiliar. They hazarded several guesses before I finally extracted myself. My question must have been the most exciting occurrence of their day. By the time we were done I felt tired and off balance, so I let the bagger help me with the groceries, though I wished I were able to decline.

I have a Southern accent myself, of course, but it's not the twangy kind you hear from the mountain people. It's no longer quite the genteel kind, either, like my mother had, the Scarlett O'Hara or Blanche DuBois kind, which is good for talking about the heat and ordering mint juleps and saying, "Oh, my." In my years in Nashville my accent faded, so that now it's down to cadence and those long Southern vowels. At least that's what I think. One of my grandnieces, who lives in (of all places) Delaware, tells me I have "the cutest" accent. I dislike this, which may explain why I dislike her. I like the other one, her sister, who says my cap of white hair makes me look "cool." It seems strange that I should care, at this late date, about "cool." But there you have it. I wear my hair cut tight to my head. My glasses are turquoise and I have a bright red coat. I am a cool old lady.

My face—what can you say about that? It no longer looks exactly like my face. And my ears have grown enormous. If I live much longer I'll be able to use them to fly.

And what of Jennifer Young? I wager her ears are still normal sized. Beyond that I can't hazard a guess as to what she looks like, except to say she's a white woman with blondish hair. I wonder how old she is. I wonder what she's done with her life. I wonder what she's doing with it here. There are only so many reasons to live in this place, in the woods, in the tiny towns. The Mountain birthed its longtime people, who seem to have no choice but to stay. The university brings the students and the professors, and the quaint old cottages in the Assembly and the big built-to-order houses in Clifftops bring the vacationers and retirees, those of us who flee up the Mountain into silence and cooler air and frequent sightings of woodpeckers and fawns. I myself moved here twenty years ago, one of the elderly evacuees of the working world. Those are my people—the no-longers, the once-weres. Jennifer Young is too young to be one of us. Perhaps she's a professor of something or other, and her being here is easily explained.

But nothing is ever easily explained, is it? Nothing is ever easily explained.

Noise

Is the woman still there? Yes, she is. Today, like each of the last several, she's there every time Jennifer glances out the glass doors to the deck. A white-haired figure on the other side of the pond, sitting and sitting and sitting. It's early spring and the light is beautiful—perhaps the woman just enjoys the outdoors. But Jennifer had never noticed her until the morning she waved, and now there she always is. As if she's watching. As if she's waiting for her.

She forces herself to slide the door open. To step with confident purpose onto the deck will vanquish her paranoia. She strides to the railing and waves, because if the woman is watching her, maybe this will embarrass her inside, but the woman doesn't wave back and now Jennifer can see, squinting, that she has her head bowed. She appears to be reading. She's an old lady who likes to sit outside and read, that's all, and yet Jennifer wishes fervently that she would go away. Behind her inside the house Milo bangs cars together on the floor of the dining room, that little-boy cacophony, but out here on the deck it's utterly quiet. It's a humming silent sound.

She chose this place, this mountain, this rental house, because of a conversation she had more than twenty years ago, at a party on a rooftop, during her brief sojourn in New York, when she was still trying to be a dancer. A girl from her dance class, a girl whose name and face she can no longer recall, told her about Sewanee, where she'd gone to college. "It's like Brigadoon," the girl said, and when Jennifer looked puzzled, she explained, "From an old movie, about this village that appears every hundred years. Whenever I go back, it's like no time has passed. Everything's exactly the same. And in the winter, when there's fog on the Mountain, it feels like you pass through clouds to get there, and on the other side the rest of the world is just gone."

"Did you like it?" Jennifer asked.

The girl shrugged. "There's two kinds of people who graduate from Sewanee," she said. "The ones who can't wait to leave and the ones who spend the rest of their lives trying to get back." It had the ring of a practiced remark. The girl wanted to claim the first category, and yet her wistful tone persuaded Jennifer she belonged to the second. This was why the conversation had stayed with her: the girl's divisive longing, called forth by something she both loved and wanted to leave. Jennifer recognized it.

At any rate, the girl was right. Up here there is no rest of the world.

She thinks about shouting, "Hey!" across the pond. Nothing else, just "Hey!" Probably the word would echo, from the water, from the trees: *hey, hey, hey*. Does she want the woman to look at her or go away? She leaves her to her book, slides her glass door emphatically shut. Back inside she clambers onto her knees beside Milo and leans over him to pick up a car. "What do we do?" she asks, revving the car in the air. "Vroom, vroom?"

"No, Mom," he says importantly. He takes the car from her hand. "You have to go up this ramp"—built of magnetic tiles—"and then you crash the building and you get points." He goes on explaining the point system, but her interest in it isn't strong. She puts her mouth on his jawline, where she knows he's ticklish, and kisses him. "Mom," he says, giggling. "Come on, Mom." His voice has that tone of pleased annoyance perfected by little boys with doting mothers. "I need to do this, okay?"

"Okay," she says, rocking back on her heels. "You do it." She hoists herself up by a chair and then sits in it, watching him play. He is too precious to her. He is the only thing that breaks the silence. Already she can feel how someday that will be a burden to him.

"Milo," she says, but he doesn't hear her over his own noise, or he ignores her. She doesn't want to ask this question. Or maybe she does want to ask it, because she's hoping he'll say no, and then she can stop feeling guilty for making him so alone. *Do you really want to go to school?* Please say no. "Milo," she says again.

There's a preschool in the Episcopal church in Sewanee. She knows because they have a sign outside and a large, rambling playground that always draws Milo's eye. She parks the car on the street, and she and Milo walk up to the school, she holding tightly to his hand. He cried the whole drive over because he'd dropped one of his cars off the front porch and into a bush, and Jennifer had been unable to find it. But he's happy and skipping now. Children can be so very, very sad, and then that sadness can be so quickly forgotten. She wishes she knew that trick. Afraid of the tears returning, she tells him as they walk that he might not be able to go right away, there might not be room. She wonders if that's what she's hoping for. He's so happy right now, but she isn't. She doesn't want him to go to school. The thought of it tightens her throat.

They do have room, though, and seem delighted at the arrival of a new pupil. If she'll fill out the paperwork, he can start that day! At this news Milo drops his shyness—he buried his face in her hip while she talked to Miss Amber—and bounds over to the water table, where two little girls in enormous blue smocks are pushing around plastic boats. "This one is the fastest!" he says, pointing, with his cheerful assumption that people will like him. One of the girls says, "No, this one is," and Milo calls over to Jennifer: "Mom, the water's pink!"

"Cool!" she says, insisting on her own enthusiasm.

She lingers for quite some time even after she's filled in every blank and signed her name to the check. Milo seems to have friends already, potential invitees to his birthday party. He is talking to two other boys, looking down at his Spider-Man shirt, which he holds out toward them, pinched on each side. Trying not to hover, she isn't quite close enough to hear their conversation, and she wonders what he's telling them. Tommy was the one who introduced him to Spider-Man.

Miss Amber comes over to her wearing a sympathetic smile. "See?" she says. "He's doing great."

"What?"

"I wouldn't worry at all," she says. "He seems like a very adaptable little boy."

"He is," Jennifer says. Miss Amber thinks, or is pretending to think, that she's lingering out of concern for Milo. She doesn't want to disabuse her, so she says, "Well, just call me if he needs me," as matter-of-factly as she can manage. When she hugs Milo goodbye, he clings to her, the fabric of her shirt bunched tightly in his little fists, and she feels a surge of relief—he doesn't want to stay, he'll come away with her, they can go. But across the room another child calls his name, and just like that Milo is gone.

Out on the street, she blinks into the sunlight. She has no idea what to do with her freedom. How did this happen? The day began as every other day in Sewanee has, and yet suddenly she is alone. She has no job. She has no friends, and can't make any, because friends want to hear your story. Where you came from and what you're doing here. Why Milo has no father. Why she is so very alone.

Don't Leave Me

Here I am at the end of adventure. The quiet house. The woods. I sit on my deck like a bird-watcher, like a hunter in a blind, wondering if my neighbor will poke her head out. I finish one mystery and start another, this one about a young woman trying to solve her family's murder. I look up from blood and bodies to gaze at the still blue pond. Blue when the sunlight's on it, gray otherwise. This is a metaphor for something. When I grow weary of that I go inside and sit where I sit now, at my desk, in the room I call my study, though what am I studying here? This desk was once my father's, and it's imposing, as was he. Dark shiny wood, bigger than a desk has a right to be. It must weigh a great deal. I have nicked it here and there, banging it with my cane, and left a stray ink mark or two on its surface. I've cluttered it with papers and books, though at least I have no computer to offend its old-fashioned sensibility. Still, it is dignified and reproachful, which are also words that belonged to my father.

I am personifying the desk. Am I so lonely I'd like it to come to life, and sing and dance with the silverware, like in a fairy-tale cartoon? No, that's not right. Loneliness is not my problem. My problem is restlessness, forever and ever, amen. I'm restless. I want something to happen, though it's been quite some time since anything happened to me.

Jennifer Young. Jennifer Young. What are you doing here?

People used to tell me I must be looking forward to retirement, after all those years of working so hard. I worked until I was in my seventies! But some of us don't work so that we can rest. Some of us rest so that we can work. I belong to the second group, but for a while, at least, I mistook myself for a member of the first. When I bought this house, I thought my restlessness had burned itself out, and that it was at long last time to retreat into peaceful solitude, free of all the world's demands. Isn't that the end of the story, for soldiers and adventurers? At least for the ones who fail to die.

Let's talk about this house, this mountain, my paradise on earth. After I moved here I was seized by a sudden interest in local history, and there is little I don't know about this place, though I don't find the facts of it quite as interesting as I once did. I live on the Cumberland Plateau, one thousand feet up, with its caves and its waterfalls and its highways blasted through rock. So many delights for the nature-minded! Trails to swimming holes and wildflowers and other species of the picturesque. When I first moved here I was nimble enough to walk the less challenging trails. No more. When I want a view from the bluff now I have to drive to an overlook in Sewanee. I like the one with the Cross. The Cross—it's a war memorial, white, sixty feet tall. Around its foot there's a circle of spotlights, so that at night it glows and draws bats and moths of all sizes. Moths as big as bats.

There's always been religion on the Mountain, though that's not why I moved here, as the war long ago cured me of any belief in God. Sewanee is an Episcopal school, a bishop's notion. Then there's the Assembly—founded in 1882, as a summer-long Sunday school. When I first came to the Mountain, as a girl in the 1930s, we were visiting a friend of my mother's who had a family cottage there. I could have bought a house in the Assembly when I moved here, but I wasn't looking for community. What I have in this house is community's opposite. My house is on a winding road off the main highway with its two lanes and its too-fast drivers. The road to my house goes past the little airport, which has little planes that putt-putter down little runways. They remind me of the war, but in a way I like. They remind me of a movie about the war. My house was built by an old couple who got divorced, or maybe a young couple who died. I can't remember which. I know it wasn't old/died, young/divorced, because I remember that when the Realtor told me the story I felt surprised. Behind it is a pond. Around it woods. The woods are also around the pond. The only other sign of human habitation is the deck of Jennifer Young's house, and her house's brown exterior wall. When I sit on my own deck I can see sunlight glinting off the windows. But for a long time no one lived there. As for my house? My house has too many rooms.

I was born the year women got the vote. That's an interesting fact about me. I changed everything. "Things are different now," my mother used to whisper, smoothing back my hair after she'd tucked me in at night. "Things will be different for you."

My mother had married at nineteen, had three children and lost one, suffered in her marriage to my father, though of course I didn't understand that then. If there was a shadow of grief on my mother I felt it only on those nights when she whispered like that in my ear. I remember her as bubbly, irrepressible, theatrical. She dressed for dinner and called me "*chérie*" and referred to the living room as the "parlor." As a child I marveled at her endless cheer—I admired it enormously, and it mystified me. So I couldn't quite see her as human. And then I got older and she grew artificial, or my idea of her did. After that we couldn't understand each other at all. But when I was a child, and she was all marvelous gleaming surfaces, moments of truth—her whisper in my ear—just frightened and unnerved me.

For years she imagined for me the brilliant life I'd have at college, but my father was a doctor, and I wanted to go to nursing school. What I really wanted was to be a doctor, too, but nothing led me to believe that was possible. When in the end she couldn't wear down

my determination, she swallowed her own disappointment and behaved as though nursing school had been exactly what she'd wanted
for me all along. When I joined the army, that was something else. I
said, "I enlisted," and she turned ashen at the words. She looked at
me like I was already a ghost. All those times she'd said *different*, this
was not what she'd had in mind.

It's funny where your mind goes, when you get to be my age.
When my mother died I was in the emergency room with her. We'd
been in there five hours or more. She'd had a stroke. I was holding
her hand, and she kept talking about a song called "The Old Oaken
Bucket" that was stuck in her head. Was the line "*by* the well" or "*in*
the well"? Which was it? I didn't know. I had no idea, and that was
maddening to her. What was wrong with me? Finally I picked one.
After that she kept saying *don't leave me*.

Don't leave me. Anyone I might say that to is already gone.

I'm restless. Once upon a time I would have cleaned my house
from top to bottom, or perfected my garden, or gone to work. Now
what am I to do with this energy? Fly to Paris and take a lover? Jog?

In the days when I still had conversations, and people found out
I went to war, they'd ask if I'd wanted an adventure, and I'd want to
tell them no, that all I wanted was to serve my country. But I suppose
if that were truly all I'd wanted I could've stayed at home and knitted
socks. I was not pressed into service, rising to the occasion against
my will. I always wanted something more. Something bigger. Something different. Something else.

Trapdoor

They need money. Even more so, now that she's put Milo in school. Their need for money wakes her every night into midnight silence, so that she traverses the darkened hall to Milo's room, whispers to his sleeping form that everything will be all right, then goes out on the deck and looks at the starry night and wills herself to feel peace. All around her the maddening mindless thrum of insects, punctuated occasionally by an eerie, insistent owl, a sound that reminds her of the woman across the pond. They need money, so she's trying to get it, sticking in each thumbtack, asking each proprietor if she can leave a stack of her cards. At the coffee shop in Sewanee, at the café in Monteagle, at Monteagle's real-deal small-town places and Sewanee's knowingly rustic ones, they tell her to go ahead, smiling at Milo as he zooms his toy car up the side of a counter, and she puts up her flyers, with their hopeful tabs printed with her number and her name. A woman behind a café counter in Sewanee tells her she has no competition: there used to be a massage therapist in the little strip of three storefronts at the edge of Monteagle—"You know the place? Everything that opens there closes"—but a few years ago she moved away. Jennifer isn't licensed in Tennessee but up here there seems little chance that anyone will check.

She'd meant to do this task alone, but impulsively she picked up

Milo early from preschool, right before nap, which she knew would win his gratitude. He hates nap. He hasn't napped since he was two and a half. "Naps are *stupid*," he likes to say. "Naps are *jackass*." Though she knows she shouldn't let him say *jackass*, she's so amused by the way he uses it as an adjective that she finds it hard to make him stop. She loves the vehemence of his pronouncements. She loves the smile that breaks across his face when he sees her. She loves the appreciative sound he makes—*mmmm*—when she gives him a bite of something good. Where they let her hang her signs, she buys a treat for herself and Milo to show her gratitude. So far they've had real lemonade, fries, a blueberry muffin, and they're topping it all off with an ice cream cone, sitting at a little table in a café that looks like a log cabin. The ice cream is an enormous scoop of dripping chocolate that she's ceded entirely to Milo, who's struggling might- ily to conquer it. "You need to lick around the bottom," she says. He pushes his whole tongue against the top, shifting the scoop into a dangerous tilt. "No, the bottom," she says. "The *bottom*. Do you want me to show you?"

"I can *do* it," he says, loudly, and she looks away, resisting the urge to snatch the thing from him before it ends up on the floor, or in her lap. Looking away, she catches the eye of a woman at the cash reg- ister. The woman is waiting for her change, holding a brown bag of something to go, and for some reason she is turned around, looking at Jennifer. Jennifer freezes, but the woman immediately breaks her gaze, returning her attention to the girl behind the counter. Jennifer turns her own head, too, but she is in the grip of adrenaline now, adrenaline that tells her to be watchful, to be ready at any moment to flee, and she keeps the woman in her peripheral vision. The woman probably just glanced over because Milo was loud. She knows this. She should shake the habit of bracing for confrontation.

But then the woman looks again, and once her change is in her hand she approaches, fumbling with her purse. Time stretches, as in the slow slide into a car wreck. There is endless time, and yet somehow not enough time to stop what's about to happen. Milo is still fighting his ice cream cone, chasing the drips around the side with his tongue. They're faster than he is. Some part of Jennifer registers that his frustration is building, but there's no time, either, to head off the tantrum or the tears. The woman gets very close, her head cocked like she's trying to place Jennifer's face. Her expression is pleasant as she does this, but it could morph, at any moment, into wary confusion, or even horror. "I recognize you, don't I?" she says. Jennifer absorbs these words with the vacant calm of someone who expected disaster. In the last year she's developed the ability to climb down into the deepest part of herself as if into a storm cellar, pulling a trapdoor shut behind her. After three weeks on the Mountain she hasn't lost the skill. At the woman's question, she is gone. It is her body, and not herself, that answers, "I don't know."

Now the woman looks at Milo, who is growling at his cone. Nothing conforms to our wishes, not other people, not ice cream, which must insist on melting, dripping sticky down our hands. "Yes," the woman says. "I've seen you two at the playground."

"Oh," Jennifer says. She nearly sways in her seat, and puts her hand on the table. "That's right," she adds, hardly knowing what she's saying. "I recognize you now."

"My son and—I'm sorry, what's his name?"

"Milo," Jennifer says, and Milo looks up, snaps, "What?"

"That's right, Milo. My son and Milo have played together. I think they're about the same age."

"*What*, Mommy?" Milo asks.

"Nothing," Jennifer says. "I was just telling her your name."

Milo shoots the woman a look, wearing a deep, disgruntled frown. "Why?"

"You played with her little boy at the playground, remember?"

Milo cocks his head, his expression suddenly pleasant. "What's his name?"

"It's Ben," the woman says. "And I'm Megan."

"Jennifer," Jennifer says. "Nice to meet you." She'd offer her hand to shake, but she's afraid it would be trembling.

"Megan and Jennifer." The woman—Megan—laughs. Jennifer is bewildered. She's back in her body, but sluggish, as if she's been sedated. "We just need a Heather," Megan says. "Seventies names." Jennifer tries a polite chuckle.

"Where's Ben?" Milo says. He's given up on his ice cream, dropping it onto his napkin on the table, where it pools and spreads. He wipes his fingers on his pants, which doesn't get his fingers clean but does distribute the mess.

"He's at school," Megan says. "He goes to the preschool at the church in Sewanee."

"That's where I go!" Milo says. Understanding dawns in his face. "I know Ben," he says. "He has Spider-Man shoes."

"Oh," Megan says, glancing at Jennifer, who interprets that glance as question or judgment.

"Sometimes I get him before nap," she says. "He doesn't nap anymore, and it's hard on him to lie there quietly for two hours."

But Megan doesn't care about naps, or why Milo isn't in school. "We should get them together," she says. "Set up a playdate."

"Yes," Milo says, "yes, yes, yes." He's bouncing in his seat, chanting the word. Megan laughs again. Jennifer gives herself an inner slap. Be normal, she exhorts herself. Be friendly. She can almost remember how it's done. "Hmmm," she says, playacting. "I get the feeling Milo would like that."

They exchange numbers and chat for a few minutes, Milo interjecting his desire to have the playdate that day, right now, immediately. Megan is a professor of sociology. She lives in Sewanee. She's younger than Jennifer, Jennifer thinks, though maybe not by a lot. She looks younger, anyway, with her open, freckled face and her wide, far-apart eyes. She looks younger than Jennifer feels.

Megan is talking about the necessity of regular escapes from the Mountain, her family's weekend jaunts to Nashville, the benefits of a membership to the aquarium in Chattanooga, when Milo leans perilously close to Megan's nice skirt with his disastrous fingers, and Jennifer catches him gently by the wrist. "I'd better clean him up before he slimes you," she says.

"Oh, I'm used to it," Megan says.

"Still," Jennifer says, holding up Milo's hand for the other woman's inspection. "Chocolate."

"True," Megan says. She smiles at Milo. "Chocolate is very messy, isn't it?"

"Mommy can stain it out," Milo says.

"Stain it out?" Megan repeats. She flashes Jennifer a conspiratorial grin. Kids and their cutely mangled sayings. Something to post on Facebook.

"He sometimes says, 'I smell like' to mean he smells something," Jennifer offers. She imitates the way Milo lifts his head, alert as a hound dog, when he catches a scent. "'I smell like garbage.'"

"I smell like chocolate!" Milo shouts gleefully, wanting in on the joke.

"Yes, you do, bubby," Jennifer says. She stands, pulling him out of his chair, and at last the other woman releases her, promising a call. "Great!" Jennifer says. She wants to turn to someone afterward, blow out air, share her relief. But there's only Milo to turn to, and her relief is nothing she can express to him, so instead she proceeds to the bathroom to scrub him clean.

The someone she wanted to turn to, she realizes as she rubs Milo's reluctant little hands together under the water, was Tommy. She still misses him, which surprises her. She comes upon the feeling from time to time, like when you step funny and feel that particular twinge in your knee. Back again. No matter what you did to get rid of it.

Horrible Deeds

Once a week I go to the library in Monteagle, a brown little institutional box of a building. Sue the librarian expects me. She knows my habits and makes me a stack of books she thinks I'll like: always five books, always detective novels, waiting for me behind the circulation desk. You might imagine that being an old lady I like the cozy mysteries, but you'd be wrong. Spare me the cats and knitting. It was Sue's idea to start picking out books for me—perhaps she gets bored—and the first stack she presented me, two or three years ago, was full of such nonsense. I don't need my murders made adorable. Death in a book is still only death in a book, but give me an author who doesn't flinch. If a mystery doesn't walk you up to the abyss before it rescues you, it's a shallow form of comfort.

At any rate Sue knows better now. When I arrived today she had ready a good solid stack of horrible deeds. "Miss Margaret!" she greeted me, beaming like she always does. "How are you today!" I did not make a mistake with the exclamation point; that is how she talks.

"As well as could be expected," I said, which is one of my standard answers. What should I say? I'm ninety. *Fine* would be a ridiculous lie.

"I've got some good ones for you," she said. She got up from her stool to get them, which gave me time to get to the desk and heave my returns onto it. In the past she's come out from behind the desk and tried to take them from me, but when politeness didn't work I snarled at her and now she doesn't do it anymore.

She plopped her books next to mine. This is one of the best moments of my week, seeing those two stacks side by side: something accomplished, something to anticipate. Perhaps it is the best moment. She lifted the top book, by Tana French, and displayed it as proudly as if she'd had a hand in its creation. "This just came in," she said. "Hasn't even made it to the shelf yet. I know you like her."

"I do," I said. "Thank you."

She went about the business of returning and checking out, and as she did my mind drifted. She talks while she works, but she's really talking to herself—saying my name as she types it in, and so forth—and so I don't really listen. She used to tell me all the local gossip, but I never responded with more than a flat, "I see," and eventually she stopped. She knows everything about everyone, Sue, and has little ability to discern what's interesting. I wondered if she'd heard about my new neighbor. My eye fell on the computers they keep for public use—near the front, to my dismay, as when I go to a library what I want to see are books—and it struck me that I could look up Jennifer Young on the Internet. It's a common name, though, I imagine. How would I know which Jennifer Young she was? What could I find that would really interest me? My detective novels would be terribly boring if all questions could be answered by an Internet search. It must be hard, these days, to imagine a mystery.

I don't have the Internet here in my home. If I did I'd probably look her up. Jennifer Young. We are curious creatures and can't be expected not to satisfy that curiosity when the answers are so readily available. A child doesn't really want to spoil the surprise of her Christmas presents, but if she knows where they're hidden in the closet she'll have no choice but to look. The world has forgotten that there is more pleasure in wondering than knowing. A quick answer—the year someone was born, the reason for hail—is such a dull satisfaction. Why do you even want to know? That's the true mystery.

At any rate I was thinking about Jennifer Young, and so when Sue spoke it seemed like telepathy. "Have you found anyone?" she asked.

I was startled. "What?"

"Weren't you looking for someone?" She pushed the new stack in my direction. "To check on you now and then? To keep you company?"

"No," I said, with no small amount of indignation.

"Are you sure? I could swear you said you were. Last week. You told me that."

"Sue, are you getting old?"

She laughed. "Miss Margaret," she said. "Every day."

"Perhaps you've been talking to my doctor."

"Oh, Dr. Bell doesn't gossip. You know that."

"Do I?"

"Miss Margaret, you are wicked. She didn't say a thing. Well, if you didn't tell me that then I must've dreamed it."

"I don't know why you'd dream about me," I said.

"Well, I think about you, all by yourself out there."

"I live five minutes from here."

"I know, but you're all alone, out in the woods. My mother fell, and—"

"I'm not going to fall," I said.

"I know, but—"

"I'm not going to fall."

She sighed. "All right, Miss Margaret. And I'm sorry if you get an unwanted call, because I did tell someone I thought you were looking for help."

"Who?"

She lifted her chin to indicate the bulletin board by the front door. I never look at it, being both uninterested in and immune to the usual exhortations to go to church, buy a house, do something charitable, or join a club. I followed her gaze, confused. "She put a sign up there," she said. "I can't think of her name—I guess I am getting old—but she said she'd rented Barbara's old house, which puts her near you, so maybe that's why you came to mind."

"Jennifer Young?"

"Yes!" she said. "You know her?"

"No," I said.

She looked at me a moment, awaiting an explanation I had no plans to offer. "Well," she said, "she does massage, and she's new here and just getting started. I thought she might be willing to come and see you, from time to time, if you needed that."

"I don't," I said.

I do not like to be treated with the restrained patience one must show a petulant child, and so I was quite annoyed by the way she was looking at me, by the careful way she said, "I know you don't." She flashed a quick smile to signal her withdrawal from the field. "She seems like a nice lady. A tiny bit shy, I think. She has a cute little boy. I hope she likes it here."

"Where did she come from?"

"I don't know." Sue cocked her head, considering. "I don't think I asked. That's not like me! She's a little . . . I said shy. So you know me. I just chattered."

"About me."

"Well, not just about you! Miss Margaret, my goodness. Don't be mad at me. You know I mean well."

I relented. "I know," I said. "It's all right." I slid the books to my chest and said, in my sweet-old-lady voice, "Thank you for these."

We said our goodbyes, but I lingered near the front door, pretending to look at the carrel of new releases. I was waiting for Sue to be busy, and once someone finally appeared at the desk to occupy her attention, I stepped to the bulletin board. LICENSED MASSAGE THERA-PIST, the sign said. IN-HOME MASSAGES. Then those tear-off strips, printed with a phone number and the name Jennifer Young.

Now I sit here at my desk knowing I could call this person, my new neighbor, if I wanted to. I have her number right here, on the little slip of paper, and, just in case I lose that, copied into the Rolo-dex I keep beside my phone. If I want to, all I have to do is pick up the phone and call.

In the Beginning

She was fourteen when she first knew him, and not an old fourteen. She'd never kissed a boy, unless you counted a sloppy encounter during a game of Truth or Dare, which she didn't. He was a junior. He had long legs and thick, unruly hair. At seventeen he already carried himself with an air of amused experience. He was good at eye contact. He had an all-inclusive smile. Everybody wanted to be near him, even—or especially—the ones who were too nervous to approach. Truth and beauty, he was truth and beauty, the beauty part probably more important than the truth, or at least what made the truth so interesting. Was he even, objectively, as handsome as he seemed? It was hard to tell, impossible to be objective in the face of his charisma. To Jennifer her longing for him seemed natural, inevitable. She made no effort to explain. Above his right eyebrow was a beauty mark—probably he would have called it a freckle or a mole, but she studied it surreptitiously every day and she called it a beauty mark.

It was geometry class that offered her this opportunity. As a freshman she should have been in algebra, and as a junior he should have been in trig. She was good at math; he was bad. She used to imagine the story would unfold the way it did in teen movies and TV shows— she'd be asked to tutor him, they'd meet after school, he'd grow to depend on her until suddenly he'd realize she was all he needed. She believed that she sensed something beneath the careless smile and the cool, a powerful undertow of longing and hurt. She imagined scenes in which he confessed his deepest emotions, told her she was the only one he could talk to, really *talk* to. The words would be all the more affecting because they were so hard for him to say. It didn't happen like that. For months they sat in desks next to each other without exchanging more than a sentence or two. For months she perfected the art of watching him without appearing to watch him. She was good, he was bad, but they both liked the back of the class.

There was nothing particularly interesting about her, at least not at school. In the dance studio, she was a star. But that was her secret life, and she kept it secret. Dancing was for her a deep privacy. This despite the yearly public recitals. In rehearsal Miss Suzanne was always having to remind her to look up and out, to watch herself in the mirrors. She succeeded in school without attracting attention, or at least not attention that outlasted a teacher's occasional unsuccessful effort to get her to speak up in class. She always nodded a lot and said she'd try, and then she never did try. She couldn't really understand the urge that made her more eager classmates wave their hands. If she spoke, everyone would look at her. If she didn't speak, what had been lost?

Her mild, forgiving parents didn't mind that she was shy, though they sometimes remarked—mildly—that it seemed odd for a shy person to want to be a dancer. She didn't like to explain herself—no matter what she said, it always sounded *wrong*—so she only nodded, or sometimes shrugged, or once, irritably, said, "You always say that," her eyes fixed resolutely out the front passenger window of her father's car.

"It's not a criticism," he said that time. "Just an observation." He hesitated. Her parents were never anything but supportive, spending their money and driving her to lessons without a word of doubt. They'd both had difficult parents, and they'd told her directly and indirectly that they wouldn't make her life any harder than it had to be. She could hear in his voice that it cost her father something to press on. "It's not an easy road, is it? I just want to be sure you're sure."

"I'm sure," she said. She was sure. She was sure beyond sure, and maybe that was why she couldn't be sure of anything else. A person came equipped with only so much certainty, so much confidence. She'd spent all of hers in one place.

This was how it happened: She had a friend whose older brother was often pressed into chauffeuring them both, very, very much against his will. He was driving them to the movies. It was a Saturday night in January. He took the scenic route, cruising the usual gathering places—the parking lots of churches and fast-food establishments—in search of people he knew. In the front seat his sister scolded and protested, threatening to kill him if they missed the previews. In the backseat Jennifer leaned her forehead against the window and stared at things until they blurred and faded. Trees, streetlights, people, cars. She couldn't bring herself to care whether they missed the previews. It was her friend who wanted to see this movie. What she herself wanted seemed very far from here.

The car stopped, her friend's voice rising as she socked her brother in the shoulder. "Hey!" the brother said, in protest, and then, "Hey, man," out his window, and a deep male voice drawled back, "Hey."

Jennifer knew that voice. Suddenly she was hot inside her coat. An exchange took place, which she followed with such intense concentration that she couldn't process any of it. Then he was in the backseat with her, bringing the whole world with him, taking up all the space. Oh my God. Tommy Carrasco.

The car started back up. "Geometry," he said to her, in a low voice that came to her under the increasingly loud argument in the front seat. She nodded but didn't speak. He studied her. He looked at her in a way that was at once flattering and intimidating. "Why are you looking at me like that?" she heard herself ask. "Do you want to sleep with me?" Her tone was matter-of-fact, the question just a question. What had possessed her to ask it? She had wanted to know. She could feel heat in her cheeks, but her hair was long and the night was dark, and she told herself he couldn't possibly notice her blush.

He laughed, a surprised laugh, and leaned his head back against the seat. She'd made him break his gaze, but she didn't think about that triumph until later, recounting the incident to herself. At the moment she had her eyes fixed on his neck, caught in a vampiric urge to put her mouth on it. "Why are you looking at *me* like that?" he asked, and her surprised eyes darted back to his face. His voice was a murmur, warm breath near your skin, a hand on your thigh. "Do you want to sleep with me?"

"I'm only fourteen," she said.

He nodded thoughtfully, narrowing his eyes in consideration. "Too young," he agreed.

"Maybe next year," she said, and he whipped his head toward her with a comic expression of genuine shock. She grinned. She knew this self-possession, this elation, flooding through her limbs. It was how she felt when she danced, and at no other time. At no other time until now.

They didn't make it to the previews, or any of the movie at all. Tommy knew about a party, and Jennifer's friend found herself outvoted. In a dark corner of the party Tommy kissed her. And that was how they came to be.

Being with him proved only to increase her yearning. Before she hadn't known it was possible to get what she wanted and so had wanted it without much hope. But now she hoped. She hoped all the time, and it was terrifying. When he left her at her door she hoped he would come back to kiss her again. When he hung up the phone she hoped he would call her later. She hoped he would meet her in the hall between classes, he would name her his girlfriend, he would ask her to prom. And he did, and he did, and he did. She existed only to witness these miracles.

That summer she was going to dance camp for six weeks. This had been planned before Tommy, and even high on love she didn't want to unplan it. Her life was too much his already. As the time approached she was filled with a fatalistic dread. He talked about how much he'd miss her, and how they'd talk every night, and what they'd do when she got back, but she believed down deep that he'd find another girl, that his interest was a fluke that couldn't outlast her absence, that her departure would be the end. They parted with many protestations of love, and she cried, and then she climbed into her father's car and stopped herself from looking back at him. He sounded anxious on the phone that night, as if he were the one worried she wouldn't want him anymore, and he called her as much as he'd said he would, but still she doubted. Still she held herself apart. She threw herself into dance. The older girls taught her to survive on bouillon and celery and by the end of the six weeks she was skinny as a prima ballerina and buoyant with pride. She was cold to him on the phone the last week, so exhilarated was she by the conviction of her immaculate self-control.

Her parents, when they picked her up, had no comment about her altered appearance, but when Tommy saw her he took one look and said, "No."

"No, what?" she asked. They were out in front of her house. He'd driven over as soon as he knew she was home, and she'd gone out with her chin lifted to meet him, determined, this time and henceforth, not to be overwhelmed.

"No to this," he said, indicating the length of her body. "I won't let you do this to yourself."

"Why not?" She tried to sound haughty but her voice quivered.

"Because I love you," he said. He sounded angry. "I love you, and you can't do this to yourself." He put his hands on her upper arms—arms he could nearly encircle, now, with one hand—and pulled her against his chest.

He'd told her many times he loved her but until that moment

she'd never believed it. The force of the belief undid her. All those weeks of self-control—she saw what an illusion that had been. There was no self-control. There was need, only need. She sobbed against his shirt until the fabric was wet, while he stroked her hair and said again and again how much he loved her, and she had been half-alive without this, a plant without water. When she finally stopped crying, they climbed into his pickup truck and went to Sonic for cheeseburgers and tater tots.

She remembers this now, sitting alone at her kitchen table, miles and miles from there and then in her dark and silent house, drinking herbal tea while the son she had with Tommy sleeps. It's a rueful amusement to think of the coda to that dramatic scene—the pickup truck, the Sonic, the tater tots. No doubt she tore a little slit in a ketchup packet and squeezed a careful dollop onto each tot, as was her habit. Sitting on the warm leather seat of his truck, her whole body still wrung out and shuddery from crying, Tommy singing along with the radio, looking at her with his meaningful eyes. Oh, Tommy. How he could make her cry.

Subterfuge

My house has two front doors. The first is a wooden one that opens onto a screen porch I use as a repository for houseplants and the larger souvenirs from my travels, the wooden coyote from New Mexico and the china elephant from Thailand. I went through that door, leaving it open; caned my way over to the second door, the one with the screen; and looked at her through it. She smiled when she saw me, but she has a serious face, and somehow the smile did nothing to make her look less serious. Her face is squarish, until the jawline, which is well defined and declines gracefully to her perfect arc of a chin and probably saves her from looking mannish. Her eyes are green and somber. Is she really a blond? I don't know. Her hair is that blond that's dark enough to be persuasively natural. Her eyebrows are brown, darker than her hair, but light enough that the hair remains plausible.

"Ms. Riley?" she asked, and when I nodded, she said, "I'm Jennifer." She was holding a large contraption that turned out to be her massage table. Over her shoulder was a big green bag.

"It's a pleasure to meet you, Jennifer," I said. "Please come in." I could hear my accent deepening, as it does when I'm being polite. My screen door opens out, so I began to push it toward her and she shuffled her burden out of the way and we did an awkward dance that ended, finally, in both of us being inside the house.

"I might be confused," she said, resting the folded table against her leg. "I brought everything for a massage, but the woman at the library told me you needed someone to look in on you. I didn't know if—"

"I never said that," I interrupted.

"Oh, all right, I—"

"Sue thinks I can't take care of myself, but I can. I called about a massage, that's all. I don't need some kind of paid companion. I don't need any other kind of help."

"All right, then, good," she said. "Good."

"I will not pay someone to pay attention to me."

"I understand," she said.

The silence was awkward, and I was sorry for it. Sometimes I am more snappish than I intend. "We're neighbors of a sort," I said.

"Yes," she said. "Across the pond."

"I saw you out on your deck the other day," I said. "I waved."

"That's right," she said. "It's nice to meet you close up."

"And you as well," I said. I'd been hoping, I realize, for more reaction than she gave me to the news of this connection between us, but she stayed calm and businesslike. Only now does it strike me I'm lucky she didn't ask how I knew the distant woman on the porch had been she, since my story was that I'd contacted her only because I'd seen her flyer and wanted a massage. One doesn't want to tell a new acquaintance that one poked through her mail.

"So," she said, glancing around, "if you'll tell me where to set up, I'll do that, and then we can talk."

"Where to set up?" I repeated blankly.

"The massage table," she said, indicating the contraption with a nod.

"Oh. Oh, yes, of course," I said. I experienced a startling moment of panic. In employing this ruse to meet her, I had failed to consider the necessity of committing to it. In what room of my house was I willing to take off my clothes and have a stranger touch me? In no room at all. I must have looked as dumbfounded as I felt, because, trying to help, she asked, "The bedroom?"

When you live alone your bedroom becomes a sacred space. As if to stop her from insisting, I said, "The guest room," and pointed to the hallway off the right side of the living room. She obediently went that way. "Be right back!" she called out in a cheerful voice that didn't suit her.

I eased myself into one of my mother's uncomfortable straight-backed chairs. When I'm alone I sit in my armchair and put my feet up on the ottoman, but it takes me a little while to get back up from that position, and the maneuvering involved is not something I'd care to perform in front of a witness. The armchair did not belong to my parents, unlike most of the furniture in the house. When my parents died in 1982, first one, then the other, I inherited many things—the antique couch with its carved crown and spiral arms, the looming, majestic sideboard in the dining room. At the time I still lived in Nashville, in a house fully furnished by my own things. I bought this house more or less to contain their furniture, and when I moved into it, selling my furniture and keeping theirs seemed the easiest choice. But my parents owned heavy, dark pieces, mournful and grand, and so my house never seems to have enough light in it, despite the skylight I had installed in the living room.

When she reemerged she had divested herself of everything but a folder and a pen. She gave me a professional smile and came over to sit in the straight-backed chair next to mine. I realize now that I was expecting her to pay me some polite compliment on the house or its furnishings and that the fact that she didn't accounted for the slight irritation I felt as she perched beside me with the folder on her knees. The folder, I saw, had my name on it. *Maggie Jean Riley*, it said. I must have given her that name when she was asking all those questions on the phone—whether I was on medications (of course), whether I'd had a massage before (of course not). She opened the folder and poised her pen over the form inside. "I started filling this out when we talked earlier," she said, "but some things I like to discuss in person."

"Wouldn't you rather work at a table?"

"I'm fine, thank you," she said, but as she asked me questions about my aches and pains and I answered them she didn't look fine, awkwardly repositioning form and folder on her knee, the pen pressing too far into the paper. This stubbornness increased my irritation. And why had I called myself *Maggie Jean*? That hadn't been my name in many years.

"You can change that to Margaret," I said, interrupting whatever question she'd been asking.

"I'm sorry, what?" she asked. Her voice so very polite.

I pointed at my name on the folder. "That should say Margaret," I said. "Not Maggie Jean."

But you told me Maggie Jean, she should have said. Or, *Don't take that tone with me*. She just crossed out the name, neat as you please, and wrote *Margaret* in small letters above it. Why do people let me speak to them so rudely? If they'd let me get away with less, I might think what I said mattered more. A few years ago one of my grandnieces tried her hand at my dead sister's recipe for strawberry-rhubarb pie. I was allowed only one bite before she called for my verdict. "I've had better," I said. No one slapped me, or snatched the pie away, as I deserved. They laughed.

I insisted on paying Jennifer Young up front, even though she said people usually did it after. I wouldn't let her bring me my checkbook either. I made her watch me cane into the study to get it and cane my way back once I had it. So excruciatingly slow! When she could have popped there and back with time to grab a smoke besides. When you're young you have to invent tasks to fill the time, while I can kill an hour just making myself some tea.

She had to help me onto the table. I took off my clothes by myself in the room. She said I could take my underwear off if I wanted to. This was a strange thing to be told. I left it on. I wanted to get on the table by myself, but I couldn't manage it, probably because I tried to do it too fast, trying to outrun her threatened knock. I wrapped myself in the sheet, as she'd instructed, and she came in and helped me up. This was all so humiliating that I wanted to weep. It's not as though I'm unaccustomed to being poked and prodded. I accept medical treatment with the not-quite-there dignity the sick and the elderly do their best to master. I suppose I just hadn't wanted her first knowledge of me to be knowledge of my fragile, frustrating body. I hired her to do exactly what she was doing without expecting her to do it. Perhaps I imagined she'd recognize all I'd wanted was a pretext for meeting her.

Lying facedown on that table I was so tense I must have looked like a prisoner awaiting torture. I could feel her presence behind me, although she didn't speak. I braced against her touch. After a moment I felt her lay her two palms flat on me, one on each of my shoulders. I thought she would begin to move them, but she didn't. Then I thought she might say something, but she didn't. I could feel the heat in her hands. I waited for her to do something. I opened my eyes and looked at my carpet and closed my eyes again. I watched each second pass like you watch each single, persistent drop from a leaky faucet form and fall. Suddenly the strangest thing happened— something in my shoulders let go. It was like caving in. It was like my shoulders had been brick and now they were pudding. I had had no idea.

She exhaled. "Good," she said, and I felt as pleased as a child to have done what she wanted. "You keep a lot of tension there," she said.

"You have to keep it somewhere," I said, trying for insouciance.

She didn't answer. She began to move her hands, gently, down my back. I must have drifted, honestly, because I don't remember much else until she pressed a spot in my lower back, and a shock went through me, some kind of electrical pulse. I startled. "Hmmm," she said. She rubbed a series of circles around that spot.

"You remind me of someone," I said. I blurted it, stupidly, like the place on my back had been a button that released that thought. She stilled. I felt the wariness in her body, even without being able to see her. "An old friend," I said. "Someone I knew a long time ago."

"Oh," she said, but flatly. It was another moment before her hands resumed their ministrations.

It's intriguing, isn't it, that that comment frightened her? I don't know what that means but I'd like to. At any rate I see now why I've taken such an interest in her, from the moment I saw her across the pond: I recognized a mystery.

She had me roll over and went to work on my legs and feet. My thoughts dissolved. I drifted away.

Later I woke to find myself alone in the room. I got down from the table carefully, and dressed, and went out to find her back in the chair she'd chosen earlier, making notes on her form. She stopped when she saw me and closed her folder. "How do you feel?" she asked.

I nodded. I couldn't manage to speak. She rose and met me where I was. "Let's sit down." She put a gentle hand under my elbow and guided me toward the chairs. I could feel her hesitating over which one to plant me in.

"The armchair," I said, and she eased me down into it, and then, without asking, lifted my feet one at a time and put them on the ottoman. It took me a moment to notice that after I was settled she disappeared. I lifted myself out of the chair a little so that I could look round for her.

She came toward me out of my own kitchen, holding a glass of water. "You should drink this," she said. "I hope you don't mind."

"Mind?" I accepted the glass. My arm floated it to my mouth.

"Me rummaging in your kitchen."

"Oh," I said. "No." I smiled dreamily at her. "I feel as though you gave me a sedative."

She smiled. "It can be like that sometimes," she said. She pulled her chair over and perched on the edge of it, leaning forward with her eyes on me.

"I'm sorry that chair is so uncomfortable," I said. "Like something from an old schoolhouse."

"That's fine," she said. "How do you feel?"

"I feel wonderful," I said. I couldn't help confessing this. "I feel like I'm melting into the chair."

She nodded, seriously, like a doctor hearing my symptoms. "Nothing feels bruised or achy?"

"Nothing," I said. "Absolutely nothing."

"Are you still able to get in and out of a bath?"

Normally I would've found this question intrusive. I just said, "I have a rail."

"Good," she said. "You might want to take an Epsom salt bath, to keep from being achy later. I was gentle, but since you're not used to massage . . . And drink lots of water."

I raised my glass to her and then dutifully drank from it.

"Can I get you some more?" she asked, and because it was so pleasurable to be tended, I let her. Then she went into the guest room to pack up her table. I dozed a little, I think, because the next thing I knew she was touching me on the shoulder. "Are you all right in that chair?" she asked, her voice low like she was trying not to wake me. "Or would you like me to help you up before I go?"

"Oh, I'm fine," I said. "I hope you don't mind if I don't get up." Her table was folded and waiting by the door.

"Not at all," she said. She straightened and looked at me as if giving me one last chance to speak.

I said, "You do remind me of that friend, you know."

"I hope that's good," she said.

I nodded. I fumbled for my water glass on the side table and took another sip.

She said, "Let me know if you—"

But I interrupted. I blurted, truth be told. "I was in the war."

She nodded as if this were to be expected. But I hadn't meant to say that. "Which one?" she asked.

"The second one," I said. "World War Two. I met my friend in basic training."

"Basic training?" She looked puzzled, which was gratifying, because from puzzled it's a quick step to curious.

"We were nurses," I said. "Army nurses. They put us through basic training, like soldiers, even though in the war we never pitched tents or did close-order drill or any of that. Ours was at Fort Bragg."

"In North Carolina," she said.

"Right," I said. "Her name was Kay." To my astonishment, my eyes grew watery.

She nodded again, that irritatingly serene acceptance. "Was she killed?"

"No!" I was so startled I nearly shouted. I wiped without grace at my eyes. "No, she wasn't killed."

"Oh," she said. "You lost touch after the war?"

"Yes," I said, and then suddenly I didn't want to say any more. I looked into my water glass.

"Where did they send you?" she asked. "After basic training?"

"England," I said, still watching the water. "Then France, and from there into Austria and Germany."

"So you were really *in* the war," she said.

"I really was." I said this snappishly, I think, because after that she didn't ask any more questions. She repeated her advice—bathe and hydrate, let the water wash it away—and said her goodbyes. I stopped her after she'd opened the door. "Can you come back tomorrow?" I called.

I couldn't see her from my position in the chair, but I felt her hesitation. After a moment she said, "Tomorrow?"

"Yes. Would you, please?"

She said she would. I'm embarrassed by how much I'm looking forward to it. It's evening now, and she was here in the morning, but the effects have not worn off. How nice it is to go a few hours without pain. And tomorrow she will come again.

Let Ugly Be

Jennifer goes to Megan's house for the playdate, despite her prefer-ence for a neutral site. The original plan had been to meet at the fire pole playground, but it's raining, and Megan offered up her home like it was nothing. Jennifer hopes that this playdate doesn't go well. She doesn't want to have to reciprocate.

They are sitting on Megan's couch, the boys doing God-knows-what upstairs, with excited chatter and occasional thunks and thuds. "What do you think that was?" Jennifer asks, for the second time. She's going to have to resist the urge to pose this question every time they make a noise.

Some parents would shrug and say, "Who knows?" Once upon a time Jennifer would have. Megan smiles sympathetically and says in a confiding tone, "I'm not allowed to go see." She settles back into the couch, tucking her legs up beside her carefully, so as not to spill her mug of peppermint tea. "It's my own rule. It's so easy to hover, when you only have one."

Jennifer nods. She, too, is holding a mug of tea, nearly full. Megan handed it to her moments ago, after a prolonged period in which she studied photos in the living room while Megan made the tea in the kitchen, calling out chatty remarks from time to time. Jennifer knew she should go in and offer to help, or at least talk companionably, instead of just calling back, "Oh, really?" through the doorway. But she hadn't been able to resist delaying this full-on conversational engagement. She'd imagined that time spent with Megan would be time spent distracted by the children. She hadn't meant to go to the other woman's house, hadn't realized there would be an upstairs playroom, didn't want to be in this position of intimacy on the couch, blowing on her tea.

"We're having a *lot* of discussions about whether to have another one," Megan says. "Of course being a sociologist I have to read all the studies—pros and cons of being an only child. Sebastian just says, if we want one we should have one. But it's not as simple as *want*, is it? It's about what's best. What's best for Ben, especially. Only children get more attention of course, and there are so many benefits to that, and all the old notions about how they're cripplingly self-centered— well, the studies show those are mostly untrue. But on the other hand siblings are important. I don't want to deprive him of what has the potential to be one of life's most important relationships. And he'll have these old parents, with no one to help him take care of them, no one who really understands what his childhood was like."

"I'm an only child," Jennifer says.

"Oh!" Megan offers a wincing smile. "Did I just suggest you're cripplingly self-centered?"

"No, you said that's untrue."

"Well, you're an excellent resource. Only child with an only child. You know it from both sides."

"I guess so," Jennifer says. In truth Milo is not an only child. Even if she wanted to explain this—which she doesn't—she wouldn't, be- cause she doesn't want to say Zoe's name aloud. She has a supersti- tious feeling that to say her name would conjure her. "I think I agree with . . . Sebastian? It's about whether you want another."

"Sebastian's my husband."

"I figured that."

"I don't plan children with other men." Megan grins. "Actually this whole place is a free-love commune. That's why you came here, right?"

Jennifer doesn't know what to say. She isn't good at banter. She musters an uncertain smile.

Megan sighs. "Really the opposite is true. It's kind of a traditional place. Coats and ties. Nuclear families. Guardian angels."

"Angels?"

"Yes, the Sewanee angels. You tap the roof of your car when you leave the Domain to take your angel with you, then when you go back through the gates you tap the roof again to release it."

"What's the Domain?"

"All the land the university owns. I thought it was a funny name when I got here—so dramatic—but now I don't think twice." She cocks her head. "Is *it* the right pronoun for an angel?"

"I don't know much about angels."

"What did people do before cars? Tap the roof of their carriages? Smack their horse?" Megan touches her lightly on the shoulder. "But I'm making it sound like I don't like it here and I do."

Jennifer nods. She sips her tea and Megan does, too, and now Jennifer really should think of something to say. She comes up with: "What does your husband do?"

"He's a photographer. Weddings and babies, mostly. He has a studio in Chattanooga."

Jennifer points at a framed picture on the side table, Megan with baby Ben. "Did he take that?"

Megan turns to look. "He did. He's so good at portraiture. But he also does art photography. Not so much lately, which is a shame." She jumps to her feet. "Come on, I'll give you a tour."

Sebastian's photos are of city streets—startling in the nature-centric context of Sewanee. They're black-and-white images of urban blight, hand-tinted in incongruous bright colors, an ancient neon sign on a closed-up theater rendered a bright salmon pink, the boarded window below it turned new-leaf green. Megan walks her down a hallway hung with his work, pointing out this and that. Jennifer makes murmuring sounds of interest and praise, but at the end of the tour Megan looks at her with a clear expectation of something more, and asks, "Isn't he good? He was going to stack these in the attic but I insisted we hang them here."

"They're great," Jennifer says, though what does she know about art? She doesn't know if they're good; she's not even sure she likes them. They make a garish beauty of the ugly. Maybe sometimes you should just let ugly be.

"I know," Megan says, studying the one at the end of the hall like she's never seen it before. "He's still taking them, but he doesn't really show me. He says it's just a hobby now." She leads Jennifer back to the living room. Over her shoulder she says, "I think once you're a photographer you never leave your camera at home. Even if you leave your camera at home. You can't help seeing the world in shots. If you don't take the picture when you see it you *abandoned* something."

"Is that something you study?" Jennifer asks.

Megan turns, looking puzzled. "What do you mean?"

"What people's jobs say about them." Why is Jennifer asking for details? As if Megan were someone she's trying to get to know.

Megan gives her a surprised, appreciative smile, like Jennifer's smarter than she thought. "You're right, I talk about that a lot. No, I write about sports and gender, or at least that's the book I'm writing now. My tenure book, I hope. What do you do? I haven't asked."

"I'm a massage therapist."

"Oh!" Megan's eyebrows shoot up with interest. "And what does that say about you?"

"I—"

"Or maybe that's a hard question to answer."

"I'm not good at talking about myself."

"Well, that's a kind of answer," Megan says. "You don't have to talk to give a massage."

"No," Jennifer says. "Though sometimes the client wants to talk."

"Really? Whenever I've gotten a massage I've just tranced out."

"Some people are like that. But some people—" She hesitates, sorry to have turned the conversation toward herself. "Sometimes when you work a knot, you trigger something."

"What do you mean?"

"Emotion lives in the body," Jennifer says. "A sore place can be anger or grief."

"And you can intuit that?"

"Sometimes." She thinks of the moment of contact with Margaret, the resistance under her skin, the longing that pulsed against it. Something about the old lady—her anger? Her grief?—makes Jennifer turn the memory aside.

Megan thrusts her arm out, and Jennifer instinctively steps back. "I'm not trying to hit you!" Megan laughs. "I want to see what you can intuit about me. I'm really sore right here." She runs a finger up and down her right forearm.

"Ah," Jennifer says. "You type too much."

"Is that all?" Megan makes a playful expression of disappointment. "How boring."

Her arm is still out. "I'm not a fortune-teller," Jennifer says. But then she puts her hand on Megan's arm. She presses her thumb along it. "You are really tense here." In fact Megan's tendon is so tight Jennifer's thumb slips off it, and Jennifer senses that the tension there radiates throughout Megan's entire body, as if Megan, who seems so easy with herself, is actually permanently braced against a blow. "Are you stressed about something?"

"Oh," Megan says lightly. "Always." She steps back, pulling her arm from Jennifer's grasp, like she's the one reluctant for intimacy.

But maybe Jennifer misread that reluctance, as five minutes later Megan is relating a morning phone call with her mother, apparently a critical and controlling person who never lets Megan get a word in edgewise. As she talks, Megan gets a sharp edge of anger and frustration in her voice and then, trying to pull back, accuses herself of overreacting, of being too sensitive. "My mother just wants the best for me," she says. "But it would be nice if she found it possible to believe I might be the one who knows what that is."

Jennifer feels a sudden sharp longing for her own mother, for both her parents, her sweet bookish uncritical parents. Before she and Milo came here, they stayed with her parents for months. After the police finally gave up, in a kind of aggressive backing away that made it clear they still didn't believe her, her parents grew cheerful. Her father resumed his habit of singing hits of the seventies—John Denver, Gordon Lightfoot, Cat Stevens—as he tidied up the house. She stopped him one afternoon as he was straightening magazines on the coffee table, in the middle of the chorus of "Sundown." She put a hand on his arm. He turned to look at her, surprised at the touch. They were not a physical family. The love between them was strong, but its expressions were tentative. She said, "Dad."

He looked worried. "Yes?"

"Aren't you ever going to ask me if I did it?"

"Did what?" he asked, though of course he knew, so she didn't answer. She waited. He looked at the magazines in his hand, gave them a final tap, then laid the neatened pile carefully down. He shook his head. She waited for him to say he didn't need to be told she was innocent to know it was true. He said, "No, I'm never going to ask." She could tell by the determined way he said it that he'd come to that decision quite some time ago. He'd decided not to seek the answer, which meant part of him thought it might be yes.

She cried. Her father put his arms around her and she wept against his chest. She might've been a child. All he wanted was to give her comfort. She wondered later if he took her weeping as confession. What it was, really, was heartbreak. Because at that moment she understood—completely, thoroughly understood—that no one in that town, not even her parents, would ever be able to separate her from that question. It didn't matter who she'd been before. Now she was what the answer made her, and since *yes* could never be uttered and *no* could never really be believed, she would forever be the woman who might have. She was the woman whose own daughter thought she could. She imagined the moment—at ten, at twenty—when Milo would want to know whether she killed his father. And she knew she couldn't let him become that. A person who had to ask.

Clues

Today is Tuesday, not that it matters. Today she made her third visit to my house. I don't care about the days of the week anymore, except as they help me know when to go to the doctor and when not to expect the mail. I had an appointment yesterday, which is why she couldn't come then. "You're doing very well, Ms. Riley, considering," Dr. Bell said.

"Considering what?" I snapped, though I knew damn well.

"Your age," Dr. Bell said mildly. She doesn't react, that doctor. She and Jennifer Young must have gone to the same acting school. What a pleasure it would be to really piss somebody off, just to see my existence fully register on someone else's face.

Massage is like a drug, and a heavy dose of it. I can't keep myself present on the table, or fight the rolling fog of calm and goodwill her poking and prodding induces. I didn't really try today, honestly. How often do I get to forget my body? My body is too much with me. "Late and soon," as Wordsworth has it, though of course he's complaining about the world. "Getting and spending, we lay waste our powers," etc. Thanks to Mrs. Smith, my tenth-grade English teacher, I still have that poem memorized. But Wordsworth and I do not agree on our difficulties. The world I can more or less get away from, as I think I've proven, and there's so much of nature around me I'd be hard-pressed to long for more. Sometimes I wish the birds would shut the hell up. It's not the world I can't escape but my body. Not its demands so much at this stage, but its complaints and limitations. Its resistance and its pain.

After today's massage, I came back to myself more quickly than I did after the first two, which I regretted. Perhaps massage, like a drug, is something you get used to. I think she knows, already, that I like her to sit for a few moments afterward, or perhaps this is something she does with all her elderly clients, knowing that part of what they pay for is a little bit of company. It's her routine to give you a glass of water and ask how you're feeling and remind you to take it easy, as though it were even possible for a person my age to take it hard. Today I was determined not to let her leave at the conclusion of all that. In anticipation of my own dazed state, I'd prepared a question that would keep her, and I asked it, feeling pleased that I hadn't let the question slip away when I floated off the table into memory and dream. "What do you think of life here?" That was the question. Not a yes-or-no, you see.

"It's peaceful," she said. "I love living on the water, even if it's just a pond."

"You don't find it boring?" I asked. "Or lonely?"

"Lonely?" She shook her head. "I don't like people," she said. She smiled immediately afterward, as if this were a joke, but it struck me as the truest thing she'd said to me so far.

"What about your little boy?"

"Well, I do like him," she said.

"No, does he like it here? Does he like the woods?"

"The woods? We haven't done a lot of exploring there. We've been to all the playgrounds. I guess I'm warming up to the idea of the woods."

"Are you frightened of them?"

"Frightened?" She has a habit of repeating part of your question. Perhaps this is a way of giving herself time to consider her answer.

She exhaled, wearing a small frown. "Milo's not very careful with his body yet."

"He's too young to value it," I said.

"Yes." She sighed. "I worry about the pond. I lock the doors at night so he can't slip out. But if I could I'd fence it off." She looks out toward my deck, the water beyond it. "Sometimes I think I shouldn't have rented that place."

I was delighted by this confession—not because of its substance, but because it was personal information offered without my asking. I debated whether to ask why, in that case, she'd chosen the house. She is so careful, so guarded. There are locked doors in conversation with her, and no way to tell when you're approaching one. Before I could decide she changed the subject. "But it's a beautiful place," she said. "An easy place to be."

To be what? I wanted to ask. "And you like the house?"

"It's quirky, but we like it."

"I've been curious about it," I said, "living across the pond from it all these years. I knew the woman who lived there before you."

"Oh?"

"Yes, her name was Barbara. We got along. I don't know why we never came to be better friends."

"Mmmm," she said.

I pressed on, perhaps too forcefully. "I've never seen the inside," I said. "Have you changed it much?"

"Not really," she said. "Not yet. We've only been here a month."

I waited a beat, but nothing else was forthcoming—by which I mean, no invitation to tea. "I wish Barbara and I had thought to visit. We just stuck to waving at each other across the water. It does seem a shame."

"But maybe it isn't," she said. "Maybe you liked each other better with the pond between you."

I didn't want to agree with that. There was a silence, and she shifted forward in her chair, a prelude to departure. I still wasn't ready for her to go. "I've lived here twenty years," I said. "Before I retired I was the vice president of a hospital in Nashville."

"Oh?" she asked, politely, holding still.

"I bet you wouldn't have guessed that. People don't assume a woman my age had a career, but I did. I kept on working after the war. I went back to school for my doctorate. I was head of all the nurses at the hospital."

"That's impressive."

"I haven't spent my life teaching Sunday school," I said. "I got a PhD. I published articles. I've slept in a foxhole. I've sat on a hill in the dark and watched the tracer bullets go by. I landed on the beach at Normandy."

"Really?" Now, at last, she looked at me with real interest.

"D-Day plus thirty-eight. Bastille Day—July 14."

"What was it like?"

"What was it like?" I used her trick of repeating the question—not on purpose, but because suddenly I wasn't sure how to answer. Now that I had introduced this topic, what did I want her to know? "It was a mess," I said.

"You must have a lot of stories."

"Of course," I said. "Doesn't everyone?"

"I meant about the war. Everyone doesn't have those."

"No," I said. "Everyone is lucky."

She let a silence lapse before she spoke. "I'm sorry," she said.

"For what?"

"Bringing up a painful topic."

"You didn't. I did." I didn't like her mentioning my pain. "I don't mind telling my war stories. Nobody asks."

"What about your family?"

"I told them some things. I wrote letters home. But all the people who got them are dead."

"There's no one left?"

"One nephew, two grandnieces," I said. "One of them I like."

"No kids?"

I shook my head. "I haven't left much of a record of myself."

What a serious face Jennifer has. She looked at me like this was terrible news. "You should write your stories down."

I didn't know what to say. Why would I do that? Who would I do it for?

After she left, I couldn't concentrate on my book, an old Martha Grimes I'd somehow missed. Though it took considerable, exhausting effort, though even now my right elbow hurts from that effort, I dragged my army trunk out of the guest room closet. It's where I keep all my memorabilia from the war. My souvenirs. I used to have real souvenirs—empty perfume bottles, framed postcards of girls from different regions of France—but I divested myself of all that bric-a-brac long ago. Here's what remains: the letters I sent home to my parents; the frayed, folded map on which I tracked my movements; a photo album I never open because I pressed a flower inside; my scrapbook. I pulled out the scrapbook, which is a heavy, fragile thing these days. It's probably sixteen inches tall, more than a foot wide, with a cover made of fake boards, complete with wood grain. On the front it has a drawing of two mallards in flight, one large in the foreground, one small in the back. Above that are the words *Scrap Book* in an old-fashioned cursive. *Scrap book* used to be two words. Now it's one. So many changes happen without our noticing, without our say-so. The pages are crisp and brown, decorated with menus and postcards and pictures held in place by photo corners, or slipping out of them. All the things I thought worth saving. So brittle now. I turned the creaking pages carefully until I found the first picture of Kay.

These photos are tiny. They're snapshots, "snaps" we called them, from the forties, three-inch-by-two-inch black-and-white rectangles with thick crimped white borders. And my eyes are not what they used to be. So I can't swear by the resemblance. Kay's hair was dark, a rich brown, almost black, not blond like Jennifer's, and she wore it rolled back, pinned, and curled, as was the fashion of the age. Her eyes were dark, too, and mischievous, and she had a sardonic grin, a way of flashing it at you like she knew exactly what you were thinking. These things I remember without the aid of photographs. I'd forgotten how slender she was, how small she looked encased in men's coveralls and a gas mask, how short. When we stand together in a photo I look a good five inches taller, and I was only five six myself, before I started to shrink.

Still, I think it is Kay she reminds me of.

Ghosts

When she's alone at night, that's when Tommy visits her. Or, more precisely, that's when she lets him come. The rule is that she's not allowed to think of him during the day, though this is a rule she sometimes breaks. He's there all the time, leaning against the curtain, insisting she notice him. She can see the outline of his form, and all day she looks away, looks away, looks away, and then at night when the world is stripped bare and the woods are humming she relinquishes effort. She lets the curtain rise. Sometimes he stands there as he was at the end—the eyes never quite focused, the redness in the nose, the hand that shook at ten in the morning. Sometimes he is as he was at the beginning, in their mutual enrapture, in the days of wonderment. Which is worse?

She'd been right, back when she watched him from the corner of her eye, to imagine Tommy was more complicated than he seemed. His easy physicality, his cowboy boots—she'd expected a father in the military, a broad-shouldered sergeant, or a contractor, maybe someone who worked with livestock. But his parents owned the local supermarket and two others in neighboring towns. They both had business degrees. Tommy's house was one of the nicest she'd ever seen, bigger and plusher than her own perfectly nice one, but he almost never had his friends over, preferring to shoot hoops in their cracked driveways, hang out in their cramped untidy basements. Most of his friends had the kind of dad she'd imagined for Tommy, before she met his father, and saw his polite and distracted smile, his glasses and his suit. Tommy's parents didn't want him to work in the summers—they said there was plenty of time for having a job—but he did it anyway. He told her this with indignant pride. He'd been working for a guy who remodeled kitchens since the summer after his freshman year. The guy wanted Tommy to go into partnership with him after he graduated. This, not college, was Tommy's plan.

Tommy could tell you anything you wanted to know about his boss—how in high school he'd been a rodeo bull rider, where he'd met his wife—and he had an equivalent level of knowledge about the janitors at school, the cashiers in his parents' stores. They'd run into the guy in charge of produce and she'd stand there smiling while Tommy talked music, sports, how the produce guy had a kid who was learning to drive, can you believe it? Tommy talked and laughed and she smiled politely. He'd have his arm around her waist. His fingers would brush her skin just below her shirt. His thigh would brush her thigh. She didn't mind standing there while he worked his charm. He was so good at it. She can't pinpoint the moment when her admiration became resentment, though she knows they were married by then. She thought it was sweet that he liked everybody, until it struck her that maybe he just needed everybody to like him. He always had to be the bartender's best friend.

The first time they had sex, she was fifteen. It was right after his father went to have a mole checked, and they told him in six months or less he'd be dead. Even if she hadn't wanted to sleep with Tommy, which she very much did, how better to demonstrate that she was alive and would never leave him? When his father was still at home, Tommy would pick her up and they'd drive around and then they'd park somewhere and he'd take her face in his hands and search it. Then he would kiss her. That was always how it started. She never asked what he was looking for, just succumbed to relief when again and again he found it. Then once his father was in the hospital, she'd hold Tommy's hand during the increasingly awful visits, and then they'd go back to his house, so often empty now, and climb into his bed. Tommy's mother didn't care if she spent the night. Her parents cared but didn't try very hard to stop her.

One night she woke to the sound of Tommy whimpering in his sleep. She put her hand on his head—hot, damp with sweat—and he stirred, then settled without waking. For a moment she was filled with a profound understanding of her purpose. Then came a wave of painful, incomprehensible agitation. She got out of bed and, unsure what was wrong, unsure what to do, went down to the kitchen for a glass of milk. Tommy's mother was sitting at the table, drinking a brown alcohol. It smelled like paint thinner. "Want a drink?" his mother said, then laughed in a sad kind of way.

"I'm getting some milk," Jennifer said. "Is that okay?"

"Is milk okay?" his mother said. "Milk!" She put her face in her hands and laughed again.

Jennifer poured the milk. She wanted very badly to leave but to do so seemed cowardly. So she eased into a chair at the table. It had been a mistake to leave the safety of the bed, and she felt all the panicked regret such a mistake occasioned. If Mrs. Carrasco didn't look up by the time Jennifer counted to one hundred, she'd allow herself to go back to bed, where Tommy would stir and pull her close against him and say in her ear how much he needed her. That was, once again, all she wanted. She got to sixty-five before his mother lowered her hands and leaned in, her expression so intent that Jennifer's discomfort ballooned. She took a quick glance down at her sedate pajamas. There was no open button. There was nothing to see. "I shouldn't be letting you do this," his mother said. "You're so young. It's irresponsible of me."

"No, no—" Jennifer started.

"But I see how you make him feel better," his mother said. "And I can't resist. I'm sorry."

"It's okay," Jennifer said, confused. "All I want is to make him feel better."

"Be careful," his mother said, closing her eyes. "I think you mean that."

Jennifer did mean it. Why wouldn't she mean it?

"Where did he come from?" His mother shook her head and opened her eyes again. "In high school I was such a nerd. How did I produce a boy like him?"

"His father?" Jennifer ventured, because his mother was staring at her like she owed her an answer.

She laughed, a sharp, quick sound. "No. I always thought that's why they don't get along. Tommy's every boy who gave him shit in high school. Every boy who took the girl he liked to the prom."

"Oh," Jennifer said. Tommy always said, "My father doesn't like me," casually, as if it didn't matter, and Jennifer always said, "That's not true, you know that's not true," but maybe it was true. His mother seemed to be saying it was true.

"Who wouldn't rather go with Tommy to the prom? Look at him. I'd rather go with Tommy to the prom. Clearly you know what I mean."

"I love him." Jennifer was torn between indignation and dismay. Did Tommy's mother think that was all he was to her, a good-looking boy? "I love him," she said again.

His mother flopped back in her chair and sighed. "I know you do, honey." Her voice had softened. "And he loves you. He just adores you. You two are so in love it's like looking into the sun. His father says . . ." She shook her head. "But sometimes these things last." She said this as if to herself. Then she seemed to remember Jennifer. She straightened up and gave her a motherly smile. "Go on back to bed now," she said.

Jennifer obeyed, though the whole thing was terribly, excruciatingly weird. She'd just been ordered by her boyfriend's mother to climb back into bed with her boyfriend. She lay there blinking at the ceiling, feeling for the first time that in spending these nights with him she was doing something wrong, feeling for the first time, but not the last, that when it came to Tommy she might not be the best judge of what the right thing was.

He stirred again, and this time she didn't touch him. After a moment, he rolled toward her and pulled her against him, as tight as he could, as tight as possible. He murmured in her ear, "Where'd you go?"

From her vantage point in the future, in a house in the woods, at her own kitchen table, Jennifer looks back and imagines that in that moment she had a prophetic vision. In that moment she understood that Tommy's need for love would be impossible to satisfy. She saw that she'd spend years and years trying to convince him, finally, that he was loved enough, and when that didn't work she'd spend years and years trying not to love him anymore, but the habit would be so deeply ingrained, so *primal*, she wouldn't be able to stop. She would never be able to stop.

Do you, Jennifer, take this man?

She thought when she came up here to the Mountain she'd be without him, truly without him, for the first time in twenty-seven years, as if she could tap the roof of her car to set him free, like the denizens of Sewanee send their angels home. But maybe ghosts are less cooperative.

Her parents tried to separate them once, sending her to New York right after high school to become a dancer, when what they really wanted was for her to go to college. Not that they ever said it was about him, of course. If they disliked him, they never said so to Jennifer, though she could see in the looks they exchanged that they discussed it when she wasn't around.

She was a lyrical jazz dancer, not the best in the world, she knew even then, but she could make people watch her. This was something she could do only when she was dancing, an unconscious ability she didn't know how to control. Her parents put all their hopes on the notion that she still wanted something besides her boyfriend, and off she went to New York City, eighteen years old and knowing no one. It seems like she must have been brave but she doesn't know if she's ever been brave, so she wonders now if it was fear that drove her, the same fear that drove her parents: that her love for Tommy was terrifyingly total, that if she stayed with him she'd never be a separate person.

She signed up for a beginner class with a prominent teacher, and he saw something in her, made her a scholarship student and then part of his company. Who knows what might have happened? What did happen is that she came home for a visit, and Tommy was there at the airport. He dropped to his knees right there at the gate and pulled out a ring. Everybody applauded.

The dance teacher called and asked her to come back, but it was like that possibility already belonged to another life. For a long time after she and Tommy got married, she forgot New York, and the time apart. She remembered being with Tommy like she'd never had a single doubt.

Who would she have been without him? She has wondered this, now, for ten years or more, and she thought when she came up here she'd finally find out. But this is a fantasy. Let go of your hopeful delusions. She'll always be the person Tommy made.

Fairy Tales

This morning I felt restless and impatient, wishing my appointment with Jennifer were at nine instead of three. If I weren't so old I would've paced the room. I was even too restless to read, which is distressing, as without my mysteries what would I do with my time? The one I tried and failed to read today is from a series about a woman park ranger. She is resourceful, this woman, and unable to escape adventure, but I couldn't concentrate on her and all the problems she knows she must solve. I gave up and called one of my grandnieces. The one I like. Her name is Lucy, after my sister, which I can't hold against her. She has told me the name is making a comeback, like many other names from my childhood, though apparently not mine. But when they chose that for her, it seemed old-fashioned. She is an anomalous Lucy, misplaced in time. When she answered the phone I said, "Why don't you pay more attention to me? I have all this money."

She laughed. Not in a mocking way. In a surprised, amused way. A fond way. She always laughs at me, this Lucy. The original Lucy never understood my sense of humor. She never understood my anything.

"Are you offering to pay me for attention?" she asked.

"I'm thinking of changing my will in your favor," I said. This was a lie. I already changed it, years ago, and most of what I have will go to her. Who else would it go to? There isn't anybody else. I left a little something to her parents and her sister but I just don't like those people.

"That's nice," she said. "But I'd rather have you around."

"You don't care if I'm around. You never come see me."

"Margaret," she said. "I have three kids and a full-time job and I live on the other side of the country. The last time we came to visit you couldn't wait for us to leave."

"I don't know why you think that."

"Because you told me! You said, 'I like seeing you, but by the end I can't wait for you to leave.'"

"I didn't say that."

"You did. You said if you were around my son any longer you were going to have to smack him upside the head."

"I don't know why you let him behave the way he does."

She sighed. She said, "I don't know either," which is her way of saying she's not going to discuss how she raises her children with me. Of course she's under no requirement. I'm not her mother, not even her grandmother, and what do I know about disciplining a child? Besides that I remember being disciplined. After she brought it up, I did recall how irritating I found her children the last time they came, especially the little boy. She was patient with both of us, my good Lucy. I told the child to shut up in a restaurant, and she asked me politely not to use that phrase. She waited until the children weren't around. I said her grandmother and I were raised to be seen and not heard, and she said, "That was eighty years ago," and I was stunned into silence by the enormity of that number. The weight of it, the *distance*. There have been so many wars since I was a child.

I shut up, back then, and today. Or at least I changed the subject. "Do you still have that family photo wall?" I asked her.

"Of course," she said. "My collection's not quite complete, though. I'm still missing your grandmother."

"I'll send you some photos," I said, though I have the feeling I've promised her this before and then failed to deliver. She is our family archivist, with a wall in her living room devoted to portraits in black and white. She is the one who might care about the old letters, the diaries, all my little treasures. She listens to my tales of family history with what I think is genuine interest. But still it's not real for her; how can it be? How can she picture my early life in anything but black and white? There I am posed before a tank in shades of gray, when actually there was olive drab, there was blue sky and bursting green, there was bright red blood. And my hair was much darker than it looks in those pictures. There is no record of the exact shade of my hair. "You're lucky," I said to Lucy, "to have your memories preserved in color."

"I love black and white," she said. "Though maybe it makes things seem a little less real."

This is why I like her: she understands what I mean. "They were real," I said.

"I know," she said.

"Any story I told you would just seem like a fairy tale."

"I remember you telling me about getting a permanent in France, the shop windows blown out, and you're sitting there practically in the street, with that machine like snakes coming out of your head. All the MPs stopping to talk to you. That was very vivid."

Oh, she was right. That was what happened. Later I saw one of those MPs and he asked how my hair turned out. I had to take off my helmet to show him, and he said he'd been skeptical when he saw me looking like Medusa under that machine but clearly he was wrong, and we talked in a slightly wistful way about the importance of optimism. I can feel that moment. It's still there. "I didn't know I told you that. I didn't know I'd told you anything about the war."

"You've told me several things."

"Why?"

"I asked!"

"But do you care?"

"Of course," she said.

I could feel her exasperation through the phone. I'm sorry, Lucy, but I have to ask. I have trouble believing you, you see, even though I'd very much like to. Perhaps because of how much I'd like to. "You could come see me without the children."

"I'd love to," she said. "Let me try to figure that out." She said she'd call me soon, and I said all right and let her go. I resisted the urge to say that she better make it snappy because I might die soon. I hope she gives me credit for resisting, though maybe, being so much younger, she doesn't understand how hard it is not to spend all your time thinking about how soon it will end.

Before Jennifer came I moved the scrapbook from my bedroom to the coffee table in the living room. I left it open to a page with a picture of Kay.

When I emerged from the guest room after the massage, Jennifer was standing by the coffee table, tilting her head to look at the pictures. I admit I was pleased to see the success of my little stratagem. She glanced up and flashed a quick smile. "I was just looking at this," she said, as though that weren't perfectly obvious.

"By all means," I said. I made my way over and settled on the couch, patting the cushion beside me so that she came around the table and obediently sat. I pointed at Kay. "This is the one you remind me of." I watched her face intently as she leaned in for a closer look. I don't know exactly what I was hoping to see. She studied the photos closely, like she was memorizing them, and then she asked, "Can we go back to the beginning?"

I was startled by the question. "The beginning of what?"

"The scrapbook. Do you mind if I look at the whole thing?"

"Oh! Not at all." Of course, I was pleased that she wanted to.

The book is held together by a large piece of leather twine, looped through holes and tied in a knot at the front. At the top the twine has broken, leaving a dangling end. There were once hinges on the cover, but two are broken, one missing completely. The book is in danger of complete collapse. The first page is brown—from age? Or was it always brown? I no longer remember—and water-stained and marked at the top right corner $2.75 in some long-dead clerk's neat handwriting. "Two seventy-five!" Jennifer said, touching the number with her fingertip like it was a sacred relic. Then she turned the creaking page.

The next two pages have photos, laid out neatly, held in place with photo corners, labeled underneath in my handwriting—what it used to look like before it took on the shaky, old-lady quality it has now. Six photos to a page. Below the first it says *Probie. September 1938.* "Probie?" she asked.

"That's what you were called in your first year of nursing school. For *probationary*."

"So that's you?"

"That's me," I said. It is me, rendered the size of my thumbnail and dressed like a doll in a long white skirt, my hair slicked to the side, long black stockings and black shoes. All the photos on this page are of me or me and my friends—a row of identically dressed dolls, sitting on the stone steps between the white columns out front of the school.

"You look happy in this one," she said, pointing to the last one on the page, me alone, standing just to the side of one of the columns. I picked up the magnifying glass from the coffee table and my smile swam into view. Why was I smiling? We passed on through pages of doctors and nurses—*Dr. Ted Pollack, Ruth Bratton, Miss Jones (Isolation)*—until a loose envelope appeared, and she picked it up, glancing at me to see if it was okay, and pulled out a card that read *The Graduating Class of the Vanderbilt University School of Nursing request*

the pleasure of your company at a DANCE Saturday evening, May six-
teenth, eight thirty o'clock, Young Christian Women's Association.

"Did you go to this?" she asked.

"Of course," I said, though truthfully I have no memory of that
particular occasion. Now that she was interested I was willing to fab-
ricate to keep her that way.

Next she stopped on a picture of me standing atop a tank, smiling, wearing men's coveralls and a pair of giant goggles on my head.

"Kay took that," I said. Climb up there, she'd said, and when I
looked around hesitantly, Come on. Come on, Maggie Jean. Be a
good soldier and do what you're told.

From England, we crossed the channel to France. "Pretty dress,"
she said, pointing to a picture of me in a frock and Kay in her coveralls, posing in a wheat field.

"Oh!" I said. "That's a funny story. This dress I'd ordered before
I went overseas found me in France. Red silk. Shame it's not a color
photo. It looked so strange against all that olive drab. Too much. Like
Gatsby with his silk shirts."

"But you tried it on."

"I wasn't going to," I said. "It was from my old life. But Kay insisted. Then we all danced around the field while someone sang."

"Kay sounds like fun," she said, and I agreed that she was fun,
rather than explain how inadequate that word is for all Kay was to me
then: friend, sister, fellow traveler, the one who put her arms around
me when I cried, the source of comfort and support. Jennifer turned
a page and then another while I wasn't paying attention, and then I
looked down and saw my first shots of Germany, and I began to find
it harder to breathe. I said, "Are we really going to sit here looking at
this all day?"

She looked startled. She withdrew her hand. "No," she said.

I reached over and shut the scrapbook, keeping my eyes on it so I
wouldn't have to see her face. Did she think I was overcome by sor-

row? In truth I don't know what it was that overcame me. Nothing so simple as sorrow. "I suppose you're going to leave now," I said.

"I can," she said. "Are you tired?"

"I wanted to talk, but we were going too fast. You said you wanted to start at the beginning."

"I—" Two lines appeared between Jennifer's brows. Was that worry or confusion I saw?

"You said I should tell my stories."

She took a breath. The lines deepened. "I thought you wanted to leave a record of yourself."

"I said I hadn't. *Hadn't* is different from *wanted to*." She wasn't looking at me, Miss Jennifer, but in the direction of the door. Well, go on then, I thought. Nothing's keeping you here.

She said quietly, "I still think you should tell your stories."

"Why would I want to?" I demanded.

"I don't know why," she said. "I can just tell that you do."

"I don't have anything to *unburden*," I said. "I don't have anything to *confess*." I'll admit I likely said these things with a rude disdain, but I was unprepared for her to turn suddenly, a striking cat, to utter with some ferocity, "I didn't say you did."

Oh, that was interesting. And frightening, too. I will tell the truth—she'd frightened me. That whip-crack of anger in her voice! The uneasy feeling it gave me must have been what I'm only now putting in words: she is not actually calm. I have been fooled. Her calm is the mask her rage wears. I don't cower, not I, so I said, "You implied it."

She smoothed her mask. "You're right," she said. "I'm sorry."

There was a silence of some length. Finally I said, "Maybe I do want to." I said this somewhat haltingly. Because it was the truth or because it was a lie? Both. Because it was both.

"You don't have to tell me anything," she said wearily. "But I'm happy to listen to whatever you want to tell."

"I will keep that in mind." I'd inadvertently returned to a high-handed tone, and I was sorry, so I added, "I know I said I don't need a companion."

"Right."

"I don't need help to take care of myself."

She nodded.

"But what about this, this *record*? Maybe I need help with this."

"What kind of help?"

"Someone to ask me questions, to help me organize. I forget things now, you know. I get scattered. I might need someone to keep me on course, to write it all down. For my grandniece. For Lucy. She says she's interested in my stories."

She considered. "I could do that. Yes."

"You're willing to be my audience."

"I could do that," she said again.

I want to be alone. I don't want to be alone. My days pop like bubbles. There is no one to remember the things that have happened to me. I said, "I'd pay you, of course."

"No, no," she said. "You wouldn't have to."

I'd like to think she meant that. It would be nice to believe she enjoys my company, that she actually wants to hear the tales of my adventurous youth. "I insist. I couldn't ask you to volunteer. What do you think would be a reasonable rate?" She hesitated. I pressed my advantage. "One hundred dollars an hour?"

Eagerness flashed in her face, but she suppressed it. "No, really," she said.

"Is that not enough?"

"Of course it's enough," she said, an edge in her voice. She softened that edge and added, "It's more than enough."

"All right, then," I said. And then, out of a fear I had betrayed my own eagerness, I said, "I'll want a weekly invoice."

"You'll get one," she said. I heard that edge again. She is trying so hard to be sweet to me, because I'm paying her, because I'm old, but she needn't make the effort for me. I don't require sweetness. As she proved today, people are much more interesting when they have a bit of a bite.

We agreed that she'll come Monday morning. First a massage, then we'll embark on our project. Our oral history.

Unburden, I said. *Confess.* Those are the words I chose.

Please Like Me

It's very expensive to see fish in Chattanooga. Jennifer feels a queasy panic as she shells out the money for aquarium tickets, Megan cheerfully suggesting she pay the $75 more it would take to get a membership. So far Margaret is the only client her flyers have yielded. She's checked a couple of places where she hung them and found only three phone-number strips torn away. She doesn't want to need Margaret, but Margaret's all she's got. One hundred dollars an hour to listen to war stories? Just how much money does Margaret have? Enough to feel entitled to that angry Queen Elizabeth air.

It surprises Jennifer that Margaret can still make her voice that loud, still achieve that high-ranking-officer note of presumed acquiescence. Imagine what it was like to work for her. Those nurses must have stood at attention. She'd rather not think about Margaret, and finds that she keeps doing so anyway, her mind returning to what she feels when she puts her hands on the old lady: anger and grief, yes, and also guilt and loneliness. She can't exactly identify the order in which those emotions appear, like a geologist working through layers of rock. What she does is not as scientific as that. But she does wonder, with Margaret on her table, what that order is, and whether the emotion at the bottom is the root of all the others, or the one Margaret most wishes to conceal. If it's the former, Jennifer would guess guilt. If the latter, loneliness.

"I'm screwed," Megan says as they enter the fluorescent dimness of the fish tanks. She says this cheerfully, too, because that's how she says most everything. She's talking about how behind she is on her grading. It's a Sunday. Tomorrow Jennifer starts listening to Margaret's stories, something she anticipates with a potent mix of curiosity and dread. She feels a little screwed herself. Milo and Ben are a few paces ahead, shouting *whoa!* at the belly of a gliding manta ray. "I have a conference paper, too." Megan groans. "I'm just so screwed!"

"Sebastian's at work?" Jennifer asks.

Megan looks puzzled. "No," she says. "Why?"

"I just assumed."

Megan grasps her meaning. "He had a wedding yesterday," she says. "He really needed time to decompress."

"Oh, okay."

"And I love doing stuff like this with Ben. I love coming here. I'd rather be doing this than writing my paper. Or, God knows, grading."

Jennifer nods. She hasn't yet met this decompressing Sebastian. Sebastian! Who in America, in *Tennessee*, is named Sebastian? Between his name and the sympathetic talk of his artistic exhaustion Jennifer might imagine him tall and wan, pressing the back of his hand to his forehead, but she's seen pictures and knows he's short and well built with large lovely eyes in a squarely handsome face, and strangely incongruous red hair that he's in the process of losing. Watch out for the men with beautiful eyes, she thinks. Take a good long look into those eyes! You will never be enough for all the longing there. Can't you see the inextricability of devotion and betrayal, of sin and apology?

But Jennifer's own history has left her jaded, seeing struggle where likely none exists. Megan's life is attractive and well organized, if you set aside the nagging question of a second child.

Milo pauses in front of the jellyfish and Jennifer stops beside him. Ben runs on ahead, Megan chasing after, calling, "Slow down!" The jellyfish pulse beautifully and stupidly in their tank. "Look, Mom," Milo says.

She doesn't want him to call her Mom. She'd like to stay Mommy a little longer. "Pretty, aren't they," she says.

Megan reappears, holding Ben by the hand. "What's interesting about jellyfish," she says, "is that they look so pretty in here, but if you see them near you in the ocean they just look terrifying." She leans close to the tank. "Painful trumps pretty. Though maybe not always. My brother's dating life is evidence of that."

"What do they do to you?" Milo asks.

"They sting you," Ben tells him importantly. "They sting you *to death*."

Megan laughs. "Not to death." She looks at Jennifer. "Or am I wrong?"

"I don't know," Jennifer says. She turns to Ben. "I've been stung and I'm not dead."

Ben looks her up and down. "Where'd they sting you?"

"On my leg," she says. "Swimming in the ocean."

"Did you cry?" Milo asks.

"Oh yeah," Jennifer says. "It hurt."

"I *hate* jellyfish," Milo says angrily. "Jellyfish are *jackass*." He turns away in high dudgeon and marches over to the octopus.

"He said *jackass*," Ben says gleefully, and then skips after Milo. "Milo, you said *jackass*!"

"Slow down," Megan calls, as Jennifer says, "Sorry." Megan makes a no-worries face and follows the boys. Jennifer lingers a moment, watching the jellyfish contract and expand, oblivious of the world's opinions. She likes to watch them drifting, glowing under the tank lights. They know nothing of danger. They have no curiosity at all.

Milo says, "Mommy," and Jennifer, startled, looks down to see him watching her from a few feet away, hands on hips and a scolding expression on his face. "You have to stay with the group."

"You're right," she says. "I'm sorry."

"We don't want to lose you," he says, and she presses her lips together so she won't laugh. The preschool recently took a field trip to a nature center, which is, she assumes, where he got this language. "Come on," he says, still in his chiding grown-up voice, and then turns and sprints off, abruptly a child again, nearly knocking over a woman to whom Jennifer has to apologize.

She catches up to them by a large tank housing a swarming school of silver fish. They flash. They flit. They go this way, then that. Both boys stand with their little hands against the glass, opening and closing their mouths, glub glub, and giggling at each other. Megan says, "They're lovely, aren't they," with a weird longing in her voice, and Jennifer makes a noncommittal sound, not because she doesn't agree but because, these days, not committing is her habit.

Milo turns to Megan suddenly, his sweet little face as severe as a frown can make it, and says in the deep voice he uses when he's being serious or confessional, "My dad went fishing."

Jennifer goes hot, then cold. She wants to retort, *No, he didn't,* but she bites her tongue. For a moment she's uncertain—did Tommy like to fish? She has no memory of that. Is it possible Milo remembers something she doesn't? Is it possible Milo remembers?

Megan gives her a searching look, hovering on the edge of apologetic. "He was just telling us some things about his dad."

Jennifer tries to smile, but she can feel that the smile is a stricken, frozen one. "Like what?"

"Oh . . ." Megan is visibly nervous. "Just, you know. He drove a pickup truck."

"He did!" Milo insists hotly, as if someone's disputing it.

Jennifer puts her hand on his head. "Yes, he did," she says, trying to sound soothing. "You're right, honey." But how does he remember that? How does he know? Zoe took the truck, and Milo hasn't seen it or Zoe in more than a year. He does not remember Zoe. He doesn't even remember his own last name.

"He built things," Milo adds, like this is proof.

"That's right." Jennifer looks at Megan and says, "He did wood-work. Built-in bookshelves. Cabinets."

"I know," Milo says.

"Yes," Jennifer says. "I guess you remember." But he doesn't, he doesn't, he doesn't. He doesn't remember. That is the foundation on which this life is built.

Ben pulls back from the fish and takes off, and Milo's face lights up with excitement, Tommy abruptly discarded. He swings one arm back, like a pitcher winding up, and launches himself into pursuit. "Boys!" Megan calls. Then she sneaks a look at Jennifer, hesitates. "Is your husband . . ."

"Dead?" Jennifer says. "Yes, he's dead."

"I'm sorry," Megan says. "I didn't know. I'd assumed you were divorced."

"It's okay," Jennifer says. "It's been a couple years. Whatever Milo says, he doesn't really remember him. He was only two when Tommy died."

She can see Megan considering whether to ask another question. She thinks for a wild moment about telling Megan the story about Tommy. All of it. How they'd started out so much in love, and how things had slowly gone wrong, and how she'd tried, she'd tried, she'd tried. How whenever she resolved to leave Tommy she'd succumb to sorrow and nostalgia, yes, but mostly she could just never resist her stupid, primal attraction to him, and one of those times they'd conceived Milo. How things had gotten better for a while, because Tommy took such good care of her while she was pregnant, and then was so good with the baby. What went wrong after that. If she told Megan all of it, all of it, would she understand? Would she still be her friend? Who in the world will still want you, once they know ev-erything you have to tell?

Jennifer says, "We'd better go after them," and Megan obligingly drops the subject. She calls, "Boys!" again, and breaks into a light jog.

Jennifer stands there. She just needs a second. Just a second, and then she'll be fine. She puts her hand against the glass, and the fish flee from it. She parts and scatters them with her terrifying hand. Because she is the bad guy. She *is* the bad guy, of course. Even if Megan imagines differently, she is not the tragic figure. Tommy is. Tommy always was. Nobody saw the tragedy in being the practical one. He was the one who fell painfully short of his potential, the one who, even as he let his business flounder and drank too much and showed up late, continued to be thought of as a *really great guy*. And he was a really great guy. He'd never changed. He still felt things deeply and struggled not to show it, and he still lost that struggle, and rewarded your comforting charms with an irresistible outpouring of emotional truth. He still drank so much you worried about him, but held his liquor well enough to escape pity or scorn. He could still charm. He could still treat all his mistakes like the inevitable result of his own sad-fuckup nature, his bad choices beyond help and therefore beyond judgment. He was still sweet. He still looked at her like she was the only thing in the world.

And other people saw that, the way he looked at her and all those other things. And so she was the villain. She was the one who didn't laugh at his joke, or who looked pained when he gave in to the call to stay for another. She was the one who wanted to leave the party; he was the one who kept it going. The one who wants to leave the party is never the favored one. People thought she didn't know how good she had it. People thought she was mean. No one ever said that directly, of course. Instead, if she complained, their responses started with "at least" or "come on." Come on, he's so sweet. At least he's still into you. Come on, you're so lucky. At least he's hot. Once a close friend had said, "Well, you know, you're always mad at him—you're probably not the easiest person to live with." Even her friends liked him better. They might not have, if she'd told them about the affairs, but she couldn't bring herself to tell, because that would expose her weakness as well as his.

The third—or fourth?—time she found out that Tommy had slept with another woman, he'd left his email open on their shared desktop—something he never did—and curiosity had made her read it. It was curiosity of the kind that comes with a shiver of nausea, because you know you don't want to know what you're about to find out. She printed the email out, as calm as a secretary. When he got home that night—late, he'd had drinks after work, of course he had—she was sitting at the dining room table waiting with the email in front of her. He said, "Hey, babe," and bent to offer her a kiss that was sharp with whiskey, and she pushed the email over so he could read it. "What the fuck, Tommy," she said. "What the *fuck*." It was all she could think of to say, so she kept saying it, a hundred times, slamming down the word that described both her outrage and the thing he'd done. She went around the house saying it, picking up his things and throwing them, while he followed, alternately pleading and shouting at her to stop. Finally he grabbed her hands, and she threw him off with such force that he stumbled backward, and she took a step in his direction and hit him as hard as she could in the face.

"Stop it!" Zoe screamed. She was eleven, or twelve. She was supposed to be in bed, but she'd come downstairs, and they hadn't seen her. Before her guilt rushed in, Jennifer felt a flash of anger toward Zoe, her daddy's girl of a daughter, who couldn't even allow her the fleeting triumph of hitting him, the satisfying pain of their failures colliding.

"It's okay," Tommy said to Zoe, who had her arms around him, who was trembling, who glared at her mother like she wanted to do her harm. "It's okay, honey. I deserved it."

"Oh God," Jennifer said. She was moving toward the garage door before she knew her own intent. "Can't you let me have *anything*?"

Tommy followed her into the garage. She wrenched the car door open. "What do you mean?" he said as she slammed it shut. He rapped on the window, the garage door slowly opening at her back.

She could hear him through the glass. "What do you want me to let you have? Whatever it is you can have it."

She rolled the window down. "I'm tired of forgiving you," she said. "Just once I want to be the one in the wrong." She threw the car in reverse and he stepped away, then followed the car as she backed down the driveway. Zoe stood behind him, framed in the doorway to the house, crying, calling, "Daddy, Daddy, Daddy, come back," as her mother drove away.

They were right, the people who talked about her. He did love her. She *was* always mad at him. She was mean. Time after time a sharp word from her left him quiet and wounded, looking at her with his sorrowful eyes. In those moments she was almost on the side of the people who disliked her for wounding him, and her dislike of herself was one of the many things she'd held against him.

Zoe's preference for him—that was another one. She'd loved her father—who so openly admired her brains and beauty, who told her about problems at work and listened seriously to her advice, who engaged her in long, confessional discussions of his troubled childhood and her romantic travails—much more than her matter-of-fact mother, who bought her shoes and got her to school on time. It wasn't just Jennifer's opinion that Zoe had loved Tommy more. Zoe herself frequently said that. Even before Tommy died Zoe had treated her like an evil stepmother whose only purpose in the story was to cause misery.

If Zoe had known about the affairs, she might not have cared. Maybe no one would have cared, would have cut Jennifer slack for her sharp tongue in the face of Tommy's charm. It occurs to her now that she's been telling herself a comforting lie, assuming people didn't know. Everybody in town knew him. If they weren't his friend, they wanted to be. Once she'd tracked him down in a bar and asked a bartender to stop serving him, and the woman had said, "I'm not cutting off Tommy Carrasco."

She had developed a stoic nonreaction to all such commentary, but that night she learned its limits. At the bartender's defiant defense of the man Jennifer had to live with—the man whose boozy three a.m. entrance would interrupt her sleep, the man whose bleary hangover would keep him from doing the school run in the morning, the man whose devotion to her never stopped him from letting her down—she cracked wide open. All the ugliness rushed out. "I hope you have a head-on!" she screamed at him.

That story got told a lot, later.

But what about the time he'd taken her dancing on her thirty-fifth birthday, and they'd stayed out on the floor all night, swaying, her head on his shoulder, her palm pressed to his chest so she could feel his heartbeat and know by its steady rhythm that it was as much hers as ever, and then at some point he stopped moving and lifted her head and held her face in both hands like he'd done from the beginning of time and said, "I'm so lucky," and then he kissed her until some drunk buddy poked them, laughing, and said, "You guys are horny as teenagers"? What about that? That was a story no one wanted to tell.

In her commitment to Sebastian's decompression, Megan has planned a whole day in Chattanooga, and so after the aquarium they walk the pedestrian bridge over the river, the boys exclaiming at the many webs shimmering between the slats of the railing, half-faking terror at the fat spiders. Jennifer's interest is in the shiny, snaking river, the way it glistens in the bridge's gaps. Just right there. Just below. Sometimes when she leans over the edge of things it's hard not to feel how it would be to fall. The rush and whoosh. But no collision, no splash. As if she'd disappear before she landed. Megan has kept up a nonstop chatter, building a wall of talk between now and the mention of Tommy. Megan tries to fix things. She tries to make you feel better. She tries to erase what has been. On the other side of the bridge, in an ice cream place called Clumpies, Jennifer sits studying the T-shirts for sale—would you want to wear a T-shirt over your breasts that said *Clumpies?*—and waits for Milo and Ben to finish their cups of animal cracker ice cream and for Megan to stop talking. Just. Stop. Talking.

"Do you think we've been gone long enough?" Jennifer asks abruptly. Rudely. She is sorry when she sees the insult register on Megan's face. None of this is Megan's fault—that Jennifer broke her own rule about Tommy, that Milo was the one who caused her to break it. That Megan believes things can be fixed, while Jennifer believes all you can do is flee the rubble, the survivor's aftermath. "I just mean, do we still have time to go to the park?"

"Park, park, park!" Ben chants, and Milo joins him. "Park, park, park!"

Megan smiles fondly at them, while over her shoulder Jennifer spots a young couple frowning in that can't-those-women-control-their-children way. "I think we have time," Megan says happily, willingly accepting the fiction that Jennifer wasn't being a bitch. Wasn't saying she wanted this outing over. Wasn't saying, *Do you think we've done enough? Do you think your asshole husband is satisfied now?*

Megan gets up, herding the boys to the bathroom to wash their hands, and when Jennifer starts to rise and Megan shakes her head and says, "I've got it," offering her a please-like-me smile, all Jennifer can think about is Megan's sweetness, Megan's desire to please, Megan's fervent wish to *get along*, and what a shame it is to waste all that on her. But Jennifer needs to be the kind of person who makes friends, doesn't she? For Milo's sake. Because otherwise she's not far removed from the prickly isolation of Margaret. Look at how she just snapped at Megan. Without Milo, she'd be a younger version, rude and suspicious, alone.

Margaret obviously wanted to show her that scrapbook—but then the agitated urgency with which she slammed it shut! Like the rest of that book was a locked room in a fairy tale, a box that should never be opened. Whatever you do, don't go in there. Jennifer has been so focused on her own secrets for so long that she'd nearly forgotten other people have them, too. It's been quite some time since she allowed herself curiosity. If curiosity is back, what else might return?

Megan emerges from the bathroom, guiding the boys toward the table, and when she sees Jennifer watching she flashes her a terrifyingly genuine smile. Jennifer smiles back. The expression can precede the emotion and still get you to the same result. Smiling can conjure happiness. Studies have shown.

Lucky You

Jennifer came prepared for our interview today with a tape recorder and a notebook to boot. When I emerged after the massage, I found her waiting in a chair she'd pulled close to my armchair, the tape recorder on the side table. She'd moved another small table close, too, and laid the scrapbook on it. She sprang up when she saw me and put her notebook and pen down in her chair. "Could you get me some water?" I asked, and she went to obey. I stood with my hand on the back of her chair, looking down at her notebook. There were already words in it. I couldn't make out what they said, but I assumed they were questions. I felt a little wobbly. I thought perhaps I should have had the massage after the interview, so as not to be softened up. Because I have no intention of *unburdening*. I'm not going to tell her the story. Of course I'm not.

She came back from the kitchen and moved past her chair to set the water glass on my table. Then she rounded her chair again, coming toward me with hand extended. "What are you doing?" I said.

"I thought you might need help sitting down."

"Oh. Yes. Thank you." She took my arm and we shuffled around to my chair and then she helped ease me into it. "Sometimes it's odd having you here," I said. "I'm not used to this. Other people. Human contact."

"I think we both like being alone." She was turned away from me, picking up her notebook. I couldn't quite see her face. I couldn't quite make out her tone.

"Is that a good trait? Or a bad one?"

"I don't know." She sat. "What do you think?"

"I've spent most of my life alone," I said.

"But you like that."

"Yes."

"So lucky you," she said. "Maybe you should be glad."

She'd surprised me again. Sue at the library would have said, *But you're not alone, Miss Margaret. You have me*, with a face that exuded pity, and a desire to pat my hand. How many people would say I should be glad? Jennifer is a cave with a rock that blocks the entrance. What are the words that mean "open sesame"? I've never had a gift for them, the right words. This is perhaps obvious by now. What comes out of my mouth is too direct, too undisguised, and then the other person is startled, and I'm annoyed, or shamed, and after that the best thing is silence. For a long time I chose silence. I chose my solitude, even if now I grow restless in its echo chamber. I chose it. I would not call it luck.

She reached over and pressed the button on the tape recorder. She flipped to a fresh page and readied her pen.

I asked, "Are you divorced?"

"What?" She looked up quickly.

"You said I was lucky to be alone," I said. "I thought perhaps you were thinking of an ex-husband."

"Oh," she said. "I was."

"You've never mentioned a husband."

"No." And then she said, "Neither have you."

"Me?" I laughed in a startled way. "I never had a husband to mention."

"No?"

"I had romances." For some reason it seemed important that she know this. "I wanted to get married. I wanted children. It just never happened."

"In the war?"

"What?"

"You had romances in the war?" She wrote something down. What could she possibly have written down?

"In the war, before the war, after the war." I wanted to laugh again, like a belle of the ball, but I couldn't quite manage it. "There was a boy named Lloyd, for instance. Lloyd Kerr."

"Lloyd Kerr," she repeated, writing it down.

"Let the record show," I said, "that there was a boy named Lloyd Kerr."

She looked at me, pen poised. She has patience, that one. She could sit beside you in a foxhole and bide her time.

"I met him in basic training."

"Where you met Kay."

"That's right, Fort Bragg." I frowned.

She waited. "You could tell me about meeting Kay."

"He took me to dances," I said. "Lloyd Kerr. He squired me around. We were all very popular, you know. Not much on offer in the way of girls."

"So you dated other boys, too?"

"Oh, yes. But Lloyd Kerr is the one I remember, because he found me again overseas. He popped up out of nowhere. That happened sometimes. Once I passed another soldier I knew in a jeep; he was going one way, I was going the other. We waved. I hadn't seen him in months and months."

"But that wasn't Lloyd."

"No, Lloyd just appeared one day. Somehow he knew where I was. This was in France. He took me to see a movie in an old château we'd taken back from the Germans. *Casanova Brown*—a silly romance with Gary Cooper and Teresa Wright. They put up a screen in the entry hall. And sitting on the marble floor watching that silly movie were hundreds of dirty unshaven GIs with guns in their hands. Topsy-turvy."

"What happened to him?" Jennifer asked.

"He was in the infantry," I said. "Somebody shot him."

"I'm sorry."

"Sorry?" I repeated. I looked at her. Was she sorry? People always say that. They say it automatically. "How I found out was, the sergeant handed me a letter at mail call, and it was one I'd written to Lloyd, and across the address there was a red stamp that said *deceased*. All in capital letters. *DECEASED*." I leaned toward her. "Here's a little confession for you," I said, "since you seem to want one. I used to tell people about Lloyd, because people thought I was strange for never marrying, and so he was my excuse. My beau who died. My tragic romance. I'd say I was in love with him, but I don't even know if that was true. Poor old Lloyd."

She looked at me, so serious, a line deepening in her forehead. Was that an expression of judgment or concern? "I don't blame you for that," she said.

I sat back in my chair. "Well, I opened my letter and read it. I'd written the usual prattle: *These cigarettes are horrible – but I am slowly learning to drink beer – Our food is pretty good.* What a ninny I was. When I wrote it he was probably already dead. You know what I think about sometimes? All the things he never had any idea about, because they happened after he died. He never saw a television. He never heard of the Internet, or an iPod. He couldn't have imagined an iPod. He never even heard of Elvis! He didn't know we'd win. He didn't know that war wouldn't be the last. He didn't know about Korea. Vietnam. The Gulf War. Iraq. Could he have imagined 9/11?"

"I don't know," she said.

"That's a disappointing answer."

"I'm sorry," she said. "I don't know what you want me to say."

"Well, someone shot him dead and after that nothing mattered. That was that for poor old Lloyd."

"I'm sorry," she said again.

"Stop apologizing. It doesn't matter now." I felt angry. "If he'd lived I might have married him and had a passel of brats and a dog. Who wants that happy ending?"

"A lot of people."

"It's bullshit."

"Yes," she said. "I know."

"I don't know what else to tell you," I said. "I don't know why we're doing this. I don't know what it is you want to know."

"You told me you wanted to leave a record," she said, keeping her temper when I was doing my best to make her lose it.

"But you must want to know something, or you're only listening for the money, and then I don't want to do it, Jennifer. I won't pay for attention. I won't. I told you I won't. Tell me that there's something you want to know or this little project is over, and you can kiss your one hundred dollars an hour goodbye."

"Okay," she said evenly. "Tell me about Kay."

I felt myself flinch. "You need that money, don't you?"

Jennifer looked at me a long moment and then she sighed, sinking back against the chair. "This is too upsetting for you, Margaret," she said. "It was a bad idea."

"No," I said. "It wasn't."

"I should go."

"No, no, don't do that. I'm sorry. Really. I'm old and cantankerous. I told you I'm not used to people. I'm sorry. I'll tell you a story about Kay."

"You don't have to."

"I want to," I said. "Really. I have a story I want to tell. I'd like someone else to know it. Write it down. Come on." I waved my hand at her notebook. "Write it down."

So she did.

• • •

In Germany, when we arrived in a new town, the boys would choose a house and go in and tell the people to vacate, and just like that the place would be ours. In Zietz I stood outside a house next to Kay with my bedroll at my feet and my hands in my pockets and stared at the sky while I waited for the owners to leave, thinking, *Hurry the hell up,* not much caring, when they finally came out, that they glared at us as they went by. The man kept showing everybody a letter that said he was a member of the Christian Science Church in Boston. He said, "You're in a Christian home."

Don't steal my stuff seemed to be his point, or anyway that's what I thought at the time. Whatever his point, it was a strange thing to say, although I guess there's no appropriate etiquette for addressing the people who turn you out of your home so they can sleep there. Kay and I moved into a dining room with a balcony. When I got up in the morning Kay was gone, and I went out on the balcony and spotted her wandering the garden, touching the flowers like she'd never seen one before. As I watched she glanced around like the owner might have spies, picked a flower, and then put it in her hair.

"Not exactly standard issue," I called down, and she jumped, looked up at me, laughed.

"Everything's in bloom," she said. "Come see."

I went downstairs and out the door and let her lead me around the garden and tell me the flowers' names. At that time I didn't know much about gardening, so when she told me what the flowers were called, I said, "Red one, purple one, blue one," and she laughed again.

"Red would suit you," she said, looking around as though we were in a hat store. She put a finger to her mouth, considered me. "Yes, red." She reached beside me and plucked a large red flower, one that had bloomed long enough to look as though it had flung itself open, one right at the moment when beauty is heightened by the knowledge that it's about to fade. I was wearing my hair in two braids at that point, pinned at the back, and she tucked the stem of the flower under one of them. "Beautiful. You're beautiful," she said.

As you might imagine, Jennifer, I saw a lot of bad things in Germany. But I wish you could see—not against all that, but existing at the same time, cupped in the palm of my hand—a German garden in the spring, and Marilyn Kay with a flower in her hair, her face open as a rose and shining in the light.

The Lonely Woods

Megan wears a smile of conspiratorial delight, in her hands plates bearing an array of sweet things: pie, cookies, chocolate torte. She approaches the table by the window where Jennifer waits, and the sunlight coming in plays peekaboo with her face, now you see her, now you don't. "Can you believe all this?" Megan asks, clattering the plates onto the table. "The girl gave me the wrong things, and when I told her said just keep it, and gave me the right things, too." She slides into her chair. "It's like that Monopoly card. Bank mistake in your favor. Wasn't that it?"

"I think so," Jennifer says, though she remembers it being bank *error*.

"Bakery mistake in your favor," Megan says. "We should wait until after the food." But then she picks up a fork and takes a bite of the torte anyway. "Oh my God this is good," she says, on her face an expression of such sensual delight that Jennifer feels the moment might be too private to witness. "I never get to eat dessert," Megan says. "But I have *such* a sweet tooth."

Don't think about it, Jennifer tells herself. Don't ask what she means when she says she never gets to eat it. Don't assume it means Sebastian tells her to watch her weight. Don't suspect everyone is secretly unhappy. Don't be sad.

After her morning with Margaret, Jennifer went home and cried. It's so exhausting to be with her: the relentless niceness in the face of Margaret's prickly need, the struggle not to react to Margaret's efforts to provoke. Perhaps Margaret doesn't really exist. That house in the woods, only Jennifer can see it. It's a dream she's wandered into, a spell sent to punish her. She can almost believe this. Except Sue the librarian, a solidly real person, is the one who first told Jennifer Margaret's name. Margaret watches her too fiercely. Margaret pays too much attention to everything she says. Margaret talks, and somehow Jennifer feels as if she's the one being exposed.

She didn't allow herself much time for tears. She washed her face and practiced smiling and came to meet Megan for lunch. This is their first outing without the boys. Megan suggested it yesterday. It would give them a chance to talk, she said. That's fine with Jennifer, as long as Megan does most of the talking.

Megan takes a substantial bite of the key lime, smiles at Jennifer as it hits her tongue, and then closes her eyes with pleasure. Jennifer looks away just as a college-age boy stops beside their table, a boy with the wild curly hair and lumberjack beard many of the students sport, rich kids pretending to be mountain men. "Professor Summerfield?" he says, and Megan's eyes pop open. She reaches for her iced tea, washing down the rest of the bite. "Adam," she says. "How are you?"

"Good, good," he says. "How are you?"

"Doing well, thanks," Megan says.

The boy gives her a mischievous grin. "Looked like you were enjoying that pie."

Megan laughs like she's taking the comment in stride, but the slow flush that creeps up her neck betrays her. "It's delicious," she says. "You should order some."

"Well, I'm not much for key lime," he says, "but if you say it's good it must be true."

Megan inclines her head and smiles in both recognition and deflection of the compliment. "Are you having a good semester?"

"I am," the boy says, and launches into an eager, animated description of the fascinations of the philosophy class he's taking. He moves closer and closer to Megan as he's talking, until he's leaning against the table, and Jennifer notes with surprise that he seems to think he has a chance. She glances at Megan's face, her wide-eyed attentiveness, her mobile mouth, and wonders how often Megan's willingness to listen is mistaken for something more. Or is Jennifer the one making the mistake? Maybe this Adam does have a chance. She reminds herself that she doesn't really know Megan, and even if she did, she wouldn't know for sure, unless Megan said to her: *I am fucking that boy.* Even if Megan said, *I am not fucking that boy*, there would always be a chance it was a lie, or would become one.

"Okay, then," the boy says. He gives the table a light slap as he straightens, like it's a mount that's pleased him. "I'll see you soon, I hope."

"See you," Megan says. She smiles, smiles, smiles, but as soon as the door has dinged his departure she collapses back into her seat with a sigh. "Oh boy," she says.

"He has a crush on you," Jennifer says, and to her surprise Megan groans, "I know."

"He's cute."

Megan laughs. "Maybe somewhere," she says. "Under all that hair."

"Does that happen a lot?" Jennifer asks. "Crushes?"

"Not really. Or if it does I don't know about it. I can tell with him because—he didn't do it this time, but usually—he leads around to personal questions, like what do I like to do on the weekends, and as soon as I mention Sebastian he looks a little stricken. It's exhausting talking to him, trying to be nice without being at all encouraging."

"I can imagine."

"He's a sweet kid. Bright. But . . ." She blows out air like a horse. "I guess I had crushes on professors, even just intellectual ones. But I went to much bigger schools. I didn't have the same kind of access. I didn't run into them having lunch."

"I didn't go to college," Jennifer says.

"Oh!" Megan says, clearly shocked, and then to cover her shock she returns quickly to the topic. "Sometimes I get tired of being so recognizable. I long for the anonymity of a big state school. I'd like to be able to swim at the rec center without encountering a student in my bathing suit. I feel like I'm under constant surveillance. And anything could be used against you. *Professor Summerfield was buying prunes! Oh my God, do you think she's constipated?* I don't want them sitting in my class thinking about how I'm constipated." She sighs, then adds, "I'm not constipated."

"Okay," Jennifer says.

"I buy the prunes for Ben. He has issues sometimes." She rolls her eyes at herself. "Not that you needed to know that."

Jennifer could tell Megan a thing or two on the subject of surveillance. Furtive glances, open hostile stares. The time a woman came up to her in the grocery store, Milo a toddler kicking his heels in the basket, and said—loudly, like she wanted the whole store to hear her—"Someone ought to take that child away from you." Milo's face transformed into the look of betrayed astonishment he wore when he got a shot, and Jennifer wanted to round on that woman, wanted to grab the can of tomatoes from her cart and bash in her head. She walked away, whispering to Milo, "Don't worry, sweetie, she's a crazy lady," while behind her the woman called, "It's shameful that you still have that child. Shameful, shameful, shameful. Imagine what you're doing to him!"

What about what this woman was doing to him? That didn't seem to matter. Milo has recently learned the word *hypocrite*, and now he's trying out the concept. He asks Jennifer: Is my teacher a hypocrite? Is the president a hypocrite? Is Batman a hypocrite? "I don't think so, honey," Jennifer answers again and again, but what she really wants to say, is *Yes, yes, yes. They are all hypocrites. There is not a soul who isn't.*

"What about you?" Megan asks. "Do you go in the post office

and run into a client? And suddenly they're, I don't know, asking you about the kink in their neck?"

"Um," Jennifer says as the girl at the food counter calls first Megan's name, then hers. Megan starts to rise but Jennifer waves her down. "I'll get them both," she says. Picking up the plates, she lets out a slow breath, banishing the memory of the grocery store woman, for which Megan is not to blame.

When Jennifer sets down the food, Megan looks at her like she's decided something. "You and I should plan an outing," she says.

"An outing?" Jennifer repeats.

"Just get away for a day. Or maybe even a weekend. Farther away than Nashville. Have you been to Atlanta?"

"Funny to think of getting away from the getaway."

Megan sighs extravagantly. "Sometimes you just have to get the fuck off this mountain," she says. "Breathe some less rarefied air. Let's go somewhere no one will recognize us."

Jennifer thinks: I already did.

"Where would you want to go?" Megan asks.

"I don't think I could go anywhere," Jennifer says. "I don't have a sitter."

"Oh, of course." Megan produces another of her slow flushes, a blotchy red creeping up her neck. The places the flush doesn't touch are weirdly fascinating—like someone's pressed their fingers hard against her throat. Why is she so embarrassed? It's not as if Jennifer forgets she's a single parent unless Megan points it out.

Jennifer crunches a bite of salad. She's surprised by even this hint of dissatisfaction from Megan—*get the fuck off this mountain*. Should she ask if something's wrong? What if Megan says yes? Yes, something is terribly wrong. Sebastian screams at her and locks himself in the bedroom for hours, Megan sobbing outside the door; Sebastian beds the women of Chattanooga in his photography studio, posing them this way and that. Megan, though—she gets her own back, all her adoring students, those pretty pretty boys. From what she knows of Megan so far, this last notion seems so outlandish that it might as well be impossible, like alien life or time travel, like Megan growing a second head, or Megan's friend being a murderer. "Did I tell you about Margaret?" she asks abruptly. "My client?"

Megan cocks her head. "I don't think so."

"She's ninety, and she's a World War Two vet."

"Really! How interesting."

"She was a nurse, near the front lines. I'm doing massage for her, but also she's asked me to . . . help her with her memoir, I guess."

"About the war?"

Jennifer nods. "We started this morning—she told me a story, I took notes. But I think it's going to be difficult. She wants to talk about it, but then she doesn't."

"What do you think that's about?"

"I don't know, the stuff you see in a war."

"The people she lost."

"Right."

Megan reaches over her salad for more pie. "Maybe there were patients she thinks she should have saved."

"That could be."

"Everyone who goes to war must have those kinds of regrets."

Jennifer takes another bite of salad. I had an affair once, she thinks. She thinks it at Megan, but clearly neither is telepathic because Megan just takes another bite of pie. He was one of my clients. Megan! Can you hear me? Megan!

"Oh my God, this is so good," Megan says. "I can't believe you're not eating this."

"I will, after my salad."

"If there's any left." Megan rolls her eyes at herself. "I have the willpower of a flea."

The man, the other man, was a regular, someone she thought about mostly, preaffair, as her Tuesday at nine a.m. He spent his weekends and any other time he could get on a bicycle, and the massages were part of his whole cycling lifestyle, along with his shaved calves and the spandex she assumed he wore.

"That's why I can't have dessert in the house," Megan says. "I eat it without even knowing it. I'm at home grading papers and then suddenly I'm in the kitchen with Oreos stuffed in my cheeks."

"So what?" Jennifer says. "You look great. You're so skinny."

"Constant effort, my friend." She sighs. "Back to the salad." She playacts an unwilling, listless bite. "Mmm," she says. "Delicious."

One Monday afternoon her client called with a weird tension in his voice and said, "I have to cancel our appointment."

"Do you want to reschedule?" Jennifer asked, already reaching for a pen.

"What I mean is I can't see you anymore."

"Oh." They were both silent, and she considered the quality of the silence, debating whether to ask. "Is something wrong?"

"The truth is," he said, "I'm too attracted to you."

That was his reason! She was taken aback. She said she understood, but she didn't. It wasn't like this happened every day. She was an under-the-radar person, that was who she was, which was one of the reasons why Tommy had happened in her life like a helicopter landing in a field, why even now she couldn't bring herself to relinquish his attention.

The next day she went to the client's house at the agreed-upon time and found him home. He looked so purely astonished to see her that she was unnerved. "But I canceled," he said.

She summoned her resolve. "I know," she said.

He was eight years younger than she was and seemed younger still, she assumed because he had no children. He was a grant writer at a small science and technology company. Something to do with mechanical arms. He told her a story once about research on monkeys, monkeys controlling the arms directly from their brains. When she pictured this, she saw a row of monkeys concentrating hard on a row of robot arms, wearing on their temples those electrode things you always see on sci-fi television.

She didn't ask him many questions about his job. Honestly, she wasn't that interested. She wasn't interested in his life before her, in his family grievances or his painful breakups or what was the weirdest sexual thing he'd ever done. She felt a painful embarrassment when he brought up these topics, as if she were thirteen and a parent had just made a dumb joke in public. She liked his body—he was tall and skinny, very different from Tommy, who was all lean slouchy muscles, even now. Sex with him was pleasant and effective. Afterward she was relaxed. It was as if they'd just gone on with their regular appointments, only now he was the therapist. When they couldn't get together, she felt the sort of disappointed restlessness you endure when your babysitter cancels or a friend texts that she can't meet you for lunch. She looked forward to seeing him with an anticipation of pleasure, but she never yearned. She never slipped into the backyard with her cell phone because she just had to hear his voice.

It went on like this for a while—six months or so. She and Tommy weren't really having sex, because she refused when he was drunk and most nights he was drunk. For all she knew he was still getting it elsewhere. She more or less assumed he was. Why couldn't she just leave him? She heard the question echo inside her head, but nobody ever replied. Zoe was thirteen, then fourteen, dating her first boyfriend, who was sixteen and already driving. Jennifer saw when she met him that he stood just like Tommy—that slouch, that lowered head, that watchfulness disguised as don't-care cool. Of course. She could barely stand to say hello to him.

What happened was that the other man started to act like he loved her. Alluding to their future. Gazing at her moony eyed. Working up to the question of why she didn't leave Tommy. "You fight with him a lot, don't you?" "Your daughter's not a kid anymore, right? Not really." "You deserve better than that guy." In retrospect she sees a connection between this behavior and her own. She grew careless. She didn't always delete his texts, leaving her phone on the kitchen counter. She went to his house without even bothering to take the massage table. She carried condoms in her purse. She agreed to go out to lunch with him, right in her own neighborhood. One afternoon they went to the movies. There was no one the theater but a couple people way up in the third row. "Let's sit in the back and make out," she said, and he, agreeable boy, was willing.

Even now she can hardly stand to think of it. She had her hand in his pants—*in his pants*—and her mouth was on his mouth, her eyes were closed and he was breathing hard, his breath catching in a way that told her he was close and she was wondering if she had any tissues in her purse, and she heard, "Mom?"

Zoe and her boyfriend had ditched school. "Well," Zoe said, "I guess I'm not getting in trouble." Later, when Tommy came home, not even six and already with a buzz on, and Zoe banged her bedroom door open and said, "Mom's having an affair"—was Jennifer wrong to think that Zoe's primary emotion was triumph?

But she hadn't won, poor kid. Not even that story—not even that—could alienate Tommy. He'd cried, in a desperate choking way that made Zoe say, "Daddy, please, I'm sorry, Daddy." Over and over he said, "This is all my fault." Limp and wrung out, Jennifer sat in a chair and watched all this, until Tommy dropped to the floor in front of her and, looking up at her with those eyes and those unabashed tears, said, "I'm so sorry, babe," and then it was her turn to cry. That was Tommy. He literally fell at her feet.

She doesn't want to think about what it was to give in to Tommy. To stop resisting. Resisting was so hard. Their love was a cobweb and when she fought it she just wound herself tighter. If she stopped fighting—the pleasures of being held that tight! If she thinks about it she misses it, and then she grows angry at herself.

It was after that they conceived Milo, and then things were lovely for a while. Not, of course, with Zoe. What was it Zoe held against her most—the image of her mother with her hand inside a strange man's jeans? The sight of her father crying? Jennifer thinks it was the fact that Tommy forgave her, which, like all things, must have been Jennifer's fault.

Later, her ex-lover told the cops she'd once said she wanted Tommy to die, though that wasn't exactly what she'd said. He'd asked, again, why she didn't leave Tommy, and she'd tried to explain what she couldn't explain—she fell in love with Tommy so young, she'd surrendered herself to him. "You can rebel, can't you?" he said, and his voice was sharp and loud with frustration. "You can leave."

"You've *surrendered yourself*," she said. "You *can't* leave because you'd leave yourself behind, and that's impossible. All I can do is wait for him to die."

If she'd known what was coming, she'd never have said such a thing. At the time she wasn't picturing the man in the interview room at the police station, offering his damning paraphrase. She was lying in his bed next to him, with his naked leg pressed against hers, and he'd wanted an explanation, as people always do, and against her better judgment, she'd tried to give him one, and had learned once again that she should have chosen silence. People don't understand. This is something she needs to remember in the face of Megan's sympathetic gaze, in the face of her own bifurcated impulse, so very much like Margaret's: conceal, reveal; reveal, conceal. People don't ever understand. No one will love us if they know the worst and yet if they don't know the worst we can't trust their love. Her whole life the only person who's ever really known her is Tommy. She wishes she hadn't told Megan his name. She likes the way Megan's looking at her now, the charmed affection, the confident assumption of intimacy. *Open as a rose*, Margaret said. *Shining in the light.*

Jennifer's been silent too long, because Megan prompts her. "Where'd you go?" Megan says. "Are you thinking about your client? Margaret?"

Jennifer nods. She pictures Margaret, alone in the lonely woods.

Banished, or in hiding. Under an enchantment, maybe of her own design. Her house is so quiet, quieter even than Jennifer's. The grandfather clock, though it makes a noise, somehow amplifies the silence. In the guest room, two high, ornate twin beds have the grand severity of thrones. The king and queen will see you now. The dresser is squat and unfriendly. The antique mirror watches with haughty disdain. Maybe it's the silence that brings these things to life. Margaret is the Beast in the castle, before Beauty came along. Or maybe after she was gone.

"I am curious about her," Jennifer says. "About what happened to her. But I don't know if I really want to know."

Ticktock

I cannot get the world's attention. That is what it means to be old. I shout but no one can hear me. I am of no consequence. People imagine I don't know that, talking to me with their voices that pat pat pat me on the head. Feigned interest, faux concern. As if this fools me. As if you fool me, world. I know you don't give a shit.

Jennifer has touched my naked skin, seen the inside of my house, rummaged in my medicine cabinet for all I know. She caught me on tape. She wrote me down. No detective could have infiltrated better. I have been investigated. She got me to talk.

And what do I know about her in return? Nothing. Nothing! Except that there is something to know. Of that I'm certain. There is something to know. But all my stratagems for solving her mystery have ended only in exposing my own.

Oh, I would like to see the inside of her house, though I'm not sure what I think it would tell me. Perhaps I'm imagining Bluebeard's castle or the house in *Psycho*, with its taxidermied animals auguring no good. But I know from my many detective novels that a person in possession of a secret is as likely as anyone to own a television, a coffee table, a couch.

Still—and perhaps I read too many of those novels and should, at this late date, give them up for something more sensible and edifying—still, I keep imagining myself as a detective, and what does a detective want but to be admitted into the house of the suspect? Think of all the little old ladies of mystery land—Miss Marple, and the one played by Angela Lansbury on TV. We look sweet and doddering, but we are wily and clever, and everything you assume about us we use to our advantage. If she would just invite me over. We'll have a nice chat and then she'll excuse herself for one reason or another and I'll notice something—a glint of metal or a corner of a letter peeking out from under the bookcase—and I'll go investigate. I'll be drawn into some dark room where there may be clues. But she'll catch me. She'll come in and I won't know it, so engrossed in my clues, and she'll say, "What are you doing?" or "Lose your way?" in the eerily calm voice of the possible murderer. I'll stammer out some excuse—oh my! Just an old lady! Confused! I'm too old to flee so I'll have to rely on my wits to escape her.

I have been *exposed*. And still she doesn't see me. She doesn't even recognize me.

I ran into her at the Piggly Wiggly first thing this morning, Jennifer and her little boy, let loose in the aisles though he's a hazard. It terrifies me to watch him run. He contains infinite possible collisions. I picture him in my house and shudder—everything there is fragile, including me. He was begging his mother for this and that. I watched for a moment without her noticing: he wanted cookies and where she should have said an outright no she was negotiating. Him the world cares about. His needs, his wants, his *feelings*.

She looked up at last and saw me, but she didn't really see me. She gave me a polite vague smile. There I was a few feet from her, a woman whose naked skin she has touched with her hands, and *she didn't recognize me*.

Jennifer, I think about you every day.

She was saying my name. She was saying, "I didn't recognize you for a second. Out of context." She was pushing her cart closer to mine, telling the little boy over her shoulder to put down the cookies and come on. She said something about having forgotten she was supposed to take snacks to his school. I wasn't really listening. I was still in the moment when she looked at me and had no idea who I was. What more do I need, to convince me how little I matter?

The rest of the morning I was teary eyed, the world filmy, the pages of my book hard to see. I sit in my armchair and reread Agatha Christie. Behind me the clock ticktocks. It's a grandfather clock that belonged to my parents, ponderous and loud. Its low and solemn voice counts each hour that passes; how else would I know to mark them off?

After a while I called Lucy. Lucy is a doctor, which gives us plenty to talk about. She's in general practice. She could've gone into a luxury-car specialty, but she was already married by then, and knew she wanted a family, and so that is what she chose. Her husband is a decent man, I guess. He does something with computers. I don't know what exactly, but truthfully I don't really care. He matters to me chiefly as he advances or impedes my access to her.

"What if I buy you a ticket?" I said to Lucy when she answered the phone. "Will you come see me then?"

There was a slight pause. "That's sweet of you," she said. She sounded a little stiff, and it occurs to me now that perhaps I offended her, assuming her hesitation was financial.

"I'll spring for first class," I said, and she laughed.

"It's not really an issue of money," she said. "It's an issue of time."

"You could come for a weekend."

"I could. But the kids are in all kinds of activities now, so leaving Austin alone with them really complicates his life, and you know I often have to round on Saturdays, so being away takes some planning."

"Maybe you'd just rather not come," I said. "Your life is very important." This time I knew I'd offended her. Even if I hadn't heard it in the silence, or the careful control in her voice when she spoke again, I knew because I'd done it on purpose.

"That's not the case," she said.

"Those children won't thank you for dancing attendance on them, you know," I said. "Applauding everything they do. What are you teaching them?"

"Margaret," she said, and then she seemed at a loss.

"Life is not soccer games and trophies," I said. "Life is an uphill battle against idiocy and despair."

"Margaret," she said. "I will look at my schedule and get back to you."

"I won't be around much longer," I said to her. "There are whispers. Don't talk to me about time."

She said I'd hear from her soon, but who knows. She hung up unhappy with me, I know it, and that wasn't my original intent, though it seemed to become my intent over the course of the call. I should call back and apologize but I haven't, and I won't.

My parents taught me that the world is unfair. These parents now, including my Lucy—what they try to teach is the opposite. We like to share, etc. A lifetime of disappointment awaits their children. My parents used to whip us with switches when we were bad, switches we'd have to select ourselves from the yard. Across the street was a boy named Jimmy. He and I were always getting in scuffles. My mother told me that if a fight kicked up between us, I needed to come straight home. The next time it happened I tried to obey her, but his father held my arm asking what had happened, what we were fighting about, insistent even though I kept saying, "I need to go home, I need to go home." It was a weekend and both my parents were there. Though my father was not the daily disciplinarian, not the maker of rules, if he was home you could be sure he would go to great lengths to enforce my mother's.

When the man finally released me, I went home to find both my parents in the parlor. Not all the details are clear in my memory—how did they know I'd been fighting with Jimmy? Somehow they knew. My mother said, "I told you to come straight home," and my father said, "Why didn't you do what your mother told you?" I explained, but my father said I needed a whipping anyway. He said if they whipped me, then Jimmy's parents would feel compelled to whip him. I saw my mother's hesitation, but my father ruled our house, and she took me in the bathroom and hit my bare legs with a switch. At first I refused to cry, but then I thought that I'd better go ahead so she'd stop, so I did and she did.

My father wanted his victory. He cared about that more than he cared about causing his own child unjustifiable pain. My mother, my lovely mother—she knew he was wrong but whipped me anyway.

Tell that story to your children. That, my dears, is the world.

Please Don't Tell

Jennifer is trying to remember all the names. Erica, Juliana, Leigh Anne. Jodi, Nicole, Susan. These are the people at Megan's party, what Megan called her "girls' night in"; she says hello to them one by one. Megan's friend Amanda—appointed Jennifer's guide while Megan tends to hors d'oeuvres in the kitchen—dutifully introduces her. Samantha. Shivika. Terry, who hugs her. "I'm a hugger," Terry says in her ear.

"Okay," Jennifer says, startled, patting the other woman's back.

"You should have told her that before you hugged her, Terry," Amanda says.

"That's true." Terry pulls back and gives her a look of playful apology. "I should warn, then hug."

"But you'd lose the element of surprise," Jennifer says. The other women laugh. They laugh! Jennifer made a joke. Is it possible she might enjoy this party, which she's been dreading for days and days?

Tommy always liked a party.

"Leigh Anne!" Amanda calls, waving the woman over. Amanda wants the scoop from Leigh Anne about the meeting of some committee, and Terry asks things like, "What did Karen say?" and from this Jennifer deduces that the three of them must be colleagues. Professors, she assumes. Terry turns to her at one point and says, "Sorry, this is so boring." But Leigh Anne is saying, "And I promise you, you will not believe what he said next . . . ," and Terry can't resist diving back in. Jennifer doesn't blame her. They all care very much about whatever they're discussing. They're all completely absorbed.

Jennifer stands on the other side of the looking glass, where she always ends up, where she's always been, and what she'd really like to know is, is she cursed or did she do it to herself, and is there a difference? Either way, she believes she understands something these women do not. The ordinary is a mask worn by the awful. What we accept as normal is a play in which we've all agreed to take part. They don't know it's a play, or they willfully forget. She can't forget. She just keeps watching, bemused by their commitment to the performance, forgetting to say her lines. Why can't she change this about herself, as easily as she changed her name? Stack the past away like boxes in the attic. Be one of these women, remake herself in their image—be cheerfully annoyed with the preschool teachers, discuss the last book she read. Lighten up.

"There you are!" Megan cries, appearing before her wearing a pinkish glow. She pulls Jennifer a little farther from the other women. Her smile is larger than usual, her gestures more expansive, and from this Jennifer deduces that she is drunk. That she is a happy drunk. That before too long she'll be saying things to Jennifer like, "You know what I like about you?" On her face that drunken-epiphany expression, stupid and profound.

It's true that these thoughts have an edge. There's no help for that, resistant as she is to drunkenness as charming innocence. But she thinks the thoughts with affection, nevertheless. She's fond of Megan. Of course she is. She gives Megan a hug. Which, frankly, surprises her as much as it seems to surprise Megan.

Megan says, "Whoosh!" as though Jennifer squeezed her tight, and then squeezes Jennifer tight, and plants a loud kiss right by her ear. She pulls away to look Jennifer in the eye, trying for serious. "I'm a little drunk," she says.

Terry must have given her the hugging idea. Jennifer thinks it's been some time since another adult hugged her, and it must have been nice to be hugged. When an adult and a child embrace, one hugs and one holds on. She'd forgotten that those are different things.

"Are *you* drunk?" Megan asks.

Jennifer shakes her head.

"Oh! That's right. You don't drink," Megan whispers. "You told me that." She takes hold of Jennifer's sleeve and swings her arm gently from side to side. "Are you going to have fun?"

"You mean without drinking?"

"That. And in general."

"I am," Jennifer says. "I swear."

Megan gives her another serious look. "People will like you, you know."

Jennifer wants to look away. There's a tingle in her cheeks like she might blush. She tries to hold Megan's gaze, but she just can't do it.

"Sometimes people find it hard here," Megan says. "It's just so small, and everybody knows everybody, and I think sometimes when you arrive it's like the party got started without you and everyone already has all their inside jokes." There's an edge to Megan's voice, some remembered hurt. "But it's really a welcoming place," she says, earnestly, almost pleadingly. "At heart it is. If you want to you can belong here."

Jennifer doesn't know what to say. What she feels is *seen*. How does Megan know that she's wondering if she can belong? If she should? How can Megan see that she wants to? Does she know how it terrifies her? The wanting to.

Megan, bless her, doesn't require an answer. She releases Jennifer from eye contact, aiming a shy smile at the floor. "I really am drunk." She laughs a little breathlessly.

"Hey, y'all," a voice says beside them, and Amanda is back, with two other women in tow. So far she seems to be the sardonic one. There's a brassy one, and an intellectual one, and an uptight one, and an empathetic one, who reacted with too much sadness when she asked about Jennifer's husband and Jennifer had to say he died. Jennifer will avoid this last one. Amanda she likes. She thinks they could be friends. Amanda says something wry about a TV show, and Jennifer laughs, and Megan beams at them both like a proud matchmaker.

What will they call Jennifer, the women at this party? The watchful one? The sad one? The one you just can't get to know?

But she rejects this kind of thinking. She will not curl into herself like a snail. It's just she's never talked much at parties. She's never had to. She can see Tommy beside her, telling one of his slow-drawl stories, and everybody watching him with an avid collective longing, and how beautiful he is, how beautiful. She can't begin to replace all that was lost in him. She wonders—did his voice allow her silence, or insist on it? Two more people have joined their circle now, and they're laughing at a small-child story, and Jennifer could tell one, she has plenty of them. Now is a moment when she could be the one to speak.

"Milo," she starts, and they all look at her with such goodwill. They are all so willing to listen. Behind her from the staircase comes a male voice, a voice calling, "Megan!" and Megan's head snaps up. Looking at Megan as she calls out, "Yes, honey?" it's impossible not to think of a dog's quivering attentiveness. Or perhaps a rabbit's. Is it obedience she sees in her friend or fear? Wait—is there any difference?

"Could you come here a sec?" the man—Sebastian—says, in

a voice that is carefully neutral. A voice with a vibration in it—so familiar it seems to chime in with a chord that's always ringing in Jennifer's head. She turns to look at Sebastian but the wall blocks her view of him. Megan flashes a brightly sheepish smile and calls out, "Sure!" starting toward him even as she speaks.

Megan gone, everyone shifts uncomfortably, as if struck with the sudden realization that without her they have nothing to say to each other. Amanda nudges Jennifer. "I think you were about to tell a story," she says.

"Was I?" Jennifer says, though she knows she was. The story doesn't seem funny anymore. It needed to be told on a wave of good humor and goodwill.

"Let me consult the record," Amanda says. She makes a show of looking at everyone. "Who was taking the minutes?"

"Oh no," one of the others says. "I forgot my . . . wait, what are those things called?"

"What things?" Amanda asks.

"Those typey-typey things. You know, that court reporters use."

"Oh, good question," Leigh Anne says, and the others murmur that they don't know, and then someone ventures a guess, and someone else digs for her phone to look it up, and the conversation deflates until Megan reappears, dragging Sebastian with her.

"Sebastian wants to say hello!" Megan announces brightly, though his expression makes clear that this is patently untrue. He does say hello though, making eye contact with an air of painful duty, his mouth a flat unhappy line. His eyes are as pretty as they looked in the photos Jennifer saw, maybe more so. They're one of those unreal colors, a green so pale and shimmery you think there must be contacts involved. He should just shave his head, because his patchy hairline mars the effect of those eyes, while baldness would probably augment it. But possibly Megan doesn't want the effect augmented. Who knows to what uses he puts his powers. Jennifer shakes his hand, giving him a firm grip, a brisk "Nice to meet you."

"He wants us to be careful not to be too loud," Megan says. "He just finally managed to get Ben down."

Sebastian shoots his wife a look, and Jennifer wonders which one of those statements annoyed him. Does he not like her unmasking him as a scold? Or does he not like the implication that he mismanaged Ben's bedtime? It's nine, a little late for a child that age, not that Jennifer is one to talk. She's only just arrived at the party mostly because she lingered at home coaxing Milo into bed, while the teenage babysitter Megan recommended sat on the couch texting furiously. "Well," Megan says mildly, in response to his look, "I didn't say the request was unreasonable."

"No," Sebastian says. "You didn't say that."

"I'm a little drunk," Megan tells everyone, lifting her glass. Amanda lifts hers, too, and they clink, and Sebastian frowns.

"What are you drinking, anyway?" he asks Megan.

"Vodka!" she says.

"Is that a good idea? Vodka? Why not beer? Why not wine?"

"Oh, sweet," Megan says. "He's worried I'll have a hangover."

"She sometimes gets carried away with vodka," he says. "I don't know if you've ever been with her on a martini night . . ."

"What does *carried away* mean for our mild-mannered Megan?" Amanda asks. "Will she dance on a table?"

"Dancing on tables is apocryphal," one of the others says. "No one ever dances on a table."

"Megan might," Sebastian says grimly, and there's a brief enigmatic silence.

"Well," Megan says in a small voice, looking into her drink.

"Just take it slow," Sebastian says.

"Okay, honey," she says.

Just as Jennifer thinks he'll make an exit—*turn on his heel* is the phrase in her head—he startles her with a flash bomb of a smile. Oh, look what's in his arsenal! Suddenly all the women are smiling back at him. Even on Jennifer's face, a traitorous, responsive smile. "Have a good time, ladies," he says, and then he does indeed go, and they all watch him walk away.

"He doesn't like me to drink," Megan says sheepishly. "He thinks I'm embarrassing."

"Embarrassing to yourself?" Jennifer asks. "Or embarrassing to him?"

"Both I guess," Megan says. And then, in a rare display of waspishness: "But mostly to him."

"What's he afraid you'll do?" Amanda asks. "Besides dance on the table?"

"Oh, say something stupid," she says. "He especially hates it when I get facts wrong. Like, I relate something I read on the Internet, but I get part of it mixed up. He hates that."

"Why?" Amanda asks.

Megan shrugs. She's starting to look sad now, and Jennifer thinks the conversation should probably be over, even if she has a nagging urge to insist on its continuance. "Some people see their spouses as separate from them," Megan says. "And some people see their spouses as an extension of them, and that informs their attitudes and behavior."

"You are such a sociologist," Amanda says, making everyone laugh. Just like that, the party mood returns, but Jennifer can't recover so easily. It would be easier if she drank. She used to like a cocktail as much as anyone, but at some point she stopped drinking, hoping to encourage Tommy to do likewise, and then once she lost hope for encouragement her refusal became a reproof. Without Tommy there's no reason not to drink. There's no one to measure herself against, no spouse to embarrass or be embarrassed by. No, listen—she *can* be a different person without Tommy. Tonight, at this party. Just to try it out. Like smiling until you're happy. She can pretend until it comes true.

She goes into the kitchen, where there's an array of bottles on the counter. She has no idea what to have, uncertain as a teenager trying to fake sophistication. She's got a bottle of vodka tilted back so she can read the label when the door swings open and Sebastian comes in. Jennifer feels caught, a feeling that intensifies when he raises his eyebrows and says, "Good reading?"

"I can't decide what to have," she says. She doesn't want to look at him, feeling both hostile and unaccountably nervous. She pretends to read the label on a bottle of gin.

"It's best to have a particular drink," he says. "Then you never have to decide. Then you just go in and say, 'The usual.' And if there's no bartender, you say it to yourself." He goes to the fridge and fills a glass of water. Jennifer waits for him to leave, but he doesn't. He leans against the counter and sips. Then looks at her. "I take it you have no usual?"

"I don't drink," she says. "My usual is nothing."

"You don't drink, but you're trying to decide what to drink?"

"You don't have to call my sponsor. I just don't drink."

"Oh, that's not where my mind went," he says. "I was wondering if you were celebrating or upset, to want a drink when you don't drink."

"Why assume it's one of those?"

"Because you didn't say, 'I don't drink often,' or 'I only drink sometimes.' You said, 'I don't drink.' So what would make you drink?"

She looks at him now. He's flirting with her in a way she suspects is automatic, habitual. It's not in the words; it's in the way he's lingering, the slightly insinuating tone, the concentrated force of his attention. What a dangerous force, male attention. What terrible things women do to get it, or to make it go away. "I don't really have a reason," she says finally.

He nods at a big glass punch bowl on the kitchen table. "That's a champagne punch," he said. "I made it. It's good, but I have to warn you it goes down easy."

Jennifer shakes her head. "Too sweet," she says. "I don't like sweet."

He studies her. "How about whiskey?" he asks. He steps over and reaches past her to open a high cabinet. Inside are a number of graceful bottles gleaming with golden-brown liquid—so Sebastian isn't just a drinker, he's a connoisseur. "Megan's not a bourbon gal," he says. "Not that I'd really want her to put these out."

"Gal?" Jennifer repeats.

"I'm from Missoura," he says. "I'm allowed to say *gal*."

"Are you from 'Missoura' in 1952?"

"Hey now," he says. He pulls out a bottle, handling with care. "How about this one? It's wheated. Smooth but not boring." He picks up a cocktail glass, pours, and hands it to her. He doesn't care that she never said she wanted it. She takes a sip. It burns her nostrils, though it's gentle on her tongue. It reminds her of Tommy. It tastes like everything she's ever given up. "Like it?" he asks.

She nods. She does like it. She takes another sip.

"You've been hanging out with Megan a lot lately," he says.

The hint of accusation makes her wary. She feels herself taking a step back. "Yeah," she says.

"So let me ask you something," he says. "Do you think she's an alcoholic?"

"Do I think—" She stares at him. This was not what she was expecting, not the question, not a discussion of Megan at all. He'd had every appearance of being about to cross a line, to touch her, make some move that would ratify her dislike. "No," she says. "We're usually together with the kids, during the day. She drinks herbal tea. I've never seen her have a drink before tonight."

He nods, his expression pensive. "It's not easy, always being the bad guy," he says.

"I don't imagine that it is," Jennifer says, and though she understands him, though she knows exactly what he means by that, her tone is sharp, and so is the look he gives her.

He pours himself a whiskey from the same bottle and holds it up to the light before taking a sip. "She's very sweet," he says. "And everybody loves her. I saw how you were looking at me earlier. Believe me, I know I'm the asshole. But that doesn't mean I'm always wrong."

Megan comes in then, laughing at something someone said in the other room. "You know it!" she shouts back, and then she sees them and smiles a shy, delighted smile. "You two!" she says. She comes up next to Jennifer and hugs her around the waist, resting her head on her shoulder. "What are you drinking? You're drinking! Sebastian, did you give her the good stuff?"

"Of course," he says.

"Oh, you're lucky," Megan says to Jennifer. "He doesn't break that out for just anyone. That's the good stuff." Still leaning against Jennifer, she starts patting her, as if in comfort, on the arm. "I'm glad you're here," she says. "I'm glad you're having fun."

"Stop hanging on her like a spider monkey," Sebastian says.

Megan flinches. She steps hastily away, flashing an apologetic smile at Jennifer. "Sorry, sorry," she says. She reaches out as if to pat her again, then thinks better of it. "I'm a little handsy when I'm drunk."

"I don't mind," Jennifer says.

"No, no," Megan says, turning herself in a half circle. "No, no. Just came in for—ah." She grabs an open bottle of red wine from the counter. "Back into the fray!" she says.

She's gone, and Jennifer looks at Sebastian. "See," he says, meeting her eye. "I'm the asshole."

"I can see that," she says.

He straightens his spine, clips off each cold word. "She does drink too much. You barely know her. You have no idea what it is to be married to her."

She can't stop herself from asking. "What's it like to be married to you?"

"You might think she's the world's best wife," he says. "You might think I'm so lucky, she's so sweet, she's so accommodating. But everything we do is on her terms. I don't want to live in this crappy little nowhere. I can't stand it here. The Southern sweetness. The small-town know-your-business clusterfuck. The goddamn *crickets*." Over the course of this speech, he's begun to lean toward her, his antagonist, and she's been bracing herself for she doesn't know what. But suddenly he collapses back against the counter. "Fuck," he says. "I don't even know you."

"No," she says. She's clutching her glass hard. "No, you don't." Her throat is tight. She downs her whiskey so quickly her eyes water. "Do you cheat on her?"

"Why?" he says. "Are you offering?"

She makes a sound of disgust, and moves to go, but he's fast, and he catches her by the wrist. "Please don't tell Megan I said that," he says, with such sudden sincere vulnerability that she nods, despite herself. Despite herself, which seems to be how she does everything. Is she being cowed or persuaded? Either way it's weakness, and there is nothing she fears and dislikes more than her own weakness. *But I love you*, Tommy would say. *I'd die for you. You know that, don't you? I would die.* She runs from him, from both of them, back into the heat and noise of the party.

She expects to find signs in Megan of the scene in the kitchen— a sheepish smile, damage in her eyes. But Megan is laughing exuberantly in a crowd of people, her face shining. Maybe Megan is not easily damaged. Maybe she hides the damage well. She catches Jennifer's eye and skips over to her. "There you are," she says. Sebastian's criticism notwithstanding, she picks up Jennifer's hand and laces their fingers together. "I missed you," she says. And then she kisses the back of Jennifer's hand with a loud smack and leads her back into the group, where Jennifer—unsettled, uncertain—no longer wants to be.

Smile, Jennifer. Maybe Megan isn't the safe haven you thought she was. Smile anyway. Maybe the floor sloshes beneath her, but her feet are planted, her grip is firm on your hand. Can you bear it, Jennifer? Complication, imperfection? The possibility that you might be understood? Or would you rather be alone?

Nobody Loves Me

This morning I got what I wanted. I resorted to devious measures, but this is nothing that should surprise anyone at this point. I'm not sure why it still, a little, surprises me. A good detective has to be devious. If you're a good detective, devious is the same as clever, manipulation an admirable skill. We call a flaw a virtue when we like the results. I called her number, and when she answered, I asked her if she had an egg I could borrow. I don't know why I didn't think of doing this before. I said I was baking cookies. Though I don't bake cookies, or anything at all, which of course she couldn't have known. She said she did have an egg. She said it slowly and as if against her will. I said I'd be right over and hung up before she could change her mind. I thought she might call back to say that she'd bring the egg to me, because I believed—and still believe—that she didn't want to let anyone inside her house. So when the phone rang as I was gathering my things, and I saw her number on the caller ID, I didn't answer. I let her think I was already on my way. Slow, perhaps, but unstoppable.

She met me at the door with the egg in her hand. I hadn't prepared for that eventuality, and for a moment I was sure I was thwarted. I was so disappointed that, I am embarrassed to say, I wanted to weep. I took the egg and thanked her. I shuffled myself in a half circle, pivoting on my cane, and then I happened to look down at the concrete porch and before I could even register the idea it gave me I'd already dropped the egg. "Oh no!" I said. I stared at the egg— its gooey splatter—because I was afraid if I looked up I wouldn't look sufficiently sheepish. And she'd know.

"Oh, that's okay," Jennifer said, her voice motherly with irritation and forgiveness. "I've got more."

"I'm so clumsy," I said. "My father always said I was clumsy. He used to make me sit down and grip the sides of my chair so I couldn't fall down or break anything." This is true, but I have no idea why I told her, or why my voice cracked like that when I did. Perhaps it was this pathetic little moment that compelled her to invite me in.

It's strange how the petty continues to upset you, even after you've been to war. The funny look someone gives you, the invitation you didn't get, the long line at the post office—these things don't cease to affect. A human mind is not a still pond into which the world drops an occasional stone. It's an ocean—waves and currents, the big and the small so mixed together it's hard to say which is which. *You're so clumsy.* I can talk about gut-shot soldiers without crying, but I told Jennifer that story and tears sprang to my eyes.

Her house was a mess. It is my nature to pass judgment on a messy home, as it is, for good or ill, my nature to pass judgment on everything. But even a less critical person than I might have been taken aback at the sight of that living room. She escorted me to a chair and left me in it while she went to fetch a paper towel to wipe off the egg that had splashed on my ankle and my shoe. So I was able to study the chaos at my leisure. Let it suffice to say that that child has a great many toys.

It's a strange little house, like a toy itself, built with haphazard creativity from more than one set. There are only three rooms on the first floor, a doll-size kitchen, a bathroom, an enormous living room. Why make that room so large, the kitchen so minuscule? And then put a huge stone fireplace in the center of it, and an open spiral staircase behind that? I wonder that Jennifer doesn't worry the boy will fall through the slats on the stairs and crack his head on the stone. Upstairs is a loft. You can see a couch and a TV there, and then what look like bedroom doors on either side of the open space. There's a deck off the back of the first floor, which I knew, but I'd never seen it from this side. The wall going out to it is all glass, with doors, and through those doors I could see the trees and the pond, and beyond that my own house. From this distance it wasn't pretty. No visible windows, and the roof is low, all the colors dark as mud. I had the fanciful notion that it was hunkered down there at the edge of the trees like a hunter wearing camouflage.

The little boy was watching me from the loft. The moment I realized it, he shouted, "Mom!" My Lord, it was loud. I felt like someone had clanged cymbals by my ear.

Jennifer emerged with rags, one damp, one dry. "What, Milo?" she called up. Rather pleasantly, for someone who'd just been shouted at.

"Who is that?" he demanded.

"Her name is Ms. Riley," Jennifer said. "She lives across the pond."

"Ms. Riley?" he repeated suspiciously.

"Come down and say hello," his mother said. She knelt in front of me and began to wipe the egg off my shoe with the briskly dutiful air of a paid caretaker. Frankly, it embarrassed me.

"I can do that," I said.

"I'm done." She pulled herself up to her feet. The movement looked effortful, but still it was more than I could have managed. I bet she imagines she's getting old.

The child had somehow appeared behind her. I'd been too flustered by Jennifer at my feet to hear him clatter down the stairs. I thought he might hide behind her and peek out at me, as I've known small children to do, but he's a bold little thing. He came right up close and studied me.

"Hi, Milo," I said.

"Hi," he said. Then he looked at his mother. "I didn't know she'd be so old!" He said this cheerfully. No insult implied.

So I laughed, at the comment, at the look of embarrassment on Jennifer's face. "Your mother should have warned you," I said.

"Milo," Jennifer reproved him, but he looked at her with incomprehension and said, "What?" Then suddenly he cried out, "Zoom!" and dashed in a circle from living room to kitchen to living room and then back up the stairs. This time I heard the clatter.

"Sorry," Jennifer said, dropping into the chair next to mine. The rags she let fall to the floor. I wondered how long they'd stay there.

"He speaks only the truth," I said. "It's a wonder he's not terrified of me."

"There's no reason he should be," she said forcefully.

I felt an argumentative urge to disagree. I don't know why. You'd think I'd know everything about myself by now, but every now and then I'm brought up short by the opposite realization. At any rate I felt almost angry at her. "My grandniece gave me a book for my birthday," I said. "Pictures of old ladies. Stuff about how beautiful they were. Maybe it's because I'm old, but I don't think old age is beautiful. I think they look awful."

She didn't answer. I could see from a sidelong glance that she looked pensive. I like about her that she doesn't speak when she's not sure what to say. I like about her that she didn't say, *Oh, no, you're beautiful,* or some other painful and condescending thing. I'm too old for insincerity.

"Do you see your grandniece often?" she asked. It felt sudden, and I was a little startled.

"No," I said. "Not often. I have two, but I only like the one."

"I have the feeling you don't like many people."

"Oh, *people*. I used to like them. It may be hard to imagine now, but I used to like to throw a dinner party."

"Not me. I hate parties of all kinds." She said this with a weird anger in her voice.

"Well, don't worry, I won't make you go to one."

She didn't answer. She pressed a thumb and finger against her forehead, like people do when they have a headache.

"I used to be awash in friends," I said to her silence. "I used to date. I made delicious desserts, especially strawberry-rhubarb pie. And coffee cake. I made a good coffee cake."

She nodded, though I don't think she was listening.

"I was a good cook. I could have made a good little housewife, if anybody'd cared to employ me." It's odd, I know, but I felt defensive after I said this, like she'd been the one to suggest no one had ever wanted to marry me. So I said, "I almost got married. I wanted to."

"I know," she said, in a neutral tone. I went on talking.

"His name was Lloyd," I said. "He died. He died in the war."

"You told me about him."

"I did?"

"It's on the tape." Then, as if realizing she'd been rude, she said, "I'm sorry to be abrupt. I'm not feeling very well."

"It was a long time ago," I said sharply. I was annoyed that I'd repeated myself, trying for the umpteenth time to draw some reaction from her. I went there for a glimpse behind the curtain, and there I was again, pulling it back on myself. "I don't think about it now." She was silent again, and I said, "Some things happen and some things don't. It hardly matters at my age which is which." Silence. Oh, she is good at silence. I wanted to get her to talk, so I told her what all mothers like to hear: "Your son is a cute little boy."

She smiled. She couldn't help herself. "He's my reward," she said.

"Your reward?"

"Maybe that's a bad way to put it."

"Put it however you like. I have no stake in it."

"In what?"

I waved one hand. "In children. In how people talk about having children. Why would I judge? What do I know about it? I never had any. Never even approached having any." I wondered if she would ask if I'd wanted to have children, as people sometimes do, with a pity in their voice that I find presumptuous, because they assume the answer will be yes, and they're preemptively sad for me.

"I can't imagine that," she said instead. Not with compassion—you poor old dear—but with wonder. Wonder I don't mind. Who doesn't feel some wonder at the sight of a life so utterly unlike her own? Proof that something else was possible.

"You haven't explained what you meant by *reward*."

She pressed her fingers to her head again. "For surviving," she said.

I felt a flicker of excitement. Here was something real. She'd said it with the weariness of truth. I kept my voice level. "Surviving what?"

"Everything that went wrong."

It wasn't enough, it wasn't enough, but it was more than I'd ever gotten. I waited. A good detective knows when to let the silence do its work. Who knows what she might've told me if Milo hadn't reappeared, bringing with him an enormous amount of noise. It's rather like being shelled—the approach of a small rambunctious child. You hear the noise growing closer, and then there it is, louder than anything, rocking the world. He emitted some sort of strange roaring, growling sound—I'm not sure what it was supposed to be. His idea of intimidation. He had a big dark blanket flung over him like a hooded cape. He stopped roaring and looked at us, hands on hips. His little face within the shadow of his cape was lowered into a glower. "I am Dark Flame," he said.

"Dark Flame?" Jennifer repeated. Her whole demeanor changed when the child came in the room. She leaned toward him. She smiled. "Are you good or evil?"

"I'm morally ambiguous."

Jennifer concealed her smile behind her hand. "We've been discussing that concept," she said to me. "Because of a character in a book."

Children are frightening, aren't they? He really did look like a treacherous creature, a little caped goblin, a devil child. He looked like something that might ruin your life. His mother asked, "Are you magic?"

He growled again, swirling his cape. "I have the power to break hearts."

Jennifer laughed, genuine and involuntary.

"Please don't break mine," I said.

"I can't break *your* heart." He dropped his blanket and giggled, a little boy again. He thought I was teasing him. "You're *old*."

"Milo," Jennifer warned.

"It's all right," I said. "I am old. I've outgrown heartbreak. Right, Milo?"

But he wasn't listening anymore. He'd zoomed away, his parable delivered. You can outgrow heartbreak only when you don't love anyone anymore, and maybe not even then. That's the thought I had, except it came to me like this: Nobody loves me. Nobody will ever love me again. Those two sentences rang in my head, crisp and clear. Like they were a revelation, though they shouldn't have been. My throat closed as if I would choke. As if I stood at the edge of the pond, pockets full of stones.

My hand was resting on the top of my cane, which I'd held on to, even sitting down, as though I might be asked to leave at any moment. I tell you this because of what happened next: Jennifer reached over and put her hand on mine. I nearly jumped, I was so startled. When was the last time someone had touched me without expecting payment? When was the last time someone had shown me a kindness, any kindness at all, that wasn't *dutiful*? Why did she do it? Because I told her about Lloyd, forgetting I'd already told her about Lloyd? Or had my voice wobbled on the word *heartbreak*? Why do I ask these questions? Why does it matter to me *why*?

Here came Milo again, back for his blanket cape. Jennifer took away her hand. "Hello, Dark Flame," I said, trying to play along.

"My name is not Dark Flame!" he shouted.

This despite the blanket back on his head. "Well, how was I supposed to know?"

"So who are you?" Jennifer asked, with a sweetness that was perhaps supposed to counteract my lack thereof. "Are you Mr. Ninja?"

"Mr. Ninja?" he repeated incredulously. "No!"

I said, "Are you Milo Young?"

He looked at me with narrowed eyes. "That is not my name."

"What is it then?" I smiled at Jennifer in what I hoped was complicit delighted amusement at the antics of her child. But she wasn't looking at me.

"Milo Carrasco!" he shouted. "Milo Carrasco!" He dragged the "o" out into a wolf's howl, and ran away trailing blanket and howl behind him.

"I was expecting something more dramatic," I said. "Child of Chaos. Wolf Boy." But then I looked at Jennifer, who was staring in the direction he'd gone.

I've performed a lot of triage. I would've pegged her as gut shot, if she'd come in on a stretcher with that look on her face.

"Carrasco," I said. "Where did he get that name?"

She jumped. I think she'd forgotten I was there. She shot me a quick glance, swallowed, tried to smile. "Who knows?" she said. "Who knows with kids."

"Indeed," I said. "Who knows."

After that she wanted me to go, though she tried not to show it. She chit-chattered and smiled—she of the neutral impassive politeness, the quick flares of temper like flashes in the dark. Who was this twittering creature, anxious as a bird, asking me if I needed anything besides the egg, if I wanted a cup of tea? I don't even think she knew what she was saying.

Well, I am not one to overstay my welcome. Nor do I like the sight of a strong person made weak. In truth I am like a child: determined to take something apart to see how it works; dismayed, then, to find it in pieces.

I nestled the egg she gave me in an empty space in a carton. Because of course I actually had eggs. One always has eggs.

The look on her face when the child said *Carrasco*. When Rumpelstiltskin heard his name, he tore himself in two. Is that what happened to you, Jennifer? Oh, Jennifer, don't you know that a good detective, given a clue like that, has no choice but to follow it?

In the End

They were at the top of the stairs. Or she was. She was on the landing. He was balanced on the top step, one hand braced against the wall. He was in a walking cast because he'd broken his ankle stepping drunk off a curb. They'd been fighting all morning and all she wanted was for it to stop. She'd gone upstairs to escape him—he'd been shouting that she'd never really loved him, in that way he did when he had no other argument to make in the face of her complaints. When his apologies weren't enough, he'd try to make it her fault—his drinking, his cheating, his sorrow and guilt—and then when he couldn't he'd sob. He'd beg forgiveness. He'd say he wished he was dead and she'd have to comfort him. She'd have to put her soothing hands in his hair. She felt too tired for that, she felt well beyond tired. So she'd tried to escape.

But he'd followed. He'd followed quickly, despite the way the boot on his foot hobbled him, and he seemed so vivid with anger that though he'd never hit her in all their many years together her heart was a rabbit in her chest, and she had the thought that maybe he loved her enough to kill her. "You can't leave," he said. "You know Zoe will stay with me. And you can't take Milo. I won't let you. I won't let you go."

"How will you stop me?" Her voice was strangely calm. She heard curiosity in it. She really wanted to know.

He shifted his weight, but he still looked unbalanced. He'd always been so at home in his body, even when he was drunk beyond sense, that it was strange to see him off-kilter. "I don't think I'll have to," he said. "I don't think you can do it."

She stared at him. He seemed so certain.

"You've never been able to before," he said. "All these years, you've never been able to do it."

"I can do it," she said.

"You can't," he said. "Stop trying. You'll never leave me. I know you won't. You don't want to. That's the problem. You really don't want to go."

He reached for her. Who knows what he intended? To hold her tenderly? To beg forgiveness? To grip her wrist like a handcuff and tell her, *You are mine, you have always been mine?*

She had a flash of pushing him, watching him tumble down the stairs. For a moment she thought it had happened, but no—he was still standing there, angry and forlorn. Slowly he let his hand fall to his side. She'd stepped back before he could reach her.

"You won't go," he said. Strangely, he said it sadly.

He was right. She knew he was right.

But not long after that he died.

Margaret

Shall we continue with your story where we left off? he says.

I've forgotten just where that was, I say. This is not quite true, but I wish to see if he has really been listening to me, or just pretending to.

—Margaret Atwood, *Alias Grace*

The Ordinary Extraordinary

Once upon a time there were two girls. One was named Marilyn Kay, but everybody called her Kay, and the other was named Margaret Jean Riley, but they called her Maggie Jean. They were young girls, nurses. It was wartime, and the posters said someone needed them. When they got to the war, it wasn't quite what they'd expected. When is war ever quite what you expect? For months they'd been getting ready. Basic training in North Carolina, field school in England, even sleeping in their bedrolls in mud near the channel—all this had taught them next to nothing about what would happen to them.

All their lives they had known things, Kay and Maggie Jean. They understood each other, the two of them, because many of the things they'd known were the same. When they were children they knew their mothers loved them and were reasonably sure their fathers did too. They knew their sisters didn't like them much but in certain moods could be fine playfellows. They knew what they read in books. They knew they were smart. They knew their multiplication tables. And then when they were student nurses they knew such a host of things. Even before they'd learned how to insert an IV they knew what time they had to be up in the morning, what time they had to be back at the dorm, what chapters they had to study for the next day. After they found jobs they knew their patients' names, what their vitals had been the day before, what meds they'd been given, even what they'd had to eat. It was all right there on the chart. In basic training they knew what bed they were going to sleep in that night. In England they knew not to say *bum* and what was meant by *biscuit* and where they could find the pub.

Then they got to the war. They got to the war, Jennifer.

This is how it is when you keep moving from the ordinary to the extraordinary and back again: the world expands to include a fleet of ships; a coastline; the sky, black with planes; and then contracts to the wet heat of your clothing, the taste of salt water in your mouth, and later the routines of helmet baths, amputations, waking to the whoosh and smash of shells, and all of that is ordinary, ordinary. The very ordinariness of it is the strangest thing you could have imagined.

I suppose the idea with training for what you cannot imagine is that when nothing else holds, when the world becomes a place you've never seen before, that training will keep you moving. Certainly we'd never practiced clambering down the side of a ship on a net, but we'd had plenty of practice in doing what we were told. The net must have swayed a little with the weight and movement of other bodies, but I don't remember fearing I would fall. I remember I kept my eyes on the men still on the ship, and they grew smaller and smaller to me, as I must have done to them.

At the bottom I got in a smaller boat, a landing craft, and Kay was in there, too, and a few of the other nurses. I kept my eye on Kay. The night before, during the crossing, she'd fallen from a top bunk and done an injury to her back. She'd made me promise not to tell anyone. She was afraid the chief nurse would have her checked out, find some reason she wasn't in shape to go on. The other girls in the cabin—Ada Dawson, Nina Hagenston—had been asleep, and when the noise woke Nina, Kay claimed she'd just dropped her helmet. Lucky it was Nina who woke, as she wasn't the type to ask questions, such as what Kay was doing splayed out on the floor. I was sure she'd pulled something, or at least bruised herself badly, and that carrying all the weight of our equipment must have been twice as hard for her as it was for me. But she gave no sign that anything was wrong.

When we got near the beach they lowered the ramp on the front of the landing craft and we walked into the water. I had never been so hot, hunching through the water to the shore. It was like a steam bath inside my gas-impregnable clothing, and I was so weighted down with blanket and tent, gas mask and canteen, first aid kit and shovel that once I got out of the boat I couldn't stand up straight. The equipment was arranged very carefully—you had to do it just so to make it fit—and it was all very well as long as you kept your feet but if I'd fallen on my back I would've been lodged there like a beetle. When I think about it now, I don't know how I made it down the net in the first place with all that stuff hung all over me. Someone told me to go and I went, and that is what it is to be in the army, and sometimes just what it is to be alive.

What a mess that beach was, the sand churned up by feet and tires, strewn with vehicles and equipment, crisscrossed with lines of soldiers. If there had ever been anything beautiful about the spot it was gone, and if there would be anything beautiful again I couldn't imagine it. Ahead of us up the hill we could see the concrete bunkers the Germans had built, squat and unlovely even if you hadn't known how deadly they were. Behind us in the water the massive bodies of the ships.

Though the front line was only a few miles into France, the beach itself was safe. We walked up it and over the dunes with less fear than we'd had on our infiltration course way back in basic training. Only thirty-eight days before men had been slaughtered in that place by the thousands.

Dead bodies? No, there were no dead bodies. I just said this was D-Day plus thirty-eight. We didn't wade through the floating dead, as I've read the nurses did who got there first. Do you wish I had? Would that be a better story? That's not much of a thing to wish on someone. What I saw over there had horrors enough.

What I remember is that we hit the beach and had to climb a hill—*that* I remember well because it was so difficult. It was very hot. The foxholes were already there when we got to the top—I never had to dig a foxhole the whole time, after all the practice we had in basic training—and we slept in them that night and damn near froze to death. "Holy cow," Kay said beside me when we flopped down at the top of the hill, and I laughed, though not because anything was particularly funny. For twenty-four years my life had been so small I could carry it in my pocket. Here I was in France, part of a thing so large it was beyond imagining. I was at war.

I've slept in a foxhole. I've sat on a hill in the dark and watched the tracer bullets go by. I say these things with a certain degree of amazement. Looking back it seems like someone else's life.

I woke up just before dawn. I thought I'd heard something—a shell, an explosion—but now all was quiet. I'd slept balled up so tightly I didn't know if I'd ever be able to straighten my limbs out again. I wanted badly to try—suddenly my whole body seemed beset with an unbearable cramping—but what if I really had heard something? I waited. And waited. Maybe I'd dreamed it. I gave in to the impulse to stand and all the bones in my body popped and cracked at once. I looked down over the beach. In the early light it looked like a graveyard, like all the vehicles had been abandoned to rust, like all the men were dead. I knew the fighting was ahead of us, now, but gazing at that beach, imagining what it had looked like a month ago, it seemed like everything that was going to happen already had.

On the other side of me a nurse named Evelyn was fumbling endlessly in her pack, muttering, "I know it's in here, somewhere, or did I put it in the—" She cut herself off with an "Aha!" and turned to me in triumph to display a compact and a lipstick. "Found 'em," she said. She flipped the compact open, studied her face in its mirror, sighed, and applied her lipstick with a steady hand.

People used to like to give me books about the war, imagining, I suppose, that I wanted to relive it, and in one of them I read about a nurse who used to let the soldiers watch her put her lipstick on. She said, "It reminded them of their mothers." I thought, Yeah, sure, that's what it reminded them of. I mean, were we really that innocent? Or were we just pretending? It's hard to look back on that time without imprinting on it everything I know now. I can't recollect it in what may have been its original purity.

In the foxhole beside me, Kay stirred, and then let out a startled sound—a hurt sound.

"Kay?" I whispered.

She didn't reply for a moment. I couldn't see her face. I could hear her breathing, which sounded to me like the breathing of someone trying not to acknowledge pain. "Good morning," she whispered back.

"You're pretty banged up, aren't you," I said.

"Maggie Jean," she said. She got to her feet so that she could look down at me. "Don't ever say anything like that again." She studied my face, not smiling. "Don't say anything like that to anyone."

I was hurt, I have to say. She didn't trust me. She thought I might go to the chief nurse about her. Maybe it was silly of me to be affronted. But I was affronted nevertheless, and I turned away so I wouldn't have to look at her.

That was a strange day. We spent hours waiting for transportation. Twice the chief nurse made us all line up and do calisthenics. Kay stood at the back and did her best to fake it, waving her arms in a feeble imitation of jumping jacks. I looked around to see if anyone else had noticed, and then made myself stop looking. She struggled on, and I did my best not to watch her, not to appear concerned. I jumped and kicked and swung my arms from side to side, and the chief nurse shouted out, "One, two, one, two," in her stentorian voice, and down on the beach a few people stared up at us and wondered what the hell was going on.

When we weren't busy jumping around like lunatics, we sat and sat. I couldn't absorb the reality of anything outside each moment. I was hot. The clothes I'd been wearing for three days were stiff with dried sweat and salt water. I was hungry, and then we broke out the K rations, and the crackers were tasteless, the fruit bar so tough and chewy I had to work my jaw over it like a cow. The water I washed it all down with had a sharp chemical taste from the purification tablets. The other girls were sweetening the water with the lemon crystals that came in envelopes in the ration boxes, so I did that, too. What was real—a sip from a canteen of sweet, warm water, the taste of lemon mixed with chlorine, the way the chlorine lingered in my mouth.

I remember at some point Kay said, "I'm sorry I was short with you earlier. I know you wouldn't say anything. I just . . . I'm doing my best to pretend it didn't happen."

"I'll try not to remind you," I said.

"Will you help me? If I need it?"

"Of course."

"You'll protect me?"

"To the death," I said.

Carrasco

The fog is on the Mountain. For the first time Jennifer understands what that girl meant all those years ago in New York City—a place that, from the vantage point of this window on the foggy woods, now seems like a fanciful notion. Afraid to drive in these conditions, she has kept Milo home from school and canceled her appointment with Margaret. Margaret seemed quite put out at first, but then subsided into understanding, telling her it was of course best to be safe. In truth Jennifer's glad to have an excuse not to go back today. Yesterday's interview was strange from the beginning. After the massage, Jennifer set up her tape recorder and settled in for another irritable round of I'll Tell You, I'll Tell You Not. But Margaret only said, "Are you ready?" That was all. Jennifer barely got out the *yes* before she began.

And then when she said, "To the death," and abruptly stopped talking, Jennifer prompted her. "Protect her?"

"Keep her secret. Help her out when she couldn't manage something. Keep her from getting sent home. Protect her."

"Were you able to?"

"I tried." Margaret looked right at her. Why, whenever she does that, does it feel like an accusation? "Do you know why I'm telling you this story?"

"Because you wanted to make a record," Jennifer recited, though clearly that's not the real reason, or Margaret wouldn't have asked. She has a feeling the reason is nothing she wants to know.

"No," Margaret said. "Do you know why I'm telling this story to *you*?"

"Because I remind you of Kay?"

"No!" Margaret smacked the arm of her chair.

Jennifer tensed. "I really have no idea."

"All right," Margaret said. She leaned her head back against her chair and closed her eyes. "I'm tired now." She said this like she was dismissing Jennifer under a cloud of disappointment, a student who hasn't lived up to her promise, or won't. Refuses to.

Should Jennifer call what she feels uneasiness? Or is it actually something approaching dread? She was hoping Margaret didn't notice. Carrasco. But maybe she did. Let's imagine the worst: Margaret went to the library, armed with that name, and looked her up. Information poured forth like gold treasure from behind a secret door. Now Margaret knows everything. Every fact except the one that matters most.

Outside her window Jennifer can see trees in the foreground, the color of charcoal except where the green moss is on them, their stolid trunks thinning into branches, thinning into delicate graceful twigs, opening like hands to grasp the sky. Never in her life has she paid so much attention to trees. Beyond these are vague and smudgy trees, as in a watercolor painting, and beyond them nothing. There is just nothing there. Impossible not to see magic in this, the gray mist that disappeared the world. She can't stop looking at it.

Milo appears beside her at the window, putting his palm on the glass. "Can we touch it?" he asks.

"We can go out there. But I think it'll just feel damp."

"What's *damp*?"

"A little bit wet."

"I think it will feel like a cloud," he declares.

"What do you think a cloud feels like?"

He appraises her, catching on. "It doesn't feel like it looks."

"I think you're right."

"So what does it feel like?"

"What do you think?"

He considers, then abandons consideration. "Cows." He giggles.

"Cows?" she asks with amusement.

"Cows!" He laughs, enormously pleased with himself. "It feels like cows!"

"All right, silly," Jennifer says. "Let's go test that theory."

Outside the fog moves with them, so that as they approach an object it resolves before them into clear solidity, while beyond it obscurity reigns. They're enclosed, as in a spell of protection. "It's mystical," she says.

"What's *mystical*?"

"A little like *magical*, but different. *Magical* is bright and sparkly. *Mystical* is . . . strange."

Milo reaches out his hand cautiously, as if the air might bite him. "I feel it," he says.

"What do you feel?"

"Cows!" he says, and looks at her hoping for a laugh.

"No, really," she says. "What does it feel like?"

"Damp," he says. Then he looks at her in earnest confusion. "Why doesn't my hand disappear?"

"Well, you can't disappear to yourself."

"Why?"

She shrugs. "The fog is never right where you're standing. Not to you, anyway. It would be to someone looking at you from far away."

"Why?"

"I don't know. Magic."

He doesn't say, *Mo-om*, a reproving singsong, like he normally does when she offers this explanation. He frowns like he's taking it seriously. "So I could disappear to you."

"You could," she says. "But please don't."

He dances away with a mischievous expression, daring her. She stays very still because if she gives chase he'll definitely run. "Don't," she says. She feels a flicker of fear.

He utters a whooping laugh and takes off.

"Milo!" she shouts, running after. She could catch him easily, except that she trips on a tree root and stumbles, and once she's straightened up he's gone. Oh God. He's gone. She listens with terror for the sound of a splash or a scream. But he'll see the pond if he comes upon it. Just because she can't see him doesn't mean he's actually been swallowed by the fog.

"Milo?" she calls. She moves slowly, listening. He's doing a remarkably good job of keeping still. Not a crackling twig. Not a giggle. The fog parts for her as she approaches but doesn't reveal her son. Trees and rocks she can have, but him it keeps. "You did it, Milo," she calls, trying not to sound terrified. "You disappeared."

Now she hears a giggle. From Milo, or the changeling sent to replace him as the fairies carry him away? She walks in what she thinks is the direction of the giggle. "Milo? Please come out now. Really, Milo. I don't like it. It's not safe out here."

Silence. She takes a long breath, slows her heart, changes her tactic. She walks backward instead of forward, falls silent herself, stays very still. Waits. Droplets kiss her skin. A small wind shivers the bushes and branches and there is the sound it makes and nothing else in this muffled world—no color, no bright spangling noise. This is what it is to vanish.

Doubtless the time she waits is much shorter than it feels, because how long can a small child bear to be alone in the woods, where his mother cannot find him? A burst of sound, and then he appears, running, running toward her, and she crouches down as he approaches so she can sweep him into her arms. "Mommy!" he says breathlessly. "You disappeared to me!"

"I know," she says into his ear, squeezing his warm little body. "It was scary, wasn't it?"

"The fog is *jackass*," he says.

"You don't like it anymore?"

"I wish it didn't *exist*."

"Maybe not if you stay with me, though. If you stay with me then you're safe."

"I want to go inside."

"All right." She starts to rise, but he clings to her, so she hoists him up and carries him in, heavy though he's grown. "Milo," she says into his ear at the doorway to their house. "What's your name?"

"It's Milo," he says.

"What's your last name?"

"Young." He says it like she's crazy, like there's never been a doubt.

She doesn't press. You can create a problem in the effort to discover if one exists. She doesn't ask, *So why did you say* Carrasco? *What else do you remember? What else? What else?* Carrasco, Carrasco, Carrasco. There's bad magic in that word. You shouldn't speak it, not if you know what's good for you.

So she doesn't. She carries her son inside and makes them both hot chocolate, and they count out how many marshmallows they're each allowed.

Has everything she's done been for nothing?

Blood on My Hands

I was once a girl named Maggie Jean being driven on a truck next to a girl named Kay through the war zone of France. Soldiers trudged along the road on either side, and when they noticed us it was with a wonderment that girls of our average prettiness weren't used to provoking. In the war, we were more beautiful than we had ever been, and everything that should have been beautiful was not. Some places the trees grew together over the road and you couldn't see any place but exactly where you were, worse than being in a maze because you couldn't even see the sky. Imagine being trapped in there with somebody shooting at you from the other side. A lovely green arch under a summer sky is a death trap. Topsy-turvy. When you're in a war, everything is topsy-turvy. Men in blue overalls and berets are smoking at tables outside a café, even though the buildings on either side look like they've been punched in from the top by a giant. You put up a hospital in a cow pasture. At first it feels exciting and ridiculous, like you're players in the world's biggest game of make-believe. You've gone out in the backyard with your tent and your toy medical kits and now you're busily pretending that sooner or later the patients will arrive.

That first place, the more time passed, the harder it became to believe we ever would get patients. It rained. The latrine trench filled with water. You had to brace yourself very carefully not to slip in the mud. Ants crawled into our bedrolls. All night long we heard shelling in the distance. A whistle. A distant boom. We got up out of bed and brushed off the ants. I tried not to watch Kay for signs of her back injury, because she was alert to the slightest hint that I might be doing so. She snapped, "What?" at me more than a few times when she caught me looking at her. She always said she was fine. But then we'd be walking somewhere, and suddenly her breathing would quicken, and I'd glance over to find her staring straight ahead with a startled, almost panicked look, her mouth slack and her face pale. "I just got a little twinge, that's all," she'd say, when she was able to look round and smile and talk normally again. I'd promised to protect her, and I was itchy with the fear that I wouldn't be able to, with the fear and the boredom and the anticipation.

A few times each day I went and wandered through the tents, as if I were checking on things, though I wasn't really. There was nothing to check on. Everything was at the ready. In the shock ward and the OR, the sawhorses were lined up just so, awaiting stretchers. Two-foot locker boxes with shelves inside held the supplies. In the empty post-op tent there was one GI blanket folded neatly at the foot of each canvas cot. I wasn't the only one engaged in this pointless roaming. I saw the other nurses, the doctors—we nodded at each other, pretending that we had some purpose. It wasn't that we wanted them hurt, the injured and the dying. If we'd had any say in the matter we'd have kept them whole and far from the battlefield. It was just that it was hard living like this, clenched like a fist, listening to the shelling all night long and waiting to see if it, if the war, would have anything to do with us. Already we'd learned to tell from the sound how far away the shells were hitting, how close. It is hard waiting, Jennifer, when you're waiting for something terrible to arrive. After a while you just want it to go ahead and come.

On the third day, they came, just as I'd begun to think they never would, that this whole thing was some strange, airless vacation on the outskirts of battle. It was lunchtime. Lunch was K rations—ham and cheese mixed up in a can, and cigarettes, of course, maybe some candy. I'd choked down about half the food and moved on to a cigarette. It was very hot. Kay and I were talking to one of the doctors, Captain Richard Steigler, a kind but excitable man. I remember him saying, "I'd just like to get a little blood on my hands," and then laughing, and we laughed, too, though we weren't quite sure it was funny, or even if it was a joke.

"You could just kill somebody," Kay said. "A murder mystery would liven things up around here."

"True, true," he said. "But I—" Whatever he was going to say was lost in a sudden commotion. Wounded. We had incoming wounded. "My God," the doctor said. He looked like somebody had slapped him, and maybe he was thinking about that blood-on-his-hands line, and whether he regretted saying it I don't know.

I got up to run, realized after a few steps that I still had that cigarette in my hand, and stopped to drop it and rub it out. I remember being very careful about it, making extra sure the spark was gone, because I had a vision of the whole shebang—field, tents, everything—going up in flames, all because of me. In those few seconds Kay got way ahead of me, and I ran even faster to catch up.

It was so unreal, Jennifer. It's hard to explain how unreal. There I was, running, and certainly that was real, the slap of my feet against ground, the sound of my own breathing in my ears. But what I was running *toward*, that I could no more imagine than I'd been able to when we were waiting in England, punting down the river with the tips of our fingers trailing in the cool water, watching the blur of green along the shore. I was on central supply and operating room, so I went to my station in the OR, just like I was supposed to. There was this excitement—that seems like the wrong word but I don't know what else to call it—and we all felt it. We looked at each other and knew that we all felt it. Like we were all chanting, silently but somehow in unison: *Here we go. Here we go. Here we go.*

Outside there was quite a commotion, the roar of vehicles pulling into the compound, male voices shouting, and one—I thought I heard one, at least—letting out a quickly stifled cry of pain. Well, I had to go see what was happening, and as I ran outside I realized everyone else was doing the same thing. When had we all begun to share a mind? Outside the tent I climbed up on a crate so I could see. Three jeeps. Eight or ten stretchers. And on them men—boys. The wounded. I was looking at them, watching as the corpsmen carried them into the triage area, and still I could hardly believe they existed. When would reality kick back in? I couldn't get over the fact that just moments before I'd been smoking a cigarette, feeling disgusted by my paltry lunch, that Kay had just made a joke about murder and I'd been on the verge of a laugh. That was my life, not this.

The CO called us all back to our positions, and we went. I assumed my place at the operating table. I switched on the light, and the brightness startled me. I stared up into the light, like I'd never seen such a thing, and then dropped my eyes and shook my head to clear my vision. Captain Steigler was at my table. He looked at me and asked if I was ready. I nodded. He nodded back. They brought the first casualty in. I still had spots in my eyes, so that when I looked at him parts of him seemed to glow, and then that was gone, and I really saw him. Really saw, for the first time, what waits on the other side of ordinary life.

The first thing you notice is the dirt. Never in your life have you seen wounds so dirty. The mud, the grass, and the way it's everywhere, everywhere. And the blood. The sheer volume of blood. This boy's legs had been blown off just below the knee, tourniquets tied just above. Beneath the dirt you could see the pallor of his flesh. You could see sinew stringing down into the place where there used to be a foot, blood, tissue, little strands of muscle mixed in, a horror like you'd never seen before. You want to give in to the revulsion, Jennifer, but you can't, and so you split in two, or maybe more pieces than that, so you can do what you have to do.

He was awake. He was maybe eighteen. He asked Captain Steigler, "How's my buddy? How's my buddy?" and Steigler of course had no idea who his buddy was. There was a boy bleeding out from an abdominal wound on the table next to ours—Kay's table. Was that his buddy? I hoped not. Steigler said, "Let me get you taken care of and then we'll find out."

The boy said, "Am I going to die?" Before anybody could answer, he spotted me. He stared at me. He asked, "Are you a girl?"

I took his hand. I said, "Yes, I am."

It's such a strange thing about being female. He thought I was an angel, just because I was a girl.

Another nurse was behind him, getting ready to administer the ether, but he kept on staring at me like I had a holy glow. Then he said, "I must be all right, then. It must be safe here, if there are women. I must not be going to die. You're not going to let me die, are you? You're not going to let me die."

And I said no, no I wasn't, and I meant it, even if I was lying. I had to debride what was left of the legs. I poured water, I picked out dirt and fragments, while the surgeon worked above the tourniquet to see how much of the legs he could save. Bone fragments were embedded in his pelvis. We had to extract those to save the thighs. I'd never done anything like this before, and yet I did it.

I'd been in operating rooms. I thought I had seen some things. I'd never seen anything like this. Our next patient required an amputation. The strangest part was not the cutting through but the moment when the limb actually came off. That first day I carried a whole arm away from the table. I held it by the elbow. The fingers on the hand were still flexed, as though reaching for me, saying, *Hold on a minute, wait, wait.* The arm was surprisingly heavy. You don't think about what an arm weighs when it's still a part of the body. And then when it's off, it's waste. It gets burned with the rest of the waste.

Parts of your body can come off, Jennifer. You can have a hole in your back so big a man can put his fist inside it.

I hadn't seen anything.

Later I'd see all of this, do all of this, many times, without sparing a thought to the oddity of it all. This time I'd moved into the extraordinary but hadn't yet learned how to live there. This wasn't even a hospital as I'd ever known one, with hallways and wards and nurses in white, but a tent full of blood and guts and screaming. There should have been some other name for it, but we didn't have one and so we applied the old one, and after a while when I thought "hospital" what I pictured was a tent or an abandoned schoolhouse, sawhorses for the stretchers, and all the patients boys.

How could I know that soon, shockingly soon, I'd come to think of injuries like that first boy had as lesser ones? I'd say things like, "He's only lost both legs." Only. Because you can keep somebody with a missing limb alive longer than you can somebody with a gut wound. They bleed out slower. My boy was a low priority compared to the one on Kay's table, the one bleeding out so fast they couldn't save him, and he died. I don't know if he was my patient's buddy. I don't remember. I can't remember everything, you know, and what's more I wouldn't want to. In my opinion the human mind is a messed-up thing, the way your memory unleashes these scenes upon you, sixty-plus years after the fact, when you can't even summon up what you had for lunch today.

Some people cried, after. I didn't cry, and neither did Kay. We were probably more proud of that than we should have been. I wrote to my mother, *Am finally doing what I came over to do – It's so different it's fun.*

Topsy-turvy. But you can get used to anything.

Day after day I soldiered through the work I had to do. I cleaned dirt from torn flesh. I picked metal from someone's insides, where it should never, ever be. I cut a slice in burned skin so a twenty-year-old boy could breathe. I told boys on the operating table they wouldn't die, even when I knew they would. I lied. Then I did the next thing, and the next thing, and the next, and no matter what, no matter how tired I was or how hungry or how bone-deep weary, no matter how awful the thing I had to do, I could always do it.

I could always do it, Jennifer. No matter how awful it was.

What about you?

Magic

From Margaret's house Jennifer doesn't go back to her own but instead drives all the way into Sewanee and parks in Megan's drive. Once again she's rattled by the way the interview with Margaret ended, by the fierce, unnerving expression on the old woman's face. *What about you?* Why did she look so disdainful, so certain of Jennifer's weakness? What answer is she hoping for?

Megan opens the door, looking rumpled, a sheaf of papers in one hand. "Hi!" she says, surprised.

"I wondered if you wanted to go for a walk," Jennifer says.

Megan cocks her head and raises her eyes to the ceiling, considering. "I'm supposed to be grading papers," she says. "But you know what? Fuck that. Come on in." She opens the door wide. "I'll put on some shoes."

Jennifer steps inside.

"I won't be a minute," Megan says. She jogs toward the back of her house, calling behind her, "Sit down if you like!"

Jennifer waits in the hall, jittery. She doesn't want to sit down. She wants to keep moving. She wants to be distracted. She wants a nice big dose of Megan's normalcy. In answer to Margaret's question, she said, "What do you mean?" It seemed possible that Margaret would ask, *I mean, did you kill your husband?* But Margaret just said she was tired and wanted to stop for the day.

Megan reappears, already a little breathless. She's slipped the shoes on without tying them and now she drops to the floor to finish the job. "Where do you want to go? The Cross?"

"What's the Cross?"

"Oh, you've never been?" Megan bounces to her feet. "Well, it's a big ol' cross." She grins. "It's pretty. There's an overlook."

I could always do it, Jennifer. No matter how awful it was.

"Let's go," Megan says. "You'll like it. Who doesn't like an overlook?" She ushers Jennifer out the door.

What about you?

Megan claps her hands. "So glad you suggested this!"

The road to the Cross is a hilly one, and as you traverse its ups and downs the great white cross at its end disappears and reappears, a little larger every time. Disappear, reappear. Disappear. Jennifer looks up and watches the branches jog along against the sky, a jagged elegance.

"Something about this road makes me feel like I'm in a fantasy novel," Megan says. "Setting off on a quest. Wearing a long braid and some kind of robe."

"I can see that," Jennifer says.

Megan laughs. "Or you think I'm nuts," she says. She stumbles and puts her hand on Jennifer's arm to steady herself. Smiling, she gives the arm a squeeze. "Apparently walking can be a hazardous activity."

"Don't do that at the edge of the bluff."

"Good advice," Megan says. "I'll take it to heart."

They lapse into silence, unsure where to go after the banter. At least that's how Jennifer feels. In their time together she's counted on Megan to power the conversation. But Megan might grow weary of this. Already she might be thinking, Lord, will this woman never talk? But what can Jennifer talk about? She doesn't want to reintroduce the subject of Margaret. She doesn't want to dwell on that. That's why she's here, walking with Megan down this road. *Do you know why I'm telling you this story? Do you know why I'm telling this story to you?*

"Milo's been calling himself Dark Flame," she says.

"Oh, I like that. That's a good one. Ben just chooses preexisting superheroes: one day he's Spider-Man, the next he's Batman. I'd like him to be more imaginative."

"Milo does that, too. Green Lantern, Iron Man, Superman."

"Ben hasn't been much of a Superman fan as of yet."

"Yeah, that one was pretty brief."

"Can't blame them, right? Boring. Insufficient angst. Milo clearly prefers a superhero with a little angst. Judging from Dark Flame anyway."

"Maybe he's a villain," Jennifer says. "Milo said he was morally ambiguous."

"Morally ambiguous?" Megan laughs. "Smart kid." The Cross reappears. "There it is again," Megan says. This hill is effortful, and they climb it in silence. The Cross disappears. "And there it goes."

"How much do you think kids remember?" Jennifer asks. "I mean, how far back do Ben's memories go?"

"I'd say not far. Sometimes I'm surprised by what he's already forgotten."

"Sometimes I'm surprised by what Milo remembers."

"Yeah?"

"I don't really want Milo to remember his dad."

There's a sudden alertness to Megan. "You don't?" she asks carefully.

"Some memories wouldn't be so good." Why is Jennifer talking? Why is she saying these things? She swallows. She has a lump in her throat. "I'd rather just be able to tell him the good things, and have that be all he knows."

"That's understandable."

"I guess."

"It is! You want him to have a happy childhood. You want to give him a good start."

"But I'm lying." Jennifer risks a glance at Megan, and is almost undone by the sympathy on her face. "I'm lying to him."

"No, no, no, it's not *lying*." Megan frowns. "It's like what we do when we pretend there's a Santa. It's preserving the magic. I don't see anything wrong with him having good memories of his father."

Don't talk, Jennifer. For God's sake. Say thank you and shut your mouth. "Tommy wanted to be a good dad," she says. "But . . ." She hesitates, thinking of Sebastian's claims about Megan, and then says it anyway. "He drank too much. So you could never quite trust him."

Megan waits.

"Once I woke up in the middle of the night with a bad feeling. I woke up startled—you know that feeling?"

Megan nods, watching Jennifer with a worried frown.

"Tommy wasn't in bed but that was normal. He usually stayed up late, drinking. I got up and went to check on Milo—he was two and still in a crib—but he wasn't there, so then I panicked. I searched the house, and he wasn't anywhere. Then I realized I could hear him crying, but I couldn't figure out where it was coming from. It was like he was a ghost, like he was in the walls—" She stops with a shudder. "Anyway," she says. "I went outside, and Tommy was on a blanket in the middle of the yard, passed out. And Milo—Milo had climbed through a broken window into Tommy's storage shed. There was a stack of paving stones beneath the window Tommy never fixed, for the patio Tommy never built. Milo was in there in the dark, with the lawn mower and the rakes. He had little pieces of glass in his hands and feet." Milo's face, Milo's desperate face. When she opened the door, he looked at her with terror. The trail of blood he'd left round the shed, the bloody fingerprints on his pajamas, his diaper soaking, his plump little feet, filthy and bare and stuck with glass. She'd let that happen to him. Because she couldn't leave Tommy. Because of *love*.

"I'm so sorry," Megan says. "How awful for you." She puts a gentle hand on Jennifer's back, keeps it there as they walk.

"Somebody at the bar told Tommy about a meteor shower, so he got Milo out of bed to show him. It was supposed to be a 'rare and magical experience.' He just wanted Milo to see."

Now Megan stops walking; now she turns Jennifer toward her and embraces her. There is no choice, is there, between steeling yourself and sobbing. Jennifer steels herself. There's no way to feel just a little bit. "You poor thing," Megan says. "You poor, poor thing."

She could tell the story, the whole story. Megan would understand.

Wouldn't that be a magic trick.

We're all a little morally ambiguous, Megan. Maybe, as it turns out, even you. We all have a little dark flame. Ah, but that doesn't mean we understand each other. We do bad things and yet think of ourselves as good. Fundamentally good, you see, despite a slipup or two. Other people, though. When they do a bad thing, we tend to think they're bad.

Megan pulls back to look Jennifer in the eye. "I'm glad you told me," she says. "Because that's a miserable thing to go through, and I can't imagine you're not still coping with it. I want you to know that I'm always here to listen."

"Thank you," Jennifer says. "I appreciate that." She turns toward the Cross, which is looming now, enormous and white, so much bigger than she expected it to be. "Almost there," she says, attempting a smile.

So now she's told that story and can't take it back. Exhibit A. Offered as defense in advance of the trial, she supposes, because surely she'd never have told it if Milo hadn't let *Carrasco* slip, if her secret hadn't been momentarily exposed. She walks fast and Megan does, too, and she hopes by the time they reach the overlook she'll have thought of something sprightly to say, so that Megan feels like it's okay to resume normal conversation, to break the melancholy silence of sympathy.

Here is what Margaret might now know: That Tommy died of a painkiller overdose. That Zoe went to the police. *My mother killed him*, Zoe said. *My mother wanted him dead. She cheated on him. She lied. My father loved me too much to take his own life. My father was a wonderful man.* Reasons to investigate, the police said, and the newspaper repeated, and after that how they all looked at her! Her daughter, her mother-in-law, everyone she knew, thinking *murderer, murderer, murderer*, even after no charges were brought, so loud they should have just chanted it. Zoe Eleanor Carrasco. Her daughter. She went to the police. She gave quotes to the newspaper. That's how sure she was.

Pretty damning, wouldn't you say? For the woman's own daughter to be that sure? Even a teenager loves her mother.

The last time Jennifer saw Zoe, she showed up at her parents' house, Tommy's mother, Caroline, in tow. "We want to see Milo," one or both of them said. Jennifer stepped back to let them in, and yet still felt as though they'd forced their way inside. As if they'd shown up with a warrant, banging on the door. Milo was playing in the living room. They dropped to the floor beside him and checked him over: Zoe touching his little hands, Caroline tilting his head back to examine his face. Caroline—who'd always taken Jennifer's side, who'd tried to tell Tommy he drank too much. How could she imagine Jennifer would hurt her little boy? Before they left Zoe told her that Caroline had been to a lawyer to talk about custody, Caroline herself lingering behind with Milo, hugging him even as he squirmed, hugging him like she wanted to lift him up and carry him away. Zoe said more, but Jennifer wasn't listening. Jennifer was listing in her head all the things she'd need to pack. She'd planned her departure, then hesitated; now it was time to go. So her son would never look at her the way her daughter did. So her son would stay safe in the enchant-ment of early childhood, where incomprehension is a blessing, where memory is a rushing stream. So her son would stay hers.

If Margaret knows, what will happen next? Will she have told Sue the librarian? Probably not, from what Jennifer knows of Marga-ret. She'll hoard the secret. She'll retreat with it to her castle in the woods. And then what?

Two Girls

Kay and Maggie Jean, they lived in a world of knowing nothing. Not the language. Not how long before they'd move again. Not whether the person they were talking to would be alive the next day. Not even, sometimes, where they were. A field. A building. Sometimes that was the best they could do.

They moved. It rained. They moved again. Every day they seemed to sink deeper into the mud. They waded through it up to their knees, stood in the shower with their feet in a thick pool of it. Their pants were splattered with it, their boots caked with it, the unrelenting, unending mud.

Let me tell you something I remember, something I'll never forget. Oh, Jennifer, wait, stop—I already told you. There's no way to count the things I forget, but I do remember telling you now. About the dress that came to me in a pasture in France, the dress from my old life, and how Kay insisted I put it on, and we danced in the grass while men sang and played their helmets like drums. Heaven should be your happiest memory. Heaven should be that memory, forever, with just enough bittersweet to make it matter, to make it hurt.

I tried to protect her, I really did. I pretended she had a fever, once or twice, when she was laid up. I carried things for her. I got her pain medication on the sly. I tried. That's why she wasn't with me the night I got loaned out to another hospital—they'd asked for two nurses, and we were both supposed to go, but when the jeep came I got in by myself and told the driver I was all the chief nurse could spare. There was artillery fire up ahead and the sky lighting up a sick green as shells exploded. He took me to a filthy hospital—it'd been occupied by the Germans—and I didn't like being there. I was worried about Kay, lying in a fetal position on the hard ground in our tent. I was tired. I didn't like being in a strange place alone. I tore a German sign off the wall and crumpled it in my hands.

I don't remember the first part of my shift, before they brought the boy in. And I don't remember what exactly his injury was. You might argue that I don't want to remember, and you might be right. He was young, a teenager. A French civilian, a boy who should have been in school. Maybe he had a brain injury. Maybe he was gut shot. What I remember is the screaming. My God, he screamed. It was the most desperate sound I had ever heard, like you might imagine people scream in hell, if you believed in hell, which I don't. Hell right here. That's what I believe in.

The doctor on shift was young, too, and green as grass, and in the way people often do, he tried to make up for inexperience with arrogance. He wanted me to hold the boy down so he could do something—if I remembered the nature of the injury I might remember what the something was—and I tried, but the boy screamed and writhed as though my hands were branding irons. I remember the feel of his shoulders, the way even his skin seemed to shrink from me, the sharpness of the bone.

"He needs morphine," I said.

"What?" the doctor said. He couldn't hear me over the screaming.

"He needs morphine," I shouted. I felt like I was going to faint, although I knew I wouldn't. Whatever his injury was I'd seen as bad or possibly worse. But the screaming affected me physically. The screaming was inside my body, it was in my brain, it was moving under my skin.

"Let's get him stabilized," the doctor said, or words to that effect. I'm guessing here, because all I remember for certain is that I kept shouting that the boy needed morphine and the doctor kept ignoring me—entirely, I believe, because he didn't want to be bossed by the nurse—and the boy kept screaming and he screamed and screamed and screamed until he died.

When he died, it was like the whole world went quiet. Of course most of the patients on the ward were pretty bad off, but they were conscious, some of them, and one of them had even started yelling along with the boy, no more able to bear the sound than I had been, I suppose. But when the boy stopped screaming all sound stopped. No one moved. No one breathed. I think I know what we all felt. We were glad he'd died. We were glad he couldn't scream anymore. Maybe we thought, Thank God, and then we realized, a moment later, that we were thanking God for killing him. I don't know if the men felt bad about that. I don't know what brutalities they'd seen or committed, in thought or deed, how far they'd gone from their original notion of themselves. For me, thinking, Thank God, when that boy died—I'd go farther, but I didn't know that. Then, that was as far as I'd gone.

When sound came back, it was the doctor talking. That stupid goddamn doctor. "Nothing we could have done," he said.

I looked at him. *Nothing we could have done.* Can I remember what he looked like? He wore glasses, I know. I would have liked to slap them off his face. "Morphine," I said. I shook my head. I felt like I was choking. *"That's* what we could have done." I turned away, before I did slap him.

I went about my rounds, checking vitals and so forth. I was even more gentle, more solicitous, than usual, trying to make up for it, I guess. For what I'd thought. Orderlies came and took the boy—the body—away. The doctor—who knows what he was up to. But I can tell you that I'd not quite finished checking vitals when he came up and planted himself in front of me.

"Nurse," he said.

"Lieutenant Riley," I corrected. I didn't look at him.

He ignored me. "We need clean needles and syringes. Go to central supply."

Oh, I know exactly why he did it. It's an easy one, psychologically speaking. I'd been right, he'd been wrong, he and any of the patients conscious enough to pay attention knew it, and now he wanted to reassert his dominance, because his need to be in charge was so great it was the reason he hadn't eased the suffering of a dying boy.

Now I did look at him, the arrogant little punk whose face my memory has erased. "I'll do that," I said, "when I'm through here. And I'll do that," I said, "when you address me as 'Lieutenant Riley' and when you say *please*."

He stared at me for a long time, no doubt weighing his options, whether he'd look more foolish if he did as I asked, or if he got in a public fight with me, or if he went to central supply himself. He was a young kid, too, when you think about it, and no doubt terrified underneath it all. You could feel sorry for him, if you wanted to. But I don't. He let that boy scream himself to death, and I hope wherever he is he hasn't forgotten that to this day. And if he's dead I hope it was one of the last things he thought about. This is vengeful and it's unkind and it's the truth. I hope he has his prisons, as I have mine.

"Lieutenant Riley," he said. "Please go to central supply for needles and syringes as soon as you are able."

"As soon as I am able, I will," I said. I nodded at him, curtly, dismissing him. *Get out of my sight*, I wanted to say.

I took my time about finishing up my rounds, but I have to admit it was a relief to get off the ward, to walk quickly down a long and empty hallway, as fast as I could go without running. The trouble was, I realized after a few minutes, that I had no idea how to find central supply. The second I walked off the ward that hospital turned into a maze. How had I found the shock ward in the first place? You know, I can't remember. I picture myself walking there alone but someone must have shown me the way. At any rate, there was no one to show me now, and I walked down that first hall and turned and walked down another, and then I went down a flight of stairs, and before too long I couldn't even have found my way back to the starting point.

I poked my head through several doorways, only to find empty wards, or piles of bloody linens. I was having a hard time staying calm. The last thing I wanted was to give that horse's ass of a doctor an opportunity to criticize me, but more than that I was developing a panicky conviction that I'd never find the right place. I couldn't seem to find anybody to ask, either. At the end of a hall I thought I heard voices behind a closed door, and so I opened it.

But nobody was talking in there. The first thing I noticed, when I pushed open the door, was the smell. I knew that smell, of course, but it took me a moment to place it, because my mind could absorb neither the evidence from my nose nor the evidence from my eyes. Bodies. Bodies upon bodies upon bodies. I saw a foot. I saw a hand. Was this what the Germans had done? Or was it what we had done?

And then I saw the boy atop the pile, like an answer to that question. Flung there, it looked like, the way his arms were splayed. His eyes still open. His mouth still screaming. He'd died brutally, and this, too, was a brutality, that he'd been flung atop this pile of corpses like so much junk. Did it matter, now that he was dead? It was hard to know what mattered anymore.

Somebody touched my shoulder. It startled me, but I made no

sound. I turned to see a corpsman. He said, "Ma'am, you don't want to see that."

"I already saw it," I said.

"They'll be buried eventually," he said. "When there's time to stop and identify them. This is temporary. Come away, now. You don't want to see."

But I'd already seen. There was no making the best of that. There was only looking, and then looking away.

"Come away now," the corpsman said again, and I was all docility. I let him pull me away. I let him shut the door. I asked him, very politely, to take me to central supply.

I remember taking the needles and syringes back to the doctor, and I remember that when he took a syringe from me—snatched, more like—I snapped, "What do you say?"

"Thank you," he said, like a scolded little boy.

Later it was midnight, mealtime, and a corpsman was telling me I was in for a treat.

"We've been eating well," he said. "The Germans left behind some beef."

He offered me a plate. I looked at the slab of meat upon it, and I didn't think, Flesh and flesh and flesh. I sat down and ate it, like I was starving. I ate it all.

A jeep dropped me off. It had started to rain, and by the time I climbed out of the jeep it was pouring. I ran for our tent, and just as it came within view I tripped over a tent rope and went flat. I was covered in mud. I found Kay awake inside the tent. She didn't sleep well anymore, from the pain. "Should we start building an ark?" she asked, then, "What happened to you?"

"It's only mud," I said.

"Do you want to clean up?"

"Why bother? Why not just stay covered in mud all the time? Simpler."

"Not terribly sterile, though," Kay said. She'd been rummaging around while I'd been talking, and now she unearthed a towel, sniffed it, made a face, and handed it to me with a shrug.

I mopped at my shirt, took it off, mopped at my skin. Though we'd put Vaseline on the tent seams in an effort to keep them from leaking, water still ran down from the spots we'd missed or hadn't been able to reach. I hunched under one of these trickles and did my best to pretend it was a shower. I kept seeing that room, that boy. His open mouth. I felt like I could no longer bear it. And by "it" I mean life, I mean everything.

"Much more of this rain and we'll just float out of here," Kay said.

"I'm going to give up this futile effort, then," I said. "I'll just lie down and wait for the floods to cleanse me."

"Of mud and sin," Kay intoned.

"Of mud and sin," I repeated, more grimly than I had intended to.

There in the dark, where it was sometimes okay to ask such questions, Kay said, "Do you think you've sinned?"

"I don't know," I said. "I feel bad about something."

"What?"

"I don't know," I said, not wanting to tell her. Not wanting her to know. "Maybe it's something I haven't done yet."

"I forgive you now," she said. "Ahead of time."

I lay down, then sat right back up, yelping. Something had pricked my shoulder, something that left it throbbing with pain. A bee. A bee had stung me.

"What happened?" Kay asked.

"A bee, Kay. Oh my Lord. I got stung by a bee." I noted with detachment a certain hysteria in my voice. "I'm plagued, I'm plagued, I'm plagued."

"Shhhh," Kay said. She got out her flashlight and checked my wound. "The stinger's still in there," she said. She found some tweezers and removed it. She touched the throbbing spot lightly with her finger and for an instant it seemed to cool. What a good nurse she was. I wanted to talk to her like the boys on the tables talked to me. I wanted to say she made me feel safe; I wanted to beg her not to let me die.

"I'm going crazy," I said.

"I'm not going to let that happen," she said. "I'm not going to let anything happen to you."

I believed her. I remember that I really did believe her, though it made no sense. She sat next to me, our shoulders touching, and we listened to the rain. She told me I was lucky I wasn't allergic to bees.

I said, "I *am* lucky," and she said, "You *are* lucky." She picked up my hand and wove our fingers together. I looked at our hands. Flesh and flesh and flesh. I looked at her face. She looked back at me. And then I kissed her.

It wasn't a long kiss. It was just a little kiss, a closed-mouth kiss, on her lips, and though I felt an answering pressure, her mouth against my mouth, she pulled back almost immediately. That was the end. That was all. So many things happened because of that kiss. But it barely existed. It could so easily have been erased.

And I don't even know, Jennifer, if it meant what you doubtless think it means. You probably think I'm lying when I say this, in this age when all love must be neatly categorized. But I'm not lying. I don't know, Jennifer. I just don't know. I'd been so shaken, so upset. That boy, the screaming. I did love her. But I don't know what kind of love it was.

I saw in her face that I had changed things, and I was sorry, immediately. "Oh," I said, "I didn't . . ." But we had no language to discuss these matters. So I couldn't finish the sentence.

"It's all right," she said. But she didn't look at me. "I'm going to turn in."

She moved slowly, painfully, over to her bedroll. I wanted to offer commiseration but my tongue throbbed in my mouth, bee-stung.

I couldn't speak. In the midst of horror I'd had one person. Now I couldn't speak.

Once upon a time there were two girls. And then I ruined everything.

Jennifer, you told me I should be glad. I should be glad I've lived so much of my life alone, in the tidy confines of solitude. Maybe you were right. Maybe I should be glad.

Girls' Night

Surrounded by people—Megan and six of her numerous friends—Jennifer is doing her best to pretend she belongs there. There, and not at Margaret's house, helplessly listening. It's begun to seem to Jennifer that when she goes to that house she enters a fairy tale; Margaret's story is a spell she's casting, and at the end, when they reach its awful heart, Jennifer's transformation will be complete. And what will she be then? She's thought about quitting but can't. She needs the money. Behind this need, there's another, despite her efforts to wish it away: she wants to know. What happened to Margaret. What Margaret knows. But there will be a price for understanding. *Bodies upon bodies upon bodies.*

After their session today, Jennifer went home and took a drained accidental nap on the couch. A hand touched her side as she lay there. She could distinguish each component part of the hand, the heel against her back, the palm cupped over the curve of her side, and against her front the pressure of each insistent fingertip—a pressure somewhere between a threat and a caress. She was close enough to the surface of consciousness to be aware of herself curled up on the couch. If she knew where she was, then the hand must be real. She woke, with a jolt of terror, to find herself alone.

Even now the feeling of the hand on her side remains uncomfortably vivid. The lively talk among the other women is a welcome distraction. They're at a fancy restaurant at one end of Sewanee, occupying a table in the back. The place is BYOB, and each person, even Jennifer, brought wine, with the result that they have a great many bottles. The waiter opened half, to start, and they all filled their glasses quite full. Even Jennifer, as that seemed simpler than explaining that she doesn't want any at all.

It's their monthly girls' night. Some of the women say *girls' night* with a touch of irony. Some of them say it in a toast-making voice, a pep-rally voice. *We're gonna whoop it up.* Tommy used to talk about "the boys." Going out with *the boys*. Jennifer remembers riding in the back of a pickup truck, the driver Tommy's most sober friend. She's pressed against Tommy. His hand is on her knee. She's warm where he touches her, cool otherwise. She feels the stereo's bass in her throat. The wind makes a flag of her hair. We call ourselves girls and boys when we want to go back in time.

Jennifer is, at Megan's request, one of two designated drivers; the other—Amanda—is making a great show of taking only the tiniest sips of her wine. "The only good thing about being the designated driver," she says, "is that next month I don't have to do it."

"Oh, poor Amanda," Terry says. She leans over and gives Amanda a squeeze. "Don't you know you don't need booze to have fun?"

Megan turns to Jennifer and says, "Thanks again for driving tonight."

"Oh, you know," Jennifer says. "It's not much of a hardship for me."

"Last month it was my turn," Megan says. "I hate my turn."

Erica, who sits on Jennifer's other side, leans in. "Sebastian's the one who made the rule."

"Yup," Megan says. "We used to just see who was sober at the end of the night, but he didn't think that was sufficient."

"Ah," Jennifer says.

"That's how he talks when he's mad at me." She deepens her voice and says, "That's insufficient, Megan. That's insufficient." Another conversation catches Erica's attention, and Megan lowers her voice so only Jennifer can hear. "He hates to lose control. Hates big displays in anybody—especially himself. When Ben has a tantrum, he practically turns into an English schoolmaster. A *Victorian* English schoolmaster."

"His upbringing, maybe," Jennifer offers.

"Maybe," Megan says. "His mother's very sweet, but prone to melancholy, and his father has a temper. So maybe. I sometimes think that he might be more emotional if I were less. You know how that is in a marriage. You have to balance the seesaw."

Jennifer nods.

"But it's a good rule," Megan says. "A good rule." She turns back to the rest of the table and raises both her voice and her glass. "To our drivers, for making this all possible!"

All the women cry, "To Amanda! To Jennifer!"

It's a nice feeling, to be cheered. A smile overtakes Jennifer's face as she looks at all their happy ones. Smiling, smiling.

But then in her head she hears *Maybe you should be glad*. It's her own voice speaking, or Margaret's. And then she thinks, I'll ruin it.

Megan notices that she's not talking much, from time to time offering a fact about her to the table or asking a question that's meant to draw her out. They have a young and handsome waiter who clearly recognizes them and grins with genuine pleasure when he sees them, and as they flirt and banter no one seems to care whether his pleasure is based on their company or their large order and forthcoming generous tip. Why should they care? Why should Jennifer?

When the meal is over, they tell the waiter they might have dessert, but first they have to polish off some more of this wine.

"Good luck," he says, promising to return shortly. "Godspeed." They fill their glasses again. When Erica holds the bottle over Jennifer's original glass, still nearly full, Jennifer covers the top with her hand.

Megan is drunk. Megan is so drunk that at times she half-leans on Jennifer, and Jennifer assumes that the rest of the time she's leaning on Amanda, who sits on her other side. Her features have loosened. There's a dreamy dullness in her eyes. When the waiter brings the dessert menus, Megan puts hers down with a laugh. "I know all your desserts, but I'm too drunk to remember," she announces cheerfully. "I'm also too drunk to read." She smiles up at the waiter. "You tell me what to have."

"You like chocolate, right?" says the waiter.

Megan shakes her head slowly from side to side, but means this shake as agreement. "Who doesn't?" she asks.

"Okay," the waiter says. He gives her a knowing nod. "I'll bring you something good."

"I want something amazing," Megan says.

"Oh, don't worry," the waiter says. "It's the torte. I'm pretty sure I've brought it to you before, and I'm pretty sure you loved it."

"Did I?" Megan says, her eyes lingering on him. He moves around the table, taking more orders, and Megan leans into Jennifer and says, "I love him." She doesn't say it particularly softly. He's right there.

Jennifer shushes her gently, feeling the embarrassment that Megan is spared by the grace of alcohol. "Megan, you cradle robber," Amanda says as the waiter moves away, and Jennifer laughs along with everyone else. It's easier if she can just find this funny. "Is that your phone?" she asks, because somewhere in the vicinity something is quacking like a duck.

"Oh!" Megan laughs, swaying, as she rummages in her bag. "Isn't that funny? That means it's Sebastian." She locates the phone and lifts it so she can see the screen. "Quack, quack," she says, before she presses answer.

Jennifer scoots away as much as she can, trying not to eavesdrop. On her other side Erica and Juliana are engaged in a passionate discussion about a TV show that Jennifer doesn't watch. She tries to look interested anyway.

Suddenly Megan takes the phone from her ear and thrusts it out into the group. She presses the button that puts Sebastian on speakerphone, and they all hear him saying, "Come home now or the next time you want to go out with the girls you can forget it." They fall silent, staring at the phone.

"Okay!" Megan shouts, and then she presses end and drops the phone on the table.

Jennifer is astonished—an open display of hostility from Megan! Already she's apologizing. "I shouldn't have done that," she says.

"We won't tell him," Terry says. "Don't worry."

"No, no, I know," Megan says. "But he'd hate that I did that."

"Oh, *who cares*," says Amanda, hitting each word hard as a drum.

"I don't want to ruin your good time," Megan says. "This is not the moment for marital drama. That's not why we go out."

"You're ruining nothing, Megan," Juliana says. "There's no censorship here."

The others chime in with encouragement and support. Everything Jennifer never got when she brought up Tommy to her old friends. Her complaints always led to an awkward silence. Maybe because she wasn't as sweet as Megan. Wasn't, isn't, never has been. Maybe she was disconcertingly angry. Maybe she was uncomfortably raw. Maybe she was plain unlikable. Or maybe everybody just really loved Tommy. It comes over her that of course the right analogy isn't Jennifer to Megan but Jennifer to Sebastian. She keeps thinking about Sebastian's voice when he said *with the girls*. The way it sharpened on those words. That was how she used to sound. Tommy on the phone, the happy rumble in the background, her bitter edge as she said, "Out with the boys?" As she made the same fruitless demand: *Come home now.* She knows exactly how much Sebastian hates *with the girls*, that cheerful euphemism. Jennifer to Sebastian. Bad guy to bad guy. The one who wants to leave the party is never the favored one.

"Maybe I should call him back," Megan says.

"I can take you home if you want," Jennifer says. "And then come back for everyone else."

"No," several of the others say. Erica, drunk and forceful, slaps the palm of her hand on the table. "Fuck him," she says.

"Y'all, don't hold this against him," Megan says. "He's just looking out for me."

"Megan, you're a saint," Terry says. "I wouldn't be that nice about it."

Erica, clearly relishing the freedom of alcoholic truth-telling, says, "He's a *dick*."

Megan bows her head, torn between accepting the compliments and resisting this characterization of the man she's married to. Jennifer sits in silent struggle against her own dark thoughts, but the rest of them continue to vilify Sebastian and sanctify Megan and in the end Megan gives in to the warm bath of affirmation and announces that she'll stay. This is greeted by cheering and more pouring of wine. Erica says, "To one more round!" and Amanda adds, "To freedom!" and they laugh and clink glasses and in their triumph it never occurs to them that what they're toasting is selfish hedonism and the willful disregard of its consequences.

It occurs to Jennifer, of course. But she is toasting, too. Because she doesn't want to be the person Tommy made, the person Margaret's spell will make her, wants to will into existence the possibility that she can be different. What the other women do she will do, so that no one looking at the group could tell her apart from the rest of them. So when Erica rounds on her suddenly, points at her vigorously, and says,

"Oh my God! I keep forgetting you're a massage therapist! I should make an appointment with you!" Jennifer points back, matches her tone of drunken epiphany, and says, "You should!" Though of course she isn't drunk. But where's the harm in pretending?

"Get out your calendar," Erica says, with a grand gesture of command. She produces her own phone. "We'll make an appointment right now."

"Appointment for what?" Samantha asks.

"For massage!" Erica says. "Remember?"

"That's right!" Samantha says. "I want an appointment, too!"

Suddenly they all want appointments. Each of them, phone in hand, saying, *What about this day, what about that, oh—you took the time I wanted! No, no, that's okay, I'll just hold it against you, don't worry at all.* Jennifer schedules them all, with a reckless disregard for times she usually devotes to Margaret. She'll worry about that later. Or she won't worry at all. At the thought of slowing the pace of Margaret's revelations, she feels a lightening of spirit. Maybe she won't worry at all.

The only person who doesn't make an appointment is Megan. Megan sits quietly polishing off her wine during the general hilarity. Jennifer feels a sharp awareness of her silence, even as she schedules the others and laughs at their jokes. Why doesn't Megan want a massage?

"All right," Amanda says as they all holster their phones. "That was a job of work."

"A job of work?" Terry repeats. "A job of work?"

"It's an expression," Amanda says. "It means that was hard work."

"I know what it means. I've just never heard it outside of an old Southern novel."

"Is that a Southern expression?" Juliana asks.

"It sounds like it should be," Amanda says. "But you know, some of the terms we think of as so Southern, like really antiquated-sounding ones that have hung on in Appalachia, are really holdouts from British English. Like *reckon*, for instance, that was—"

"Jennifer can tell what you're feeling," Megan interrupts. "Just from touching you."

All heads swivel toward Jennifer. "Really?" Juliana says.

"Well, no, not exactly," Jennifer says. "Not like a psychic."

"How then?" Samantha asks.

"Explain it to them," Megan says, waving her hand. Her eyes have an unfocused look that Jennifer doesn't want to see. That she wants to pretend isn't there. She repeats what she told Megan: that emotion lives in the body, and so does memory. A betrayal in the right shoulder, guilt in the ball of the foot.

"So when you give us massages," Amanda says, "you'll be able to tell us about our emotional state?"

"Probably," Jennifer says. "If you want me to. Yes."

"Oh, that's intriguing," Amanda says. "You might tell me things I don't know."

"Yes," Jennifer says, "but usually once I say it people recognize it."

"Oh!" Erica says. "This is going to be like a treasure hunt." She turns her shoulder toward Jennifer and points. "This knot right here. What does it mean?"

Jennifer's getting nervous. She doesn't want to be called upon to perform parlor tricks. She doesn't want to expose anyone's pain. "Now, now," she says, in a mock-scold, "no freebies." Then, to show her goodwill, she puts her hand on Erica's shoulder and works the knot a little.

"Ohhhhh," Erica says, a noise of painful pleasure.

"Don't worry," Jennifer says, patting Erica before removing her hand. "We'll get that out."

"Can my appointment be right now?" Erica asks, and then someone else jokes about laying Erica out on the table and what the management would say, and how much they'd have to tip, and where the cute waiter is with the promised incredible desserts. To Jennifer's relief the conversation spirals away from her.

Later, after the passengers of Jennifer's car have said goodbye to the passengers of Amanda's, Megan leans against Jennifer and says, "What do you sense about me?"

And because Jennifer is determined not to ruin it, she puts her arm around Megan, squeezes her, and says, "That you're wonderful," and not *That you're very sad.*

I Think I'll Go

She tried for a while to pretend I hadn't kissed her. Kay, I mean. We both tried to pretend. But there had been a perfect intimacy between us, and now it was gone. She was no longer completely herself with me, nor I with her. Now our friendship was a role to play, the part of Kay, the part of Maggie Jean. Being in her company was like mourning a dead person while sitting down to dinner with her ghost.

There were exceptions. Of course there were. Nothing is ever one thing all the time. Nothing is *consistent*, least of all what a person feels. That morning in Zietz, in Germany, Kay in the blooming garden. That was an exception. She tucked a flower into my hair, touching me like she wasn't afraid, and I wanted to weep, I wanted to catch her hands and press them to my mouth, but I couldn't, I couldn't, and still I was so glad. By the time we'd crossed the border from France I'd been weary to the bone, and sick to death of my weariness, discouraged by my own discouragement. I remember rattling along in the back of a truck, past white flags flying in some smashed-flat town, and thinking with some disgust that I, too, had surrendered. Here was the end of something. Dead cattle and smashed-up towns. Here were the dragon teeth and pillboxes of the Siegfried Line, long tank traps, fields just dotted with foxholes. Here were the white flags flying, and in one little village a town crier calling the people together with a bell.

Once we passed two little girls playing in a front yard, and they were so absorbed in what they were doing they didn't notice us until we were almost upon them, and when they did they froze. Just froze, and stood there, like people in a painting. A woman—their mother—hurried out of the house. She didn't look at us, as though if she didn't look we wouldn't be there. She grabbed each girl by an arm and tugged them backward toward the house. We were rolling past as this happened. I leaned so far out of the truck to watch them, Kay caught hold of my sleeve. I saw a child's hand, still extended, and then it disappeared, and the door shut, and they were gone, and so were we. The whole thing seemed to happen without a sound, like a scene from a silent movie. "Be careful," Kay said. "Don't want to lose you."

I don't know if she really said that. I like to remember that's what she said.

Despite everything, Germany was beautiful.

The things I remember. The blooming garden. I thought maybe after that things would go back to normal with Kay. But they did and they didn't. One night at two or three in the morning we were alone on a ward when the klaxon sounded. We'd been told if this happened we were to make for the basement, but we were on a ward where none of the patients could be moved. We ran down the ward putting steel pots and helmets on the patients, whatever we could find, and then we just crouched in a corner, put our helmets on, and pretended our whole bodies fit inside them instead of just our heads. What a store of faith we put in those helmets. We didn't have anything else.

When you're accustomed to shells coming in, you can tell by the sound whether they're going to go over. You can hear them testing—the shells go too far one way, and then they try the other way, and then the third time they get you. "One," I said out loud as I heard them go too far. "Two," I said as I heard them go the other direction.

"Don't," Kay said.

Three, I said silently in my head. I waited. "Three," I whispered. But nothing. I held my breath. I let it out. I could have sworn I heard Kay whisper, "Three." But nothing came.

Kay reached for my hand. She clutched it so hard I felt my bones give way, but I didn't say a word to stop her. I said, "'But death replied: "I choose him." So he went, / And there was silence in the summer night; / Silence and safety; and the veils of sleep. / Then, far away, the thudding of the guns.'"

"Jesus, Maggie Jean," she said.

"Siegfried Sassoon," I said. "I had a patient, before the war, who used to quote poetry to me. Didn't I ever tell you that? He'd been in the First World War, and I think he was hoping to persuade me not to join. Mr. Lewis. I can't believe I never told you about him."

More shells. The first went past us again.

"One," Kay said.

"He was dying," I said. "Cancer of the neck. He was probably fifty. He was married, no kids, and his wife almost drove me crazy, because from the moment I saw him I knew he'd come to the hospital to die, and every day she'd come in and ask me didn't I think he was better. He'd been an English teacher of some kind, high school or college, I can't remember. The cancer had affected his voice, so that he spoke in this scratchy way that sounded painful. Must have been painful. But he was determined to talk. His whole life had been about talking and it was the last thing he'd let go."

I stopped talking for a moment and listened. Nothing. I went on. "The head nurse was a stickler when it came to pain meds, didn't want us to up his morphine. I mean, was she afraid he'd carry an addiction into the next life, begging morphine from the angels? He didn't complain, not Mr. Lewis, but when a patient's on your ward long enough you learn to read him, and I could tell by his forehead . . ." In the dark I touched my own, picturing the tension in Mr. Lewis's brow, the way the skin whitened around his mouth. "Once when I got near his bed I realized some sound I'd been hearing suddenly stopped. After that I started pausing a few feet away to listen to him. 'Oh, oh, oh,' he'd whisper, when he thought nobody was near. 'Oh, oh, oh.'"

I stopped again. "Go on," Kay whispered.

"I asked her—the head nurse—over and over to up his meds. She wouldn't. So I went to the doctor. He not only upped the meds, he took her to task, let me tell you. She hated me after that."

Kay snorted. "I shouldn't wonder." She sounded a little more like herself. We heard a howling overhead. "Two," Kay said.

I listened hard. "That's why I joined. Because Mr. Lewis died. I know that doesn't quite make sense. But that's why."

"You never did tell me that," Kay said, and I wondered why there was sorrow in her voice. "But I've told you," she said, "how my father didn't want me to join." Her shaking seemed to vibrate the floor. "He said I would shame him. He said if I joined I could forget coming home again." She pulled her hand from mine.

I swallowed. I didn't want her to mean that I was part of that shame. I didn't want that to be why she'd taken away her hand. "But where else will you go?"

"I have shamed him, haven't I?" she said. "He was right to try to stop me. I never should have come."

"Don't say that."

"I'm sorry that I came."

"Don't say that."

"We're going to die right here, Maggie Jean. We're going to die."

"We aren't," I said, and I took her hand and held it hard, as hard as she'd held mine earlier, trying to stop her shaking.

We heard howling again, and this time it got louder and louder and failed to diminish. When would it diminish? "Three," we said at the same moment, and then the shell hit. A life-altering sound. The walls *quaked*. Plaster rained from the ceiling. It felt like it was not just the building about to crumble around us but the entire world.

A long time after the walls stopped trembling, we stayed in that corner. Kay shook and shook and I held her hand and listened to the both of us breathing.

We waited. Nothing, and nothing. Then some distant shouting. "Is it over?" Kay asked.

"Yes," I said, as if I had any idea.

"Help me up," she said, and only then did I realize that her back was bad again. I helped her up, though my hands were trembling. And then we went to check on the patients, who were fine, or as fine as they could be, just white with plaster dust. A corpsman had died, but I didn't know him, and his death isn't why I tell this story.

I tell it because of this.

For a moment, before we went to check for damage, we stood there looking at each other, my hands on her arms as if to steady her. Her eyes were full of tears that I thought at first were from the pain and the fright. But that wasn't why she was sad. She looked at me hard, like she was never going to see me again, like she was trying to memorize my face. And then she stepped back so that my hands fell away. That was the moment I really knew I'd lost her. I don't know what I'd been hoping for, but that was when I knew I'd never have it, or if I'd had it, it was gone.

The next night was when she went out with him. I remember she didn't seem to want to go. I remember she said before she went, "I don't know about him. He's . . . pushy."

"So don't go," I said. "Stay here with me."

A strange look crossed her face then. Maybe it was the way I'd said the words. Or maybe it was just the way she heard them, that kiss, that goddamn kiss, changing everything. "I think I'll go," she said.

And I put my face back in my book, without another word. That's what I did, Jennifer.

In the morning, when I asked how the date had been, she said it was fine, but she wouldn't look at me. There was an angry scratch on her neck, a strange flatness in her voice. Do you understand, Jennifer? I didn't myself, until later. I was there and I failed to see, and maybe that's one reason why I did what I did, because in my own grief and resentment I'd failed to see. There are so many ways in which the world is terrible, sometimes you fail to spot them all.

The Ones We Love

This morning Jennifer yelled at Milo. She lost her temper—over a little thing, an everyday thing, his snatching the Cheerios box from her hand after she said no more cereal, spilling Cheerios all over the floor, then stepping on them, crunching them into a spreading dust. All of it, except the snatching, an accident. In return she grabbed his arm, pulled him close, smacked him, twice, on his behind. For a moment he looked mulish but then he burst into tears. "You *spanked* me," he said, in tones of grief and wonderment.

She knows it's not rational to blame Margaret for this. But she is tense, she is so tense, and that is undeniably Margaret's fault. *Just tell me*, she wants to demand. *About Kay, yes, and the terrible world, and why you did what you did, and what you know about me. Unwrap the bandage. Hand me a mirror.* "Do you understand?" Margaret asked, and Jennifer said, "I think—" but Margaret interrupted.

"Don't," she said. "Don't say it."

"You asked me," Jennifer said.

"So I did," Margaret said. And then she abruptly changed the subject. "Are you still spending time with that professor friend?" Why would Jennifer have told her about Megan? But she must have, because then Margaret said Megan's name. "Her husband's a photographer, you said?"

"Yes," Jennifer said.

"Maybe I should have one last portrait made. To go with this"—Margaret waved her hand at Jennifer's notebook, on her face that look of disdain—"this thing you're writing. Have you had your portrait made?"

"No," Jennifer said. "Why would I do that?"

Margaret looked at her appraisingly. "You wouldn't," she said with certainty, and then to Jennifer's surprise she smiled. "I wouldn't either, to tell you the truth."

Jennifer is reviewing this scene, thinking about Margaret, even though she's out walking in an effort to shake her off. She's on the Perimeter Trail, which encircles Sewanee—or the Domain, that humorously fantastic and yet appropriate name. She's discovered, since Megan introduced her to this trail and the access point at the Cross, that she likes a solitary walk in the woods, likes clambering up a rock where the trees open out on a view of valleys and mountains and trees and trees and trees. She likes surveying an uninhabited world. When someone approaches on the trail—you can always hear them coming, their voices and their footsteps in the crackling leaves so wrongfully loud—she has to fight an urge to dart behind rock or tree and hide until they've passed. She forces herself to stay on the path, make eye contact, smile, say hi.

"You and I," Margaret said yesterday, "we'd both like to be invisible."

"What makes you say that?"

"But then," Margaret said, "sometimes we wish we weren't."

Jennifer would've liked to deny this, but instead she looked down at the notebook, closed the cover on its words. Jennifer wishes Margaret didn't know Megan's name.

Her phone rings in her pocket and she checks the screen and sees the number for Milo's school. She pauses, panting a little from exertion, and holds on to a small tree. Right here the trail's at the very edge of the bluff, and it's a long way down. She makes herself wait one more ring before she answers, makes herself say a calm hello, as though to behave as if something bad had happened would guarantee it had.

But something bad *has* happened. Milo is fine, Milo is fine, but he's harmed another boy. "I don't understand," Jennifer says, after the first description, and so Miss Amber explains again. Her Southern accent has an edge during the second telling, sweetness that isn't sweet. "But I don't understand why he would do that," Jennifer says.

There's a shrug in Miss Amber's voice. "He says the other child took his toy, but of course that's no excuse."

"Of course not," Jennifer says blankly.

"We'd like you to come pick him up," Miss Amber says. "He'll have to go home for the rest of the day. We don't tolerate this kind of violence. That's our policy."

Jennifer has an impulse to ask what kind of violence they do tolerate, but she doesn't. She assures Miss Amber that she'll be there soon, and then she stands there clutching the tree in a daze. What Milo did today was stab another child in the face with a pencil. "Thankfully," Miss Amber said, "not in his eye."

Yes, thankfully not in his eye. But why at all? Why would her tiny child, her baby, her sweet, sweet boy, put a hole in another child's face? Because she spanked him today? This is what she knows—she with her repository of secrets, her comforting, healing touch: that none of us is good, as much as we might want to be. And yet somehow she believed that Milo would be the exception. Now, like everyone else, he's an inflictor of damage. He's left a scar.

When she gets out of her car in the preschool parking lot, Sebastian is a row ahead of her, getting out of his. She stops, surprised and unnerved, and hoping his presence doesn't mean that Ben was the victim of Milo's attack. Ben and Milo proclaim themselves best friends at every opportunity. Again and again Jennifer and Megan have shared affectionate smiles at the sight of the two boys whispering together, one with his arm around the other's waist. If Milo had to stab somebody, she would rather it be Ethan, a pushy and obnoxious child who runs up to her at pickup for the sole purpose of giving her an animal's predatory grin, baring his sharp and tiny teeth before darting away. She'd like to stand here a moment, let Sebastian walk into the school ahead of her, but that would be cowardly, and even if she waited chances are slim that she could avoid him completely in the narrow hallways, crowded with cubbies and bins of picture books. So she walks, at a normal pace, and before he reaches the gate into the playground he hears her footsteps and turns. Then she has to keep walking toward him, with him watching her, which she doesn't like.

"Well, this is a surprise," he says, when she's very close. "Was it Milo?"

"Was it Ben?" she answers.

"With the pencil in his face? Yes."

"I'm sorry," she says.

He shrugs. "You didn't do it," he says. "I assume you're not at home doing weapons training with school supplies."

She smiles, against her will. "No," she says. "But I'm still sorry. I can't imagine why he'd go after Ben. He loves Ben."

"We hurt the ones we love," he says. "Let's go survey the aftermath."

Jennifer realizes, following him inside, that she's relieved it's Sebastian and not Megan who's come to deal with this. She's afraid Megan will be terribly upset, will take this as a sign that both burgeoning friendships should be quashed. Sebastian, though, seems calm. We hurt the ones we love. Maybe he takes that for granted.

Sebastian walks right into Miss Amber's classroom, but Jennifer puts her head in the door, trying not to feel like she herself is the guilty one. Milo isn't in the room. Ben is playing trucks in the corner with another child, a Band-Aid cross high on his left cheek.

Sebastian crouches next to him and picks up a truck. As far as Jennifer can tell he's not asking about the incident. He crashes his truck into Ben's, and then Ben crashes his into Sebastian's. On the other side of the room Miss Amber is enmeshed in a hug from an adoring little girl. She looks up and sees Jennifer and her expression changes. As she comes over to Jennifer, her face is grave. "Milo's in Miss Helen's office," she says. Miss Helen is the preschool director, a woman in her sixties who is either sweet or stupid or very cleverly disguised. "What happened?" Jennifer says, because it's her obligation to know.

Miss Amber holds up both hands as if to forestall attack. "I didn't see it," she says. "First thing I knew, Ben was crying and his face was bleeding. Milo says he did it but he won't apologize. I've seen nothing wrong between them. They play a little rough every now and then, but that's just boys. I'm surprised Milo would be so aggressive. Has something been going on at home?"

Jennifer hates this question: the teacher's polite way of asking how you've fucked up your child. She got it frequently with Zoe, who behaved and tested well but often half-assed her homework. Sometimes Jennifer suspected Zoe of doing it on purpose—her messy unfinished algebra or partially plagiarized essay on Huck Finn—so that Jennifer would have to have these conversations. So that again and again she'd have to lie. "No," she'd say. "Nothing's going on at home." She says it now, and for once she's not lying. "I don't know why he'd do that."

Miss Amber makes a moue of sympathy, which may or may not be genuine. "Well, it's probably just a one-time thing," she says.

"Either that or he's a sociopath," Jennifer says. Miss Amber looks like she doesn't quite know how to respond to this, so Jennifer smiles, to signal that she's joking, and Miss Amber makes a sound that gestures toward laughter, and Jennifer says she'll talk to Milo and withdraws into the hall. Once, after Milo had been in the classroom about a month, Jennifer arrived unseen and heard Miss Amber saying to the children, "You're killing me."

Inside Miss Helen's office, Milo is slouched in a child-size plastic chair with his arms folded across his chest. Her baby, her boy-child. Her reward. He radiates defiance, and Jennifer can tell from the edge in the director's voice that she's been trying and failing to inspire remorse. "We've been talking about what happened," Miss Helen says.

"What happened, Milo?" Jennifer asks.

"Didn't Miss Amber tell you?" Miss Helen asks.

"She told me what happened," Jennifer says. "I was asking him why."

"Well, he hasn't told us that. We've asked, but he refuses to say."

Milo slides from the chair to the floor and picks two cars out of a plastic bin. In an echo of Ben, he crashes the cars together. "Ow, ow, ow," one car cries, and the other says, "Ha ha ha," and smashes down again. She could tell him not to smash the cars like that, not to act out the infliction of pain. She could make it a permanent rule. But then he'd just do it when she wasn't there to see. Is that all morality is? Concealment?

Miss Helen stands up behind her desk as if to signal that she wants the both of them to get the hell out. "Milo has refused to apologize. I've explained we need to control our bodies. We need to be sorry when we've hurt someone."

"I'll talk to him," Jennifer says. Milo suddenly launches himself up from the floor and into Jennifer. He smashes his face into her leg and clings with both hands to her jeans. He growls. Jennifer steadies herself and puts a hand on his head. "I'll talk to him," she says again, and then she crouches and picks Milo up—awkwardly, he's getting so big—and hustles him out of there as fast as she can. He's still clinging, still intermittently growling. "Milo, Milo, Milo," she says into his ear. "Why did you do it?"

"I *didn't*," he says, ferociously, as if he believes it. Maybe he can persuade her to believe it, too.

How could he stab his friend in the face, her sunny, innocent creation? How could he do that? Because he's hers? What she should do is drive away from this Mountain, flee the scene. Now there's not just her reputation to escape but Milo's as well, and in the next place there will be no preschools, no lunches, no playdates, so that no one can know them. No one can ever know them.

Back outside, she's surprised to find Sebastian and Ben lounging on the playground, as if waiting for them. She assumes Sebastian wants to see Milo apologize, so she complies with this unstated request—crouching down, looking Milo seriously in the eye, pointing at Ben. At first he refuses, but she walks him over and makes him repeat the words until they approximate sincerity. Throughout this Ben twists from side to side, as if he finds the whole scene excruciating. When it's over, he looks up at his dad. "Can we go to the playground?" he asks. "With them?"

"We're on a playground."

"No, the other playground. The one me and Milo like."

Sebastian looks at Jennifer and shrugs. A master of ambiguity. It bothers her that Ben is so quick to forgive Milo, so recently his abuser. And yet she's also glad. "Okay," she says.

They walk. Though often in Sewanee you drive a distance that short, Sebastian sets off walking without discussion. The boys run ahead of him and Jennifer lags behind, because her only previous encounter with Sebastian has convinced her that she doesn't enjoy his company.

To her surprise, when they get to the playground Sebastian starts playing with the boys—chasing them and swinging them around until they're manic with delight. She'd had him pegged as the type to hang back, checking his phone. She sits on a bench and watches him do the testosterone thing. Sometimes she plays with Milo like this, but she's too old to sustain the necessary energy long. Tommy wanted to be this kind of dad, and intermittently was, before he died. But a drunk can't be counted on to distinguish between fun and frightening. A drunk can't be counted on to gauge another person's response.

Sebastian flops down next to her on the bench, giving off heat. He makes an animal sound of weariness. He doesn't look at her, keeping his eyes on the boys. They're giggling behind the slide, planning something they clearly think is devilish and clever, but most likely isn't. "I guess that was just a blip on the radar," he says.

"What was?"

He mimes stabbing.

"Oh," she says. "I'm really sorry."

He shrugs irritably, and from this she concludes he wants no further apology. But she can't think of anything else to talk about, so if they're to converse the burden will be on him. He props his elbows on the back of the bench, not looking at her. "I need to apologize," he said. "I'm sorry about how I was at Megan's party."

"It's all right."

"Not really. It was a little early in our acquaintance to show you my worst side."

"Better than the reverse," Jennifer says. "At least then you know what you're getting."

Sebastian looks at her like he can't decide whether to be affronted or amused.

Jennifer watches herself choose to press forward. Something about him provokes her to speech when normally she'd choose silence. "Why do you live here, if you don't like it?"

"We came for Megan's job."

"Oh."

"If you're an academic, you have to go where the jobs are." He sighs. "But also Megan likes it here. She didn't really like New York."

"But you did?"

"I did. I was a real photographer in New York, and now I take pictures of toddlers in their Easter clothes."

"Oh," Jennifer says again. Then, to her own surprise, she says, "I lived in New York a little while. I wanted to be a dancer."

"Really? What happened?"

"I got married."

"Ah." Sebastian laughs. "Me too." There's a silence, and then he says, "At my wedding my aunt told me she had a piece of advice. I thought it would be something like never go to bed angry, but instead she looked at me and said, 'Endure. Endure. Endure.'" He tells this like it's funny, but Jennifer feels no urge to laugh. Maybe because she doesn't, he gives her that wary look again. "Anyway, I'm sorry. I'm sure you think I'm an asshole."

"Maybe not."

"Maybe not?"

"It was just one incident," Jennifer says. "Do you think my son's a sociopath?"

He grins. "No. Maybe not." The grin fades, and he continues, "But I have to warn you that Megan might. She gets very worked up about Ben, very nervous any time she thinks another kid might be a bully."

"Oh," Jennifer says.

"We have friends, another couple, with a kid a year older than Ben, and once we had them over for dinner and their kid bit his ear. Now I can't get Megan to hang out with them. Don't be surprised if she's weird with you for a while."

"But *I* didn't stab Ben."

He shrugs. "Your kid did. Same thing."

"But not for you."

"I'm not quite as caught up in the psychodrama of child rearing. Is your kid alive at the end of the day? Did you feed him? Did you tell him you liked his drawing? Good. Great. You've done your job. It's crazy to think you can mold them into perfect human beings, if you just make all the perfect choices. It's crazy to think you can protect them from pain."

Jennifer has a stunned, stupid feeling. The only thought in her head is: I ruined it.

"People don't think it, because she seems so nice, so open, but Megan's actually pretty unforgiving."

"I didn't realize that." Jennifer must sound stricken, because Sebastian glances at her and groans in dismay.

"Shit, I'm sorry," he says. "She might not be like that about this. I know she really likes you. She told me as soon as she met you she thought you could be friends. I'm just dumping my own crap on you again. I don't know why I keep doing that." He shakes his head. Then, to her enormous surprise, he starts to cry.

Her first instinct is to touch him, but she represses that. Her second is to look around for the boys, thinking that to see Sebastian in tears might alarm Ben, if not Milo as well. But they're still barely in sight and happily oblivious, on the other side of the playground. Sebastian's turned even farther away from her now, with his hands on his face, and she can see that he's trying to stop crying, that he's trying to hide. God, sometimes she really does feel sorry for men. Manliness—a trap they build themselves, and then invite their sons to join them in. And little boys are so tender! Milo's heart breaks much more often and more extravagantly than Zoe's ever did.

She scoots a little closer. She hesitates, but it seems cruel to leave him sitting there in tears, untouched, so she puts one gentle hand on his shoulder. He tenses, trying to throw off her ministrations. He's afraid to let go. Automatically she squeezes the shoulder a little, as she would in a massage, pushing back against the body's resistance. She feels how knotted up he is, how deep the tension goes. "Oh," she says. "You're sad."

He sniffs, scrubbing at his face. "Clearly," he says in self-mockery.

"No, I mean, you're really sad," she says. "I can feel it in your body." She works the knot a little more. "You're really sad. Maybe more than you realize, even, it's down that deep."

He swallows. "Oh," he says.

Her instinct tells her to keep touching him, because he needs the comfort. But it's been too long since she touched a man, and it seems dangerous to her, her desire to keep doing it. She takes her hands away and stills them in her lap. If he were on her massage table, she could find the buzzing, knotted places in his body, separate the balled-up threads of pain and sorrow, and he could tell her whatever he wanted to tell, facedown toward the anonymous floor. He could cry. Sometimes people weep on her table. They find relief in that unburdening. This is one reason why her clients love her, why they call her again and again, why they are so grateful. That should be past tense, of course. *Loved, called, found.* Because then her daughter called the police and the clients never called again. She says, "People who seem angry—often what they really are is sad."

"I love Megan," Sebastian says, suddenly forceful.

"I know."

"Sometimes I wish I didn't."

Jennifer says nothing. What is there to say? She can't grant wishes. *Sometimes I miss my husband,* she thinks of telling him. *Sometimes I'm glad he's dead. I don't have to wonder where he is, what he's doing, or who. I don't have to worry about all the ways he'll scar my son. I don't have to watch myself give in again and again, audience to my own relentless weakness. I thought if he were gone I wouldn't hate myself so much, which isn't true, as it turns out, but still his absence is as close as I can get to freedom. There's a certain clearheadedness now, there's a kind of lonely clarity—*

"Sebastian!" Megan calls. They both jump. Megan is visible at the place where the playground meets the parking lot, approaching.

Sebastian waves. Jennifer lifts her hand and drops it, trying not to look nervous, trying to smile. Sebastian looks at Jennifer with apprehension. "Do I look like I've been crying?"

"A little," she says. "It could be allergies."

"I don't have them," he says. "But I could maybe be getting a cold."

They watch Megan's approach in silence. Jennifer wonders if she should slide farther away from him on the bench, but Megan would see that, and it would look suspicious, in a way it's possible her current proximity to him does not. She has a despairing sense that Megan will register a new intimacy between her and Sebastian and mistake it for something it isn't.

"Hey," Sebastian says.

"Hi." Megan's a little breathless. She looks around. "Where are the boys?"

Sebastian points. "On the other side of the jungle gym."

"I don't see them."

"They're there."

Megan looks at Jennifer for the first time, flashes a tight little smile. She says to her husband, "When I got out of class I saw the school had called, so I went by there. They told me what happened." Her eyes flick to Jennifer, then back to Sebastian. "I saw your car was still in the parking lot, so I thought maybe you were down here."

"The boys wanted to play," Sebastian says. "It was Ben's idea."

"Uh-huh," Megan says. "Are they playing together well?"

"They're fine," Sebastian says.

"But how do you know, if you're sitting here talking, and they're over there?"

"Nobody's screamed."

"Uh-huh," Megan says again.

If Jennifer weren't here, would Megan unleash her fury? Would she yell? Would she say, Nobody's screamed? *What the fuck is wrong with you?*

She is here. So there's no way to know.

"I'm just a little concerned." Eye flick. "Because of what happened today."

Sebastian shrugs. "They're children. They're boys."

"Yes, but . . ." She gives Jennifer a smile that's not quite a smile, a potent cocktail of anger and apology. "What happened today was more than the usual roughhousing."

"Megan," Sebastian said, "they're fine. You have to relax. You have to let this go."

"I'm just being careful. I don't want . . . I'm just being careful."

"They're fine," Sebastian says. "Boys will be boys."

"Boys will be boys," Megan repeats. Jennifer knows that Megan is thinking about the little hole in her son's face. That she wants to protect him, not only from that but from *boys will be boys*: the abuse you're supposed to take without flinching, the abuse you're supposed to dole out. If Milo were not her child, it's possible she'd agree with Megan that Ben shouldn't play with him. But because he is, she's grateful to Sebastian for his efforts to make the whole thing go away. *Shake it off. Get back in the game.* How easily opinions shift from vantage point to vantage point. Of course we're all hypocrites. Without hypocrisy there's no survival.

Jennifer has not said a word. She can't think of a word to say. Jennifer knows now, with the intuitive certainty she feels in massage, that if Megan hears her story their friendship won't survive. It's not, and never has been, Megan who might understand her.

"If you're so worried about it," Sebastian says, "why are you here talking to us? Go monitor them."

Megan nods. "Fine." She heads off toward the playground, calling out, "Ben?"

The boys whoop with startled glee in response, dashing around the jungle gym in Megan's direction, then abruptly changing course as they get close to her. They run away screaming, and Megan obliges them by running after, making monster sounds.

Maybe Jennifer should follow, join in, apologize, plead her case. But she doesn't.

"She didn't even notice," Sebastian says. "So at least I didn't have to lie."

"I almost wish Ben would do something to Milo," Jennifer says. "In front of Megan. Nothing too bad, of course. Just push him down or smack him upside the head. Just so they'd be even."

"You *almost* wish that?" Sebastian asks.

"I wish it," she says.

Later, when they part, Megan says, "Let's get together," but not as if she means it.

Like Apologies

W e were set up across from a POW camp, living in a dirty building
full of straw. I remember watching the POWs pick lice from their
clothing. The night we arrived some of the buildings were still burning. After living in a blackout for so long it was scary to see lights at
night. A German physician came to us in a German jeep under a
white flag, and what he wanted was medicine so that he could carry
on his experiments. We gave him nothing. We let him drive away. I
remember windmills, an airfield with German planes smashed up on
the ground, roads full of refugees. Houses crowded together, winding cobbled streets, church spires dominating the town. Trees and
flowers in bloom. We were with a division and an armored outfit,
and there'd been push after push, most of the casualties caused by
twelve- or thirteen-year-old boys, all that was left to fight in Germany.

"It's such a beautiful country," I said to Kay. "I can't understand
why the Krauts won't stay home and enjoy it."

Kay didn't answer. She was lying in her cot. By then, she was always lying in her cot, every chance she could get. Things were pretty
slow right then, so she got a lot of chances. I was pacing between the
two windows in our room, half-watching the POWs. I was restless.
I felt compelled to keep Kay company, though she didn't seem to

want me to. I thought her back was worse. She had so little energy. She struggled to get up in the mornings. When I could get them, I brought her morphine syrettes. Even when she didn't ask. Like they were flowers. Like they were apologies. She said very little now, so either we were silent together, or when I couldn't bear that I chattered like a ninny.

"It's almost lunchtime," I said. "At least the army's gotten wise to itself and made some decent C rations. Frankfurters and beans are a long way from that stinking meat and vegetable stew."

"I can't eat," she said.

"I talked to some boys yesterday who were prisoners for seven and ten months. Just liberated. After they were captured they were marched for two days and nights, loaded on boxcars without food for five days. They were fed on turnip soup with meat sometimes but the meat was green, it was so old."

Kay groaned. "Don't," she said.

"Don't what?"

"Don't talk about food."

"The boy I talked to was jaundiced and had lost forty pounds." Out the window a man behind wire stared bleakly in my direction. I didn't think he could see me. "Looks like this mess won't be over before the fall," I said. "If I have to go to the CBI I'll be a section eight."

"Maggie Jean," she said. She waited for me to turn and look at her. She was sitting up now, propped on both arms. She swallowed hard, like someone trying not to be sick. "Do you know I'm pregnant?"

I didn't. I didn't know. I just stood there, gone slack. I'd been trying so hard with her, trying so hard for weeks. All that effort, like doing a rain dance in the desert. I'd exhausted myself. I could think of nothing to say.

"The night after the shelling," she said. She pulled her knees up, wincing, and hunched over them. "He held me down."

"What?" I asked.

Now she looked at me. "You know what I mean, don't you?" she asked. "Please don't make me explain."

I had wild thoughts: that I would find the man, that I should have known, that maybe she wasn't really pregnant, that I should have known. I tried to stay calm. Maybe that wasn't the right response. I don't know what the right response would have been. "What do you want to do?" I asked.

"What do I want to do?" she repeated. She shook her head. "I can't get rid of it."

I don't know what she meant by this. I've thought about it plenty since. That she didn't know where to get an abortion? That she'd tried something and it hadn't worked? Or that she couldn't bring herself to try? In some ways despite all I'd seen I was innocent, and I was inadequate. All I really understood was how inadequate I was. I wanted someone else to be in charge. "Does the chief nurse know?" I asked.

"Of course not," she said. "I wouldn't be here."

"How can you stay? Between your back and this . . . What if they send you to the CBI?"

"I can't go home." Her voice a whip-crack. "They won't have me."

"Then go to my parents," I said. "I'll ask them to take you in. Then when I get home, we can get jobs in Nashville, get an apartment there."

There was a long silence. "Why would your parents take me when even my own won't?"

"I'll tell them a sad story," I said. "You'll be a war bride. Married two months, then your husband was killed. And I'll make you an orphan, too."

"And then what?"

"And then I'll come home. There will be nursing jobs in Nashville. I still know people at Vanderbilt. We'll share an apartment. I've saved some money, you probably have, too, my parents might even help a little . . ."

"What about the baby?"

She was right—I was leaving out the baby. The baby was hard to imagine. The baby that shouldn't have existed. "I'll help you with the baby," I said.

"How will I go to work?"

"Maybe you won't," I said. "Maybe I'll go to work and you'll stay with the baby."

"Like a married couple?"

"No," I said. "Like friends."

She lay back down on the cot. She put her hands over her eyes. She said, "I don't know what else to do."

That was the tone she took from then on, when we talked about our plans. Weary resignation. I admit I sometimes felt frustrated, sometimes wanted a little more gratitude. It's not as though there wasn't any, but it wasn't what prevailed. She'd given up, I think. To her I wasn't the one who threw the life preserver. I was the one who wouldn't let her jump. I wrote to my parents, embellishing my sob story, and my sweet, kind mother wrote back, *Of course*. Kay's eyes filled with tears when I showed her the letter. That time she said thank you, or at least that's how I remember it.

I don't know quite how long we treaded water. The war was slowing, and so we weren't busy, and it wasn't hard to cover for Kay. Then the Sixth Cavalry found a concentration camp in Austria, and they sent for our unit to take care of them. You've seen pictures, Jennifer, but you've never seen a human being like this, in those striped uniforms and nothing but bones. No flesh on them at all, just skin. Oh Lord. The soldiers wouldn't let us into the buildings—the women, the nurses. They said they found dead ones in bed with live ones. The townspeople said they didn't know anything about it, but they'd requested that the camp raise the chimney because the smell of burning flesh was bothering them. Bodies and bodies, dumped in a ditch. General Patton made the men of that town bury all those people. I have pictures of that. And our chaplain said a service. Man's inhumanity to man, let me tell you.

I have tried not to let these things haunt my dreams. I have tried not to believe that human beings are evil, animals picking each other's bones.

After the camp, it began to seem urgent that Kay tell the chief nurse, go ahead and get her discharge. She kept saying she wanted to wait a little longer, but she was starting to fill out, and soon it would be apparent to anyone who looked at her, and more than that, more than that, I just couldn't bear it. I was responsible for her, and I couldn't bear it anymore, not after the camp. Later I pasted the pictures from the camp in my scrapbook, with all the other ones I took. Pages and pages of army life: A nurse washes her clothes in an empty barrel. A soldier smokes a cigarette, striking a cocky pose. Pages and pages like that, and then there they are in neat rows: A stack of dead bodies. A man like a stick figure in a striped uniform. I can't remember putting those pictures in the book, slipping the corners into their little black triangles, lining them up. It frightens me a little to think of the person who did that. The person who documented the horrific and the daily as if they were the same. The person I must have been.

So one day I said, again, "Kay, you have to tell her."

"Not today," Kay said, her usual demurral, but this time I said, "Yes, today, or I will." At that she tightened her mouth into a line. Silence. All day I waited for her to crack. I waited and waited. But we went to bed without another word on the subject.

I couldn't sleep. No matter how I positioned myself on the cot my body ached. When I finally got up Kay stirred. "Where are you going?" she asked. I pretended not to have heard.

We were in tents there. The chief nurse had a tent to herself. I knocked on the tent pole, heard a faint, "Wha . . . ?" and stepped inside. She sat up, pushing a tangle of hair out of her face. She was a martinet and we all hated her, but even she looked vulnerable at three in the morning, her cheeks oddly puffy. "What on earth, Riley?" she said. "Are we under attack?"

"No." I crouched awkwardly at her feet. It was not too late to change my mind. "I think Kay is pregnant."

I watched as she registered this news. "Thank you, Riley," she said. "You may go."

I went back to my tent. I thought Kay was asleep. But then she startled me by speaking. "You told her, didn't you," she said, without the question mark.

"You can't stay here anymore," I said. I expected anger from her, but instead in the dark I heard weeping. I rolled away from her, hardening myself. "I've arranged everything with my parents," I said, and I was the one who sounded angry. I'd gone to the camp and she hadn't. Maybe that was why. "You have a place to go. You're lucky to get out of here. You're lucky."

I'd been bringing her the syrettes. But I didn't know she'd been hoarding them. How would I know? There were days she barely spoke to me. What was I supposed to do? Refuse her help when she was in pain? Insist I give her the injections, search her things, treat her like a child, humiliate her? How was I supposed to know? What could I have done to stop her? Tell me, Jennifer. What could I have done?

You're lucky was the last thing I said to her. In the morning she was dead.

Jennifer said, "You told me she lived." I was startled. She was accusing me.

"Did I?" I said.

"When you first brought her up. You said she didn't die."

"All right, let's say she didn't," I said. "Let's pretend none of this, none of what I've told you is true."

"Is that what you want? Because I'll write it down however you want."

I'd upset her. I couldn't get over my surprise. "What happened happened."

"What happened is what somebody says happened," she said. "That's all history is."

I've been thinking about that, since she left. So we create the past, do we, Jennifer? Maybe. Maybe. But have you really convinced yourself it's quite that simple? I think you know perfectly well that the past creates us too.

See Rock City

As soon as she gets home Jennifer goes out on her back deck. She tells herself not to go out there but does it anyway. After the fog and a run of cloudy days, the sun is out, the light is bright, the leaves are green, the pond is a shimmering blue reflection. Margaret is not outside. Though what drove Jennifer out was a sense that Margaret would be watching, waiting for her, she fails to be relieved by the sight of the empty deck across the pond.

Kay died. Kay died of an overdose of pain medication. Is this story even true?

She can't listen to Margaret anymore. She can't. She tightens her grip on the deck railing, firming this decision, and at that moment Margaret comes outside. Jennifer sees the old woman register her presence, but she doesn't wave, and neither does Jennifer. They both stand there, Jennifer leaning on her railing, Margaret leaning on her cane.

Jennifer turns away from Margaret and goes inside with a resolution forming. She will not wait around for Megan to resume their friendship. She can still tell her story any way she wants.

Megan answers the phone. Jennifer's heart was in her throat, thinking she wouldn't. "Are you grading papers today?" Jennifer asks.

"No, I'm all caught up. I usually run errands on Friday."

"Are they important? The errands?"

"Not terribly," Megan says. "I just wanted to get out of the house."

"Oh, good," Jennifer says. "Because I have an idea."

Megan is reluctant. But she doesn't outright say no. Jennifer knows Megan has never been to Rock City, despite having lived in Sewanee for four years, and that she's curious. "But the boys are already at school," Megan says.

"We'll go get them. They'll be thrilled." Jennifer's behaving uncharacteristically, pushing in the face of resistance, and it's making her nervous, but she's determined. "Don't you feel like an adventure? Let's get off this mountain."

"We'll just be going up another one."

"At least it'll be a different mountain."

"All right," Megan says. Not because she wants to, Jennifer thinks. Because she hates to deny anyone anything, poor Megan. It hurts her to have to say no. Jennifer has taken advantage of this, but not with nefarious intent. With positive intent, Megan! In hopes they will have fun.

In the car Megan is turned around in her seat, talking to the boys. Keeping an eye on Milo? Watching for signs of imminent psychotic break? Jennifer doesn't know. She tries not to care. Megan's working hard at entertaining them. Do they know where they're going? Do they know everything they're going to see there? Gnomes! Real ones? the boys ask, and Megan says, with a parent's carefully obvious show of pretense, "Maybe." No, no, the boys say, giggling, they won't be real. What else are they going to see? Rocks! Big ones. A cave. Waterfalls! How much farther is it, the boys want to know, five minutes after they get on the highway and every five minutes thereafter. Why don't you count the signs? Megan suggests. Some are billboards. Some are painted on barns. Once you get to fifty, I'll bet we'll be there.

"Fifty?" Jennifer asks, and Megan says quietly, "Good round number. Can't be more than fifty, right?" Then she shouts, "There's one!" pointing out the window. SEE ROCK CITY in white letters on a barn. Jennifer knows about Rock City only because of these signs. On the long first drive to Sewanee the signs counted down her progress for hundreds of miles. An exhortation. A command. For miles and miles and miles she wondered what the hell Rock City was. "Okay, boys, you know those letters?" Megan says. "You're looking for S-E-E. Okay? Let's see who can spot the next one."

"I will!" Ben cries, and Milo says, "Me too! Me too!"

The road looks as if it intends to dump them straight into Nickajack Lake, sparkling in invitation, and then at the bottom of the incline it's all sunlight and mountains and water. In the middle of the shining lake small islands of darkly clustered trees. Trying to look without crashing the car, Jennifer fancies she sees Margaret staring out from one of those islands, a white face between the trees.

Rock City is on a twisty road, the kind that curves ahead of you so that you can see the open air beyond it and remember every second you're right on the edge of the mountain. Jennifer drives slow. At the ticket booth they purchase admittance to Rock City and its neighbor Ruby Falls, and Jennifer doesn't flinch at the cost. This whole day, nothing will make her flinch. DISCOVER JOY, the billboard just outside the turnoff said, and she's in a mood to take that seriously. Discover joy. As though no one who comes here has ever felt it before.

Megan continues bright and cheery with the boys, pointing after fairies she claims to have seen darting behind the enormous rocks or fluttering over the arched stone bridges. The boys begin to say they've seen them, too. To Jennifer she says nothing. When they make eye contact she offers a quick smile and looks away. Really, it's impossible not to think she blames Jennifer for what Milo did. If a small child does something bad, surely it's the parent's fault. What are children if not evidence of our own worst qualities? They witness them, they replicate them, they remind you again and again of everything that's wrong with you.

Don't flinch, Jennifer. Maybe she just didn't want to come today, and suspects you of knowing that, and making her come anyway. But you'll fix that by the end of the day. By the end of the day everything will be fine, and life can go on here, like you want it to.

Gnome Valley, Goblin's Underpass, Lover's Leap. Rocks shaped like mushrooms, like tortoiseshells. Gaps in the rock, long tumbles down to streams below. It's beautiful. They bounce along a suspension bridge, dizzyingly high, Megan saying, "Oh be careful, oh be careful," over and over. They photograph the boys at the sign marking the view of seven states. The boys point this way and that, claiming to be certain that smudgy mountain is North Carolina, that one Virginia. They're being so lovely together, and Jennifer keeps sneaking looks at Megan, wanting confirmation that she sees it, too.

They pause at the top of the stairs leading down to a tiny gap between two enormous rocks known as Fat Man's Squeeze. "Okay, boys," Jennifer says, ushering each of them closer to the railing. "These stairs are slick. Hold on tight."

Megan leans close behind Jennifer and whispers, "It's all very vaginal."

Jennifer laughs, a surprised loud laugh that makes Milo say, "What's so funny?"

"Nothing," Jennifer says. "Watch your step."

"Don't tell me you weren't thinking that," Megan says as they descend.

"Well, now I am," Jennifer says. She's smiling straight ahead, smiling big at the gap in the rocks. As they edge through the gap—

indeed a tight squeeze—Megan says behind her, "Now we're in the birth canal."

They emerge onto an outcropping of rock, ringed by a stone wall, with viewing machines awaiting their quarters. Blue blue sky. Jennifer says, "Now we're born," but Megan doesn't answer, hustling the boys past the machines back onto the path and then to a wooden platform for waterfall viewing, built jutting out from the side of the rock.

"Hurray," Megan says under her breath to Jennifer. "Another precipice."

"Don't worry," Jennifer says. "There's a railing. They'll be okay as long as they don't climb."

"But will I?"

"Are you afraid of heights?"

Megan winces, holds her thumb and forefinger a tiny amount apart.

"You live on a mountain."

Megan shrugs. "It's not really heights I'm afraid of. It's edges." She peers over. "They make me want to jump." She looks at Jennifer and bounces her eyebrows up and down, and Jennifer laughs.

Ruby Falls involves a long elevator ride down to a cave, and then a guided meander to an underground waterfall. After the elevator each group must pose for a photo, and Megan and Jennifer stand side by side, hands on the shoulders of the boys in front of them. "Say *squeeze*!" the photographer says.

Their guide, and the guides they pass, all make jokes: "How are you?" their guide says, and the other guide says, "I'd be fine if these people would stop following me." So many jokes that Jennifer wonders aloud to Megan if it's someone's job to write them.

"I don't know," Megan says. She seems stiff and distracted again, so Jennifer keeps her next thought to herself: how the haunting beauty of the cave inspires awe on its own, and then they try to ramp up the awe with red glowing lights and fantasy-epic music playing from hidden speakers, then undercut that effort with jokes. As if you need a break from awe. As if there is a danger in too much of it.

The guide stops them before the waterfall chamber. "You are now one thousand one hundred twenty-five feet below the surface of the earth," he says, and beside her Megan gasps. The guide utters words of caution, then presses a button that starts more fantasy music and makes the lights go out. They enter the chamber, the air filled with the sound of rushing water. The boys make ghost sounds and giggle and behind them, to Jennifer's annoyance, people snap pictures, ruining the ambiance with sharp bursts of light. A hand touches Jennifer's, and she startles, because it's not a little hand, not Milo's hand, because he's standing right in front of her and she's holding on to his shoulder. Megan's voice is in her ear: "This might be a good time to tell you I'm claustrophobic." Jennifer laughs, thinking this is more comedy, but then Megan takes firm hold of Jennifer's hand and squeezes it, much too hard for joking.

The big reveal: the music swells, the lights come up, and there it is, the waterfall. "Awesome," Ben says, and Milo repeats. Megan holds tight to Jennifer's hand.

"It's not usually this bad," Megan says to her, under the sound of water. "But we're a thousand feet down, and I'd rather not have a panic attack in front of Ben. Or you and Milo. I'm okay right here because this is a big space, but the way back . . ."

"What if you held on to me and closed your eyes? Would that help?"

"Maybe. I don't know."

"Let's try it," Jennifer says. "You can pretend you're walking through a field."

"All right." Megan sighs. "I'm sorry."

"Don't be," Jennifer says. "It'll be okay."

They walk out that way, the boys in front of Jennifer and Megan clinging to her hand behind. Past the delicate, spectacular formations and the signs that point out what they resemble: bacon, steak and potatoes, an angel's wing. "Weird, ain't it," says a man in front of Jennifer. She wishes she could come down here alone, pause and gaze up, stare a long, long time. But they have to keep moving. Past the Dragon's Foot, past the Mirror Pool. Behind her Megan lets out the long slow breaths of someone wrestling with panic. "This is our last stop before the elevator," the guide says at last, and as he goes on talking Jennifer feels a sudden sharp pang, a longing to dash back inside, to hear again that rushing water in the dark, to gaze into the Mirror Pool. But she can't do that, because Milo and Ben are in front of her, and Megan holds on to her hand.

From the elevator they're led up steps to a tower, from which there is a strangely unpretty, if expansive, view. At the first opportunity Megan hugs her. "Thank you," she says. And then for good measure Megan hugs both the boys. "Thank you," she says to each of them, and they look at each other with puzzled smiles and ask for what, and she says for being so good.

After the tower is the gift shop, where a long-haired boy behind a counter pulls out a bright red Ruby Falls folder holding the photo taken at the beginning of the tour. There they are, Megan, Jennifer, Milo, Ben—an eight-by-ten on the right side of the folder, a sheet of wallets on the left. "Twenty dollars for the big one," the boy says. "Thirty for all of it, plus you get this!" He holds up a small cheap frame that says RUBY FALLS.

Megan leans over the photos without touching them. "Cute," she says. "Let us think about it." She walks away, telling the kids to come on, and the boy shrugs, knowing that means no. He moves to put the folder on a stack of other abandoned ones.

"Wait," Jennifer says. "I'll take all of them, and the frame." She catches up to Megan and the boys and says, "I couldn't resist."

Megan laughs. She puts her arm around Jennifer's shoulders and squeezes, leans her head against Jennifer's so their temples touch. "Sucker," she says affectionately. "You have to give me one."

They drive home with the sun low in the sky. The water in the lake is a dull silver now, but the clouds are gorgeous, voluminous, dark and white, lit from behind. Megan rides in the passenger seat with her head tilted back, gazing out the window. "Michelangelo clouds," she says. "Beautiful."

The List of Sins

I've had too much activity today, I think. I had one of my dizzy spells. It went on and on, even after I sat down. I gripped the seat of the chair like my father used to tell me to. *You're so clumsy you'll fall off.* Yes, Papa, you're right. When you're young you get sick and you know there'll be an end to it, but when you're old you know a time is coming when you won't get better. I'll get dizzy and I'll get dizzy, and then I'll fly off the merry-go-round. I'm getting metaphorical, Papa. I mean I'll die.

Today is my father's birthday. He lived to be eighty-seven, which seemed so old to me then, and yet is younger than I am now. I am older than he was when he died. I am so old.

What I wanted was for Jennifer to offer to drive me down the Mountain to Murfreesboro, to see his grave, but she didn't. She wouldn't. I couldn't get her to. When she was here a few days ago, I mentioned the birthday, and my habit of visiting his grave on it. At the time I tried not to admit to myself why I was telling her this—though why? Why am I still trying to hide myself from myself? Clearly the old are not immune to self-delusion. I didn't want to ask her directly, so instead I talked at length about my uncertainty that I should be trusted that long behind the wheel, hoping she would arrive at the idea on her own. Maybe she wasn't really listening. At any rate she didn't take the hint. So my plan was to ask her directly, after our morning appointment.

But first thing this morning, the phone rang, and when I answered, it was Jennifer. "I'm so sorry," she said, "but I need to cancel today."

"You can't," I said.

Silence.

"Our appointment's in less than an hour," I said. "I've been planning on it."

"Something came up," she said. "I'm sorry, Margaret." She said it like she meant it, but so what if she's sorry? What do I care if she's *sorry*?

"What came up?" I asked.

"Milo's school has a teacher in-service day," she said. "This is all my fault, I'm sorry—I'd forgotten. I only just remembered."

I knew this was a lie. If she'd had a reason that good she would've led with it. How many times in my life have I known someone was lying and said nothing? How many times have I lied and watched the other person feign belief? We say nothing, we say nothing. Life would be unbearable without lies.

"Is that so," I said.

"Yes," she said. Her voice was cool and crisp, impenetrable. She'd make no effort to persuade me. She is a good liar. She doesn't care if you believe her.

I look forward to her visits. They are what I look forward to. *Forlorn* is not the wrong word for how I felt. This is the second time she's canceled on me. Does she fail to understand what a cruelty it is?

"Also," she said, "I wanted to tell you I think we should put the history project on hold for a while."

"What?" I said. "Why?"

"I'm starting to book other clients, and I don't think I'll be able to give it my full attention."

"That makes no sense. Why book other clients when I'm paying you to come here?"

There was a brief silence, and then she said, "To make a living as a massage therapist, I need to have a good-sized client base."

"But I'm paying you to come here."

"And I still will. For massage."

"This makes no sense, Jennifer."

"Margaret, I'm sorry. Milo's calling me. I'll see you on Wednesday at the usual time?"

I put on my sweetest, most genteel voice and said, "Of course." Then I hung up and sat there trembling. I was supposed to tell her the end of the story today, but she's bottled me up, and the feeling is unbearable. I can tell it to her anyway, when she comes here. I can insist. But it wouldn't be the same to blurt it out lying on the table or afterward when she's hustling out the door. I need her to be listening. I need to see in her face what she thinks of what I've done. Otherwise what is the point?

I drove to her house when my appointment was supposed to be. Just to see if she was there. I had in my head that if she wasn't there it would prove she was lying, though I realize now that's non-sense, as she could've taken the boy to the playground or the gro-cery store. It's impossible to be inconspicuous coming up her long gravel drive, so I planned my excuses. I took an egg from the carton and made a paper-towel nest for it inside a Tupperware container. It took me some time to decide how best to transport that single egg. If she was there, I planned to say I was replacing the egg she loaned me. She'd just think it was some antiquated politeness. In my day, and so forth. Being old has so few advantages. One must take them where one can.

She wasn't there. No car in the drive. At that moment, I still be-lieved this proved she'd lied, and I sat there taking in that knowledge. I was angry but tears pricked at my eyes. I'd told her what happened to Kay—something I'd never told anyone, not anyone. I suppose I'd thought she might say it wasn't my fault, she might absolve me after all these years. But she said I'd lied about what happened to Kay, in the aggrieved tone of the betrayed, and then she said I should just change the story. And now she'd rejected me. I can't change the story, Jennifer! Don't you think I would if I could? I can't, I can't, and you can't either.

I got out of the car. I was at her house, and she wasn't. What detective would fail to seize such an opportunity?

Of course, I had no idea whether she locked her door. Most people here don't, or anyway that's the local lore. It's the kind of place you don't have to lock your doors, they say with satisfaction. Unlike Nashville, that crime-ridden flatland, that alien planet. Unlike the rest of the world. Sometimes up here on this mountain it can feel like there is no rest of the world. All those other places we've been are just dreams we had, as life would seem like a dream from the pretty claustrophobia of heaven.

I can't believe in heaven. Even now, as death grows ever harder to unimagine.

Her door was unlocked. She must have heard the same conversations. Inside, the house was much as I had seen it before—disastrous. Not the home of someone who expects to invite anyone inside. But you never know when someone might appear at your door—a neighbor, the UPS man. You must always be presentable. That's what my mother taught me. You must always be ready to conceal.

I'm not interested in anything that belongs to the little boy. I looked for a space that was Jennifer's alone, which proved annoyingly difficult to find. Even her bedroom showed signs of the child's habitation—a tiny knight on the pillow, a discarded superhero shirt on the floor. A pair of his pajamas beside the bed, inside out, led me to wonder if she lets him sleep with her—something my parents certainly would never have allowed. All this bonding they do these days. As if what's between a parent and a child would vanish without snuggling and trips to the zoo. I can attest that one is sufficiently bonded without those things, one is sufficiently stuck.

Down the hall from the bedrooms is a small room, barely bigger than a closet, that seems to serve as Jennifer's study. Desk, computer, bookcase, two-drawer filing cabinet, in which papers have been dumped rather than filed. Also in the filing cabinet: photos of Jennifer with a baby and a teenage girl on the beach; a stopped watch; a screwdriver; an assortment of paper clips; the wheel of a toy car; an empty glasses case; a smiling Lego head; a little card of the sort that comes with flowers. *You are all that matters.*

On the back of the photo it said: *Me, Milo, and Zoe,* and the date.

Zoe, who called the police on her own mother, who marked her mother as a murderer, who pinned a letter to her mother's chest. Imagine if she is wrong. Imagine if she is right. When I looked up *Jennifer Carrasco* on the Internet and found those articles, I felt a hard-boiled unsurprise. It turns out I am a detective after all. These detectives—they always uncover the same transgressions. A murder, a theft. Another woman's husband, another man's wife. We cheat, we steal, we lie, we kill. The list of sins is short. We all do the same bad things.

You are all that matters. Was it from the dead man, her husband? No one has ever said such a thing to me. Perhaps you would keep a card like that even if you murdered the one who wrote it.

Listen, Jennifer, I know what it's like. I know what it's like to have a madwoman in the attic of your memory. The thing you can't let out. The thing you must pretend isn't there, even when you hear the knocking.

Did you know that pressure on the brain swells it until it pushes its way out the bottom of the skull? That's called herniating. The pressure can come from a depressed skull fracture. Maybe a piece of shrapnel flew through the air and caught you in the head. Different kinds of ordnances cause different injuries. A shell, for instance, causes percussive injuries, because the body gets thrown, and if it gets thrown hard enough, that's one way it stops being the person and becomes the body.

We all become the body eventually. I know that.

Sitting in Jennifer's chair at Jennifer's desk, I imagined she was dead and I'd come to clean out her house. I often imagine this scenario, except I am the dead one, my house the one being cleaned. A silent interrogation, the examination of my things. What will they think of me?

When my parents died, I was the one who cleaned out their house. My sister came from North Carolina to "help" for three days, but her help consisted mostly of letting me know which things she wanted, then sneaking off to have various items appraised. She cared only about a certain kind of value. She had her eyes on the prize. I got lost in the rest of it—the evidence of their strange and secret lives. An entire dresser drawer full of my mother's ring boxes: black cardboard; clear, cut like crystal, imprinted with something in Korean; red velvet, worn bare in patches, with a snap-open lid. When I found this last one, I thought I remembered it, presented by my father at a formal dinner party on one of their anniversaries. In one of my mother's jewelry boxes, I found the ring I remembered belonging in it—platinum with diamonds in a style that had survived to become vintage. "An apology ring," I once heard my mother call it.

Why had she kept all those ring boxes? Had my father given her all of them? Were there that many apologies?

His drawers, his desk, contained no such mysteries. Everything was organized, spare, neatly arranged, as though in anticipation of my snooping. Unrevealing, I'd say, except in the sense that it's revealing to want to go unknown.

I'm not saying my sister got everything of value. I'm no dummy. I got it appraised, too, all of it. We split things fifty-fifty. Hers she sold, mine I live with. As I write I'm wearing my mother's apology ring. It used to fit, but now it slips around my finger, too heavy and too loose.

As soon as I was back home in Nashville, I threw out all the ring boxes.

I imagine if Jennifer were dead, Zoe going through her things, she would want what I want—an answer, evidence, an end to uncertainty. When she went to the police about her mother, did she just believe her guilty? Or did she know? What I really wanted to find was a journal like this one. If Jennifer keeps one, it's well hidden. It wasn't in the desk. It wasn't beside her bed. This is as close as I came: in the middle desk drawer, beneath a scatter of scrap paper, was a pad of sticky notes with *Zoe* and a phone number written on the top one. Below that, a lightly drawn question mark, over which Jennifer had put an *X*.

Here is a catalog of my precious objects:

The letters I wrote from the war, and my mother's replies
My father's medals from the First World War
A dried flower, pressed inside a photo album
My doctoral degree, in a black frame
My first nurse's cap

Also, this: a silver spoon like people used to collect, engraved with the word *Wisconsin*. Do people still collect these spoons, arrange them in little wooden curio shelves carved to secure their handles, made exactly for this spoon-collecting purpose? I don't think so. Oh, the things that disappear from the world. This spoon belonged to Kay. Kay wasn't from Wisconsin. After she was gone, I found it. I've never had any idea what it meant, but I've kept it all these years and whatever it meant for Kay, I believe I've kept that, too. The spoon is in the bottom drawer of my father's desk. I've never been to Wisconsin, but when I think of it I imagine snow.

From Jennifer's house I took a small stone. It was on a high shelf of the bookcase in her room, which is how I know it's hers and not Milo's. It's a brown rock—smooth, shiny, close to round but slightly irregular. It contains many shades of brown, even approaching gold. I imagine she found it on a beach. She is the kind of melancholy person one can picture gazing out to sea. Sometimes I picture myself standing on the prow of the ship that brought me home from the war, the salt wind in my hair, on my face an expression of sorrow and resolve. When in fact I spent much of the journey home crying in my bunk, trying not to be heard by the other girls.

The rock is here on my desk now. It's pleasing to the touch. I'll have to hide it before the next time Jennifer comes over. One more object that no one else will ever understand.

I have Zoe's number on my desk, too, and I can't help but think of how not so long ago I had her mother's number here, yet to be called, and now my life has changed. I wonder what Zoe would say if I called her. Were I a real detective, I wouldn't hesitate. I'd think I had every right to call her and ask her what she knows.

So much depends on every choice we make. This is obvious and yet endlessly to be marveled at. So many tales of what ripples outward, so many dreams of parallel universes. Because we tell stories about the things we find impossible to bear. Then we can pretend they are only stories.

I went down the Mountain today after all. I stood for a long time at my father's grave, and told him none of this.

Offerings

Now that she has friends, or at least potential friends—now that she knows people—Jennifer is cleaning up in case any of them drop by. In case she takes a notion to invite them over. Her grandmother used to say that having someone see your dirty house was like having someone see you naked. And her mother. And her father. They were and are constant cleaners, habitual cleaners, and for most of her life she's been one, too. But she's let this house fall into an embarrassing condition, in a way she'd stopped noticing until Margaret came over for the egg and she saw it under her critical eye. Ever since, she's felt a nagging sense of duty neglected, but she's done nothing about it until today. She's in Milo's room, sorting toys into bins. She saved his room for last, because it was the most daunting. Her own room is spotless, and the bathroom, and the study—everything. She's just about ready, should anyone unexpectedly arrive.

She slides her arms under Milo's bed to feel for small items. Wherever she looks, she finds Legos. She sweeps some out and picks through them, sorting by color—an almost entirely pointless task, but she's feeling thorough. Red, yellow, blue, black, black, yellow, blue. Her cleaning has failed to turn up the stone that belongs on the bookshelf in her study. Yellow, yellow, yellow, green. She thought maybe Milo took it and she'd find it in his room.

When she's finished she tours her clean house in admiration of her handiwork. The only thing that continues to nag is the missing stone. At the bookshelf in her study, she once again runs her hand over the space where the stone used to be. It's hard not to believe, when something is lost, that you'll find it back in the place where it was, if you just look one more time.

One summer, when Zoe was four, the same age that Milo is now, Jennifer took her to the beach for a few days, just the two of them. The trip had been Tommy's idea as much as hers, and the theory was that without him there to prefer, to anticipate, Zoe might like her mother more. At first the experiment seemed like a failure, Zoe kicking Jennifer's seat so hard on the drive there that she had to move Zoe behind the passenger seat, Zoe shouting, "You told Daddy not to come," Zoe wailing that she'd left behind her favorite toy and wanted to go home. What toy it was, Zoe wouldn't say. She was skilled at manipulation but not yet good at lies.

On the third day Zoe started bringing her things she'd found around the rental cottage. A shell. A puzzle piece. A feather. A tiny gold bead. Jennifer would come upon these treasures, placed in a way that marked them clearly as meant for her: beside her coffee cup, on her bedside table, resting atop her book. It was like being courted by a cat. Jennifer was afraid that if she acknowledged the gifts out loud they'd stop coming, so instead she responded in kind. She left a dime, a lip balm, a pair of cheap shiny earrings. Once or twice she watched from around a corner as Zoe discovered her offerings. The child's delight was unmistakable, but she too never said a word. It was hard to say who was following whose lead. One day Jennifer left Zoe that stone, a souvenir of the beach, shiny and smooth, and for the remainder of the vacation Zoe carried it around in her pocket, taking it out from time to time to study it under the light.

The vacation over, they were an hour away from the beach house when Zoe started to cry. The stone was lost. She couldn't find it. Jennifer turned the car around. She had to go back to the rental office and ask for the keys. It took them another hour to find the stone, behind the headboard of the bed where Zoe had been sleeping. Zoe clutched it all the way home, and when they got there, before Tommy came out to lift his precious sleepy daughter from the car, Zoe handed it to Jennifer, her expression focused and intense, and said, "You keep this for me, Mom. So I can always find it." As soon as she laid eyes on her daddy, she was Tommy's girl again, but still, for a long time after that, Zoe had checked in with Jennifer on the stone's safety, and Jennifer had thought that meant something, and then Zoe had grown older and forgotten, and Jennifer had kept it anyway, had kept it all this time. Now it was gone.

Zoe

I always see the skull beneath the skin.

—P. D. JAMES

Life Story

In Zoe's oldest memory her father is singing. She doesn't remember
what, only that it was something sweetly melancholy, and that she
was in his lap and he was rocking her and she was very, very upset.
She no longer knows why. She was holding a doll with a tear-shaped
stain under one eye, and she remembers believing that both the doll's
tear and her father's song expressed the depths of her own sorrow.

Her father! He was a wonderful man. If she were to list her top
five memories, it would be tough to include one that didn't feature
him. If she were to then arrange those memories chronologically, as
a version of her life story, it would look like all that had mattered in
her life so far was the time they spent together. Lying on her bed in
her dorm room, staring up at her roommate's stupid posters, she can
picture this timeline. Like the ones she used to make in elementary
school, with photos and dates and titles for the appropriate milestones—My First Birthday, My First Dance Class.

They wouldn't be milestones, though. Not on this timeline. Never
mind the clichés. No birthdays, no tutus, no sitting on Santa's lap.
What should matter isn't what's *supposed* to matter but what *does*. At
nineteen Zoe already knows how much of experience loses substance
in your mind, grows foggy, fades and vanishes. From solid to smoke.
What matters are not the times when you took lots of pictures. What

matters are the times when you felt something so strongly it overrode the automatic delete. The memories that stay in your mind like a program you can run. Like a dream you can reenter. Like a hologram. Time in a bubble. There's a reason you see so much of that stuff in sci-fi. Everybody wants it to be real.

"See there?" the film studies professor who tried so hard last semester might say. "You *do* have a topic you can write about."

Would she rather her brain was a projector, and she could play scenes on the wall, watch them like a movie? Or would she prefer a virtual reality machine, letting her live her memories again? Maybe she'd like to have both capabilities, so she could switch between them at will. Sometimes she'd watch. Sometimes she'd live.

Zoe's childhood, which she thinks of as a fairly standard American middle-class one, took place in Clovis, New Mexico. In fact most of her life to date took place there, excepting a few vacations, until she came to college here. To people here, in Michigan, New Mexico is exotic, but this is beyond ridiculous. She spent no time at all roaming the mountains, learning Native American wisdom. We're talking small-town Americana, people. A town with strip malls and housing developments, sitting in matter-of-fact exposure on the flat-ass plains. There's nothing exotic about a pickup truck.

Zoe exists in a condition of irritable sorrow. Her grief is a secret to the people around her. Her irritability is not. At least she thinks her grief is a secret. Some of the adults—that film studies professor—treat her with a compassion that suggests they can spot it. Her peers mostly leave her alone, and thus she lies on her bed in her dorm room on a Friday night, while the rest of the world makes merry. She would not like anyone to know it, but she has cried about this. And yet the people who try to reach her—she pulls back from them with all but an animal snarl.

She was not always like this. Once she had many friends, she had an openness to joy. What her father taught her in childhood was how to welcome the world, to seek out delight. Her mother, her wary, closed-off mother—but she will not think about her mother now. Her father once showed her a video of her mother dancing. Zoe was little, five or six. Her father whispered, "Don't tell her I showed you this," even though her mother wasn't there to hear. It was hard for Zoe to understand that the dancer on the stage was her mother, even though of course she looked like her. But she was so *abandoned*. At that age Zoe wouldn't have used that word. But she recognized what she wasn't yet able to describe: her mother not just abandoned to beauty, but making the world more beautiful, all by herself. Her mother summoning joy. Zoe's eyes filled with tears, watching.

"Oh, look at you," her father said, pulling her onto his lap, wiping her eyes with his fingers. "Look at you, sweet pea. Are you happy or sad?"

"Why?"

"Why what, sweet pea?"

"Why can't I tell her?"

Her father watched the video. She could see he was thinking about what to say. "Sometimes we don't like to remember when we were happy."

"Why?"

"Because remembering makes us miss it, and then we feel sad." He kissed her head. "But I wanted you to see how your mother could dance."

"Could I dance like that?"

"You're her little girl," he said. "I bet you can."

Zoe closes one eye and then the other, watching how her roommate's poster shifts from side to side. It's a *Doctor Who* poster—her roommate is a major fangirl. Zoe, never having heard of the show, did ask some polite questions in the beginning, but she found her roommate's eager complicated explanations hard to follow, and then when the other girl offered to show her some episodes Zoe said no. Now her roommate has found a crowd of like-minded people, and they wear catchphrase T-shirts they find on the Internet and buy advance tickets to midnight openings of fantasy movies. Zoe probably could have belonged to this group—maybe quite happily, as she has no objection to nerds or their enthusiasms—if she'd just that one time said yes. She could be with them right now, doing whatever they're doing—her roommate doesn't bother to tell her anymore. *Sure, let's watch one.* Would that have been so hard?

Yes, that's the trouble. Yes, it would've been.

So that's one memory. Is that really a top five though? What criteria is she applying? Does *top* mean favorite, or just unshakable? She remembers sitting on the stairs until her leg fell asleep, and how scary and weird that was, because it had never happened to her before, and it hurt but it didn't, and she couldn't walk on it, numb and then prickly prickly prickly, and she cried. Who came running when she cried, that time? She doesn't remember. Maybe no one. Does that count as a top-five memory? Does she have to be crying in all of them?

And so we move through childhood into junior high and high school, and there are birthdays, and tutus. She insisted on taking dance classes, though her mother was reluctant at first. She took them all through elementary school. Then, after the end-of-year recital in seventh grade, her mother was in tears, and Zoe stormed away, certain they were tears of disappointment, and her mother caught up to her and squeezed both of her arms and said, "For God's sake, Zoe, I'm crying because you were wonderful!" The next year, when her mother said, "So I'm signing you up again, right?" Zoe said, "No, I don't want to do it anymore." Her mother opened her mouth to argue. But then she just closed it and walked away.

That was her mother. They never talked about it again.

She walked away from most fights with Zoe, her face set, her mouth thin, everything about her a refusal. She was willing enough to scream at Zoe's father, though. If the fight was with Zoe's father, she was perfectly willing to freak out.

High school was high school: classes, friends, dating. Learning to drive. A baby in the house—that was a striking development. And seeing your mother in a movie theater with some guy, performing a confident hand job. There's one that stays in the brain. She'd like to have seen the teacher's face if she turned in a timeline with that on it. But that happened before high school—she's jumbling everything up. That happened around the time she decided to quit dancing.

She has good memories from high school. She and her father chase Milo in the backyard. He's wearing a little yellow sweater. He laughs his delighted baby laugh. Her father catches him and throws him in the air and Milo screams with joyful terror, and then her mother pokes her head outside and says, "Be careful," and they all stand very still, like deer, until she goes back inside. "Baby catch!" her father says, and tosses Milo to Zoe, and she catches him with a hand on either side of his solid little torso and he looks at her with a face that says yes yes yes, a face full of trusting happiness, and she kisses him on his little nose and then turns him around and tosses him back to her father.

But this is stupid, this has always been stupid. Listing her memories, marking off her life. It's all a lot of blah blah blah. She did this, she did that. Time progressed, like it does.

And then she walked into a room in search of a hairbrush and found her father dead.

What People Do

Last night I had a dream that I'd gone to an enormous building, where all the surfaces were shiny, the floors were enormous conveyer belts, and everywhere I went someone gave me exactly what I wanted. I carried a cup that was repeatedly filled with silver liquid, like mercury.

I don't know what this means. Maybe that's my odd little notion of heaven. It was one of those dreams so vivid they compete with actual events in your memory, insisting on their realness. I look down and feel faintly surprised not to see that cup of mercury in my hands.

An actual memory: When I was small I spent some weeks quarantined in my room, sick with a fever. In the morning I listened as my father left the house and at night I waited to hear him return. My mother said that after I got better I started telling everyone, "I go to work someday," which, depending on your point of view, was either a shocking or an amusing thing to hear a little girl say. You might wonder if I became a nurse because I'd once been ill, but there's no need to apply psychology to that particular decision. There weren't many careers open to women back then.

The reason I didn't join the army right out of school is because my father kept telling me to wait. He'd been in the First World War. There was a framed picture of him on his study wall, shaking hands with some general, and the look on his face, of joy and admiration, was not one I ever saw in person. I told him I wanted to enlist long before I did it. *Wait*, he said, *wait*. He wrote, *This war is going to last a long time*. He said, and he was right, that I didn't have the remotest idea what it was going to be like. I was so innocent. Or dumb. I was still in nursing school then, and it really was like a convent. All you did was you got up and you worked and then you went back to the dormitory and you had to study, because you had classes, and then you went to bed. You didn't go on vacation, take trips, go abroad. You didn't do any of that stuff, because you didn't have any money, but it didn't matter because what did you know of another way of life? We scrubbed furniture and soaked linen. We had two weeks' annual vacation, and other than that not a single day off in three years. We had to get written permission to be out past ten o'clock. We got five dollars a month.

When I graduated, they kept me on at Vanderbilt. My friend Grace and I rented a furnished apartment with two other girls. It was so small Grace and I had to share a bed, and we took turns sleeping on the lumpy side. It's funny to think about people who were once the same as you. Grace stayed stateside. While I was overseas she got married and moved to Montana, where all manner of things doubtless happened to her. At Vanderbilt, I worked on the medical ward, although I would rather have been on the surgical one, where Grace was. There, nurses shaved skin for surgery, prepared recovery beds, changed dressings, wished people well and forgot their names. It felt like progress. People on the medical ward had diseases, cancer and pneumonia, and so many of them just wasted away.

Every day on the way to work I saw the same recruitment poster, with a nurse gazing down at her patient like she was about to kiss him, and lettering that said, SAVE HIS LIFE AND FIND YOUR OWN—BE A NURSE. I didn't feel like I was saving anybody's life. Maybe good nursing care did save the pneumonia patients, like the head nurse said, but I always felt like their recovery had more to do with natural resil-

ience, and the healing properties of time. Ever since Pearl Harbor, I'd
been living in one of those dreams where you know you're supposed
to be somewhere but you just can't get there and time speeds by
while you stand at the mirror, trying to pin up your hair. Every time I
got on the bus to go to work, especially if I was late and had to dash
for it and climb aboard disheveled with my cap bag swinging in my
hand, and all those people looked at me, I seemed to hear what they
were thinking: there I was, still in Nashville, unable to even make a
bus on time, when I should have been at war.

Then one day in 1944 I stumbled off a train into the near dawn
of Fayetteville, North Carolina. The platform was deserted and dark,
my bag was heavy, I was supposed to get to Fort Bragg. I'd expected
someone to be there to meet me, but no one was. I'd expected that
person to tell me where to go. I considered sitting down on my bag
and crying, until I imagined the look my father would give me. So
I didn't cry, I didn't wait for someone to show up to rescue me. I
dragged my bag across the street to the Fayetteville Hotel, a tall
building with a single dim light in the window, and pushed through
the lobby door. And there she was, Marilyn Kay, my fellow soldier.
Waiting for me.

Lucy called yesterday. Fairly early in the morning, considering
she's on California time.

"Hello, darling," I said, so pleased to hear her voice.

"Hi, Margaret," she said. "How are you?" There was a hitch in her
tone, a slight formality, that told me what I didn't want to know. She
could have hung up without another word and I would've known she
wasn't coming. We had to play out the conversation anyway, because
that is what people do.

"How are you?" she asked.

"I'm lonely," I said.

"Oh, Margaret, I know, I'm sorry," she said. "And I can't come
see you any time soon, and I'm so so sorry about that. I really wish I
could."

She sounded weary and sad about it, and I believed she was. I was angry at her anyway. "All right," I said.

"Is there any chance you could come out here?"

"It's been a long time since I traveled."

"I know."

Then we both were silent. Maybe I could go out there—clear it with my doctor, pack my bags. The thought is terrifying. I was upset that she'd suggested it. I don't like to be reminded that I've lost my taste for adventure.

"I really would like to see you," she said. "I love you, you know."

"That's easy to say," I said, though I of all people know it isn't. "If you really loved me, you'd come." Then I hung up.

Don't think I report any of this with pride.

As for Jennifer, she meant what she said: no more unburdening. She's come three times since she made that decree, and every time I thought she might relent, but she didn't, and trying to think how to compel her I was so tense and unhappy under her hands that I felt worse after the massage than I had before. So I said we'd take a break from that, too. Instead of looking sorry she said, "All right," and told me to call her if I changed my mind.

I have thought ever since about changing my mind.

It is easier to be alone when you've been a long time used to it. When you've forgotten the other possibility. But I don't want her to come if she doesn't want to come. That has been my position all along. The paper with Zoe's number is still right here on the desk. I took the paper from Jennifer's house even though she might've noticed it missing. Perhaps I wanted her to notice. But I shouldn't call. I know I shouldn't call.

I'm lonely, I said to Lucy. It strikes me that I've never said that aloud before. How very sad it is to be honest only when I want to hurt someone.

•   •   •

I don't know why I did it. I tried to ignore the idea. I wrote down that I shouldn't do it, like that would vanquish the urge. I made some tea and drank it. I made many valiant efforts to read my mystery. But the mystery I really want to solve is not in the pages of that book. I want to know whatever it is Zoe knows. That must be why I dialed the number, pressing each big button on my old phone slowly, as if to give myself time to change my mind. One ring, then two, and the girl answered. Her hello was abrupt, clipped, reluctant. Or did it just sound that way to me? At any rate, whatever I might have said snagged on its way out. I breathed into the phone, and then I hung up. I sat for a moment with my hand on my heart, like a startled old lady on a TV show. When the phone rang shrilly a moment or two later, I'm glad no one was there to see me jump. I answered. I tried to say hello, but I hadn't spoken a word aloud since I talked to Lucy yesterday, and the sound emerged a whisper.

"Hello?" an answering voice said. The girl's voice, of course. I can't really say more about it than that—not the sound of it, not her tone as she said the word—because I noticed little beyond my own confusion. "Is someone there?"

I didn't speak, but neither did I hang up.

"Who is this?" the girl, Zoe, asked. "The least you could do is say something."

I hung up.

Sometimes I forget the basic facts of what the world is now. Of course I know that there is no longer such a thing as an anonymous phone call. Of course she'd seen my number on her telephone. I should have anticipated all that. But many things have been true and then no longer true in the years that I've been alive. The years and years, the many, many years. Surely it's no wonder I sometimes forget.

She called back. I didn't answer. My answering machine picked up—a robotic voice, announcing my number. A beep. Her voice: "Pick up." A silence. Then: "I just got a call from this number. Is anyone there?"

"Yes," I said aloud to the machine.

There was a long, whirring silence. Then she said, "Mom? Is that you? I don't know why you would call me if you didn't want to talk to me." Then she hung up.

Dear girl, I don't know why either.

I thought that would be the end of it. But she called again. This time she didn't wait for the machine but hung up midring. Silence. The clock ticktocking. Then she called again. This has gone on ever since. The phone is a live creature. I have woken a beast.

Now it rings again. The persistence of this girl, the utterly terrifying persistence. Is it anger or desperation that drives her to insist again and again on my attention? If I were indeed her mother, and if I were to answer, what would she want me to say?

Why did I call her? I'd be hard-pressed to explain my behavior, even if you put me on the witness stand and I swore to tell the truth. Which I'd take seriously, as my civic duty, and not because I think there is a God to help me.

We all want to satisfy our curiosity, and the little voice that tells us it's wrong to peep and pry is one trained into us from childhood, and nothing natural about it. We will all satisfy our curiosity when we can, which is any time we think no one will catch us.

The phone rang for the last time at midnight, but I can't sleep. I just lie here, waiting for it to come again and break the silence.

Mountains

Suspended animation. That was her condition. And then the phone call woke her up. It's not particularly rational to feel that way, Zoe knows that. And it certainly wasn't rational to call back so many times. Sometimes Zoe is glad she has no friends, as she'd hate for anyone to be paying attention to some of the shit she does. It could've been a wrong number. But then wouldn't the person have just said so when she called back? Instead of breathing in a frightened way and refusing to speak? There was too much weirdness for a simple mistake. Also in favor of Zoe's theory is the pure clarifying conviction she feels. In the grip of it she couldn't stop herself from calling again and again.

There you have it, folks. Zoe's private, personal craziness, from which she's spared you, her resolute unfriendliness a kind of martyrdom. Even without evidence, she is certain that it was her mother who called. Her mother has never tried to contact her before, not since Zoe moved in with her grandmother in the wake of her father's death. After Zoe went to the police, she heard nothing from her mother. No accusations, no self-defense. No apologies. She saw her only the time when she and her grandmother came by to see Milo. Then her mother and Milo vanished.

But now: a phone call. And a refusal to speak, which must be proof of guilt, or if not that then some other strong emotion. An irresistible longing. An unvanquishable loneliness. Proof of something her mother feels. Proof that her mother feels something. She realizes now that this is what she's been waiting for.

She has dance class today. An exercise class is among the college requirements, and she thought she might as well take something she could manage to pass fairly easily. *Do the minimum* has been her philosophy, but today she flings herself into every kick and turn. It feels good, she has to admit. To let her movement meet the music, to get those kicks up high, to sweat. Halfway through the class she notes the teacher watching her with barely repressed astonishment. But she pays no attention. She is not dancing for the teacher. She is just dancing.

After class the teacher comes up to her and says, "Zoe, I feel like I've never seen you before."

"I've been here."

"No, you haven't."

Zoe can't really argue with this. "Well," she says.

"You have enormous natural ability. Has anyone ever told you that?"

Zoe shrugs. Yes, they have, but it seems obnoxious to say so.

"And this is your first class? It's a shame you didn't start training earlier."

"I danced when I was little. It's just been a long time."

"Well, those fundamentals don't go away. You must have had good teachers."

"My mother was a dancer," Zoe says. And then she claps her hand to her mouth.

If the teacher notes how very weird this is, she's too polite to reveal it. "You've just been taking this for your phys ed requirement, yes? Come talk to me. I'd like to tell you more about our program."

Zoe says that she will, and she thinks she might even mean it.

She has resolved not to call the number again, at least not today or tomorrow. Just in case it was a misdial. She doesn't want to stalk a stranger. But underneath that reason is another, truer one: she hopes if she gives her mother a day or two to think about it, a little silence, her mother will call her back. Zoe does her best to ignore this reason because it creates a prickly anticipation that the phone will ring, which is a little hard to live with, moment to moment, even as it's strangely invigorating. Since she got out of bed this morning, she hasn't gotten back into it once. She hasn't even been tempted.

She goes back to the dorm after dance to shower, and when her roommate comes in later, opening the door quietly, as has become her habit since Zoe rose balefully from the bed and snapped at her one afternoon, Zoe is sitting at her desk, reading about the area with the 931 area code. "Oh!" her roommate says, and Zoe pivots in her chair and says hi. Her roommate looks astonished, not even trying to hide it. That's the second person Zoe's astonished today. It's making her realize just what a walking corpse she's been, the same way everybody remarking on the weight you've lost makes you realize how fat they used to think you.

"I'm out of bed," Zoe says, because that's so obviously what her roommate is thinking.

"Yeah," her roommate says. She tosses her backpack on her own bed, then leans over Zoe's shoulder, tentatively, for a closer look at the screen. Zoe has pulled up a photo of mountains with a white scud of cloud racing along their peaks. She resists the urge to cringe from her roommate's nearness, to snap the laptop shut.

"Pretty," her roommate says. "Very *Lord of the Rings*. Where is it?"

"Tennessee."

"Are you going there or something?"

"Maybe," Zoe says, though the idea had not yet occurred to her. "Maybe spring break." She adds, because she can't help it, "My mother is there."

"I didn't know you had a mother."

Neither did I, Zoe thinks of saying, but that would be inviting questions and she's not in the habit. She says lightly, "Did you think I sprang from the head of Zeus?"

Once again, she has managed to astonish her roommate—let's just say her name, which is Anna—but this time Anna recovers quickly. "That's *exactly* what I thought," she says.

Zoe could probably think of something else funny to say, but Anna steps back as if the conversation's over—maybe, to be fair to Anna, because Zoe's never given her much reason to think she'd want to talk.

Anna goes over to her dresser and starts opening and closing drawers. Zoe returns to clicking through mountainscapes, trying to picture her mother in that environment, flown from the brown flat land to hide among the trees, with Zoe's baby brother who has turned four without his sister. It's amazing how you get used to living with a stranger, how you learn to ignore each other in such a tiny space. She hears the noise Anna's making, primping to go out or whatever she's doing, choosing a different T-shirt, but she's also removed from it, as though Anna were doing these things on a television Zoe wasn't watching.

After a while, Anna heads for the door. "See you later," she says. Zoe senses a brief hesitation, as if she's debating asking Zoe whether she wants to come along. To the coffee shop, the club, the movie, the apartment shindig. But she doesn't ask. She goes. The trouble with pushing people away is sometimes they don't come back.

Zoe sits at her desk, imagining mountains, waiting for her mother to call.

Wrong Number

Today is my birthday. I was sure Lucy would call. I'll get back to you, she said. But no. I was waiting but pretending to myself that I wasn't, sitting in my armchair beside the table that holds the phone, it and my detective novels and my old Rolodex and a notepad and a jar of pens and a lamp. I had a book but the book wasn't holding my attention—I could guess who the killer was, and my ability to guess filled me with a disproportionate despair. Even at this late date I still want to be surprised.

"Oh, hell," I said, and I picked up the phone to call her. But I was stopped by something that was either anger or grief. Or pride. I can't keep begging. Why do I have to beg? Just because she owes me nothing. Just because there's nothing I deserve. I sat with the phone in my hand until the busy signal began to sound.

The instant I hung it up, it rang, startling me. Pleasing me, too, because I was sure it would be Lucy—that as reward for resisting the urge to call her, she'd called *me*. But after I said hello, I heard what I thought was Jennifer's voice, except that her hello came back in a tone of wary confusion.

"Jennifer?" I asked.

A startled, indignant no. Then a long pause. "I'm actually calling for Jennifer. Does she live there?"

"No one lives here but me," I said.

"But someone called me from this number."

"Not I," I said hastily. I don't know if it was the right course to lie. Given time to think, perhaps I would have told the truth. Every locked door has a key that will open it—sometimes it's a lie, sometimes a lie's opposite. It's perhaps the most valuable skill a detective has, knowing which to employ. This according to the books I read.

"When you picked up you said Jennifer," she said.

"You sounded like someone I know."

"Someone named Jennifer? Jennifer Carrasco?"

"Jennifer Carrasco?" Lie or truth? It was so hard to decide. "I think you mean Jennifer Young."

"Jennifer Young."

"Yes."

"Young's her maiden name."

"Well, that's what she goes by now."

Silence. "So you do know her."

"Yes," I said. "She gives massages."

"You're one of her clients?"

"That's what I am. And who are you?" Though of course I knew.

"I'm Zoe," she said. "Jennifer Carrasco is my mother."

It was an odd way to put it. Most people, I think, would've said, "I'm her daughter," but maybe that's a title Zoe is reluctant to claim. "Hello, Zoe," I said. "I'm Margaret Riley."

"You're sure we're talking about the same Jennifer?"

"I'm sure."

"So she told you she'd changed her name. Why would she change her name and then tell people?"

"I don't know."

"What else does she tell people?"

I said, carefully, "I'm not sure what you mean."

But she didn't respond to that. "She must have called me from your house. Why would she call me from your house?"

"I don't know," I said. "Sometimes I doze off after a massage, and she waits for me to wake. Perhaps she did it then."

"I guess," Zoe said.

"Is it so strange for her to call you?"

"You don't know how strange," Zoe said. Oh, the sorrow in that last sentence! I was expecting anger in this girl. A righteous indignation. A crusader in a vengeful fury. In response to her sorrow I didn't know what to say.

"I'm sorry I called so much," she said. "I thought it had to be her number. I hope I didn't freak you out."

"Of course not, my dear. I didn't hear it. Sometimes I turn off the ringer. Telemarketers."

"Oh," she said.

"They're so insistent."

"Is this your cell or a landline?"

"This is my home telephone," I said, and then she began to tell me about the Do Not Call Registry, which she said I could join very easily online—this girl who rang my phone off the hook, telling me how to stop other people from calling. I interrupted to say that I didn't have a computer and shocked her into silence.

"I'm old," I said.

"My grandparents have computers."

"I'm older than your grandparents."

"How old are you?"

"Ninety-one," I said. As of today, I didn't add, so as not to oblige her to acknowledge my birthday.

"Wow" was her response. "That's impressive."

"Don't give me too much credit," I said. "All I've done is not die."

"Still," she said. Perhaps I imagined the melancholic note in her voice. Thinking about Zoe, I have failed to consider the grief she must feel about her father. The grief we feel when someone dies. The grief and the blame and the guilt. To tell the truth, which I'm trying my best to do if only in these pages, even now grief and its fellows are hard for me to think about.

"Well, thank you," I said. "I'm glad you approve."

"Could you tell my mother . . ." She paused. "Could you tell her not to call me again?"

"If I see her," I said.

"I don't want to talk to her," she said.

But of course that was a lie.

Oh, Zoe, I know your longing. I recognize your need. I know you'd like to kill it, but you can't. They say there's peace if you can relinquish desire. For me desire's absence has only ever left a dull persistent ache. An insistent humming insectile silence. A lonely house in the woods. But perhaps the lesson is that I never relinquished desire, and that's why there's been no peace.

What Zoe Did

She was looking for a hairbrush. That was all she wanted. She couldn't find her own. The door to her parents' room was closed. Her mother was at the mall with Milo, so she assumed her father was in there. She knocked. When there was no answer, she thought maybe he was napping, so she opened the door quietly. In the dim light she saw his figure on the bed, lying on his back, propped up on two pillows, with his injured ankle elevated by a third. Her poor father. That ankle had given him so much trouble, and her mother was a bitter, reluctant nurse. His head was turned to the side, away from her.

She crept past him slowly. Her mother kept her hairbrush on the sink in the master bath. There it was, where her mother always put it—and why don't you have a place for your own things, Zoe, so you don't keep having to borrow mine? Zoe brushed her hair, a bit hurriedly, as she didn't want to wake her father or have her mother return unexpectedly to criticize. Her hair got staticky, long blond strands floating around her, sizzling. She put the brush back in place, went to the door, thought again, went back and pulled all the hair from it, balled the hair in her hand, and shoved it in her pocket so her mother wouldn't find it in the trash. Her hair was exactly the shade of her mother's, but still this precaution was necessary, as her mother cleaned her brush every time she used it. Every single time.

She replaced the brush, moved it a few degrees to the right, looked at herself in the mirror, and, satisfied, turned to go.

What was it that told her he wasn't just sleeping? She'd tiptoed past his bed, almost to the door, before the bad feeling hit her. He was too still, maybe. Or she registered, subconsciously, that she didn't hear him breathing. She hasn't been able to figure it out, though she's returned again and again—without meaning to, without wanting to—to that moment and its question. How did she know? As if the key to the whole mystery lies in that.

First, she said, "Dad?" She said it quietly, like you do to test whether someone's sleeping. She didn't yet believe what she knew. Second, she said it again, this time louder than normal speech. She moved closer to the bed. "Dad?" Third, she put her hand on his shoulder, and felt no answering movement in his body. The phrase *as still as death* came into her head. She put her other hand on his other arm and she shook him; she said, "Dad, Dad, Dad, Daddy, Daddy, Daddy." Her voice rose and rose. His head lolled as she shook him.

Fifth, or sixth, or seventh, she put her head on his chest and sobbed. She kept feeling his chest with one hand, as if she'd find his heartbeat if she just kept searching for it. A calm voice in her head said, "You need to make a call." After a time—who knows how long a time—she said, "All right," out loud. She stood and straightened her clothes and walked around the bed to her mother's side, where the phone was. She turned her back on her father while she dialed 911. Talking to the operator, she lowered her voice, because she didn't want to embarrass him.

Now she was supposed to wait. It was dark in the room. When the people came they wouldn't be able to see. She went to the light switch and flipped it. She saw her father on the bed and flipped it off again. She put her hand to her mouth and made an animal sound. She stood there in the dark, shaking. There were pill bottles on the bed. She hadn't noticed them before, though she must have jostled them when she tried to rouse her father. She flipped the light back on. It would be terrible for the people to see the pill bottles. What would they think? Her father would be mortified.

Once she'd come home from a date to find him passed out in his truck in their driveway. She'd helped him inside the house; he was barely conscious enough to register she was the one supporting him. The next morning, she woke to an angry exchange between her parents, her mother spitting words like *daughter* and *ashamed*, and then her mother slammed out of the house with, it turned out, Milo. Her father came into her room and pulled the desk chair over to her bed and sat there with his head bowed in the early morning light and he cried and cried.

"Oh, Daddy," she was saying as she gathered up the bottles, hastily, dropping one and picking it up again. "Oh, Daddy, don't worry, it's all right, it's all right."

I'm a bad father, he'd said, that time, and she said, "You're not. You're a wonderful father. You're doing the best you can."

I love you so much, he'd said, and she said, "I know you do. I love you, too."

She had all the bottles now, but what was she going to do with them? Would the people search this room? Would they check the drawers? Would they look in the bathroom trash? She went out of the room, clutching the bottles to her chest, and in the kitchen she found a plastic grocery bag to contain them. She grabbed a few paper towels off the roll, crumpled them, and arranged them over the pills. The bag went into the kitchen trash. Now she needed to go back to the bedroom.

But would they look in the trash? The bag couldn't stay there. She fished it back out. The bag couldn't be in the house. She went out the front door. No sign yet of the people. No sign of her mother and Milo, either. On the other side of the street the neighbor's pickup truck was parked in the driveway. She ran across, with a hasty glance both ways, and tossed the bag in the truck bed. She stood there a moment, waiting to be caught. Then she looked into the bed.

The bag lay splayed in the middle, hints of orange showing through. She pushed herself up, pitched forward, and grabbed the bag, tossing it to the back right corner. There were a few pieces of scrap lumber in the truck. She dragged one of them on top of the bag, then added a second one. That would have to be good enough. She didn't want the neighbor to come outside and catch her. She didn't want the people to find her here.

She ran back across the street, forgetting to look both ways until she was already on the other side, when, though it was too late, she did it to make up for not doing it before.

Where was her mother? It was always Milo she took with her when she left.

She didn't know where she was supposed to be when the people came. In the bedroom with her father? She would rather not go back in there. *I'm sorry, I'm sorry*, he said. Maybe it was all right to be waiting outside. She found that she didn't want to go back inside the house at all. She sat down on the front lawn. Really, her legs gave way—she didn't sit so much as drop. It had been dry—it was almost always dry—and the grass was prickly and brown at the ends. She brushed her palm over it, letting it tickle her hand. She felt that it made a sound as she brushed her hand over it. Shhh, shhh, it said. It was probably not all right to lie down.

The ambulance came. She answered the questions she was asked. The paramedics went inside. *Then* she lay down. It was all right to lie down now. The blue bright sky showed her the most beautifully sculpted cloud. *Look what I made*, it said.

She put her hand in her pocket and found the balled-up hair. She pulled it out and stared at it, utterly confused. The sun sparked it, so that it shone with little specks of gold. That was when she realized this was all her mother's fault.

Orphan

This morning I went to the Smoke House in Monteagle for breakfast. I so rarely eat out. I thought it would be a treat, even if I managed only a poached egg and a few bites of bacon. A biscuit, maybe,
and coffee someone else made, and a little silver pitcher full of
cream. But all I got for cream was a small white bowl filled with
those little plastic pots with the peel-off lids. I said to the waitress,
"You used to bring cream in a silver pitcher."

"No, ma'am, we've always used these, long as I worked here,"
she said. Her name was Danielle. "I can bring you milk in a pitcher
though. It's a little white pitcher."

"How long have you worked here?'

"About five years."

"Well, I've lived here twenty, and I remember those pitchers."

"Yes, ma'am. Would you like me to bring you some milk?"

She was perfectly nice. Her hair in a long ponytail. I don't want
to be yes ma'amed. I want to be believed. It's a little thing, a little
thing. But I was so sure. Little silver pitchers. Danielle the waitress
never saw them so they can't ever have existed. My truths vanish,
loss upon loss.

The Smoke House has a gift shop, which they prefer to call the
Old General Store and have decorated with whiskey barrels and a

player piano. What the place really purveys is old-timeyness, but the specific products include jams and jellies, bacon, wood that has been carved. I poked around the shop after my breakfast. God knows why. I suppose I didn't want to go home. It's tempting, in telling a story like this, to assign yourself a prophetic sense. If I hadn't lingered like that, without purpose or cause, I would have been gone before she came in.

The moment I saw her I knew who she was. That is the truth. The squarish face declining into a graceful jaw. The somber eyes. Her hair the same blond, just as straight but longer, shinier. It has the sleek shine of gold behind glass, a gleaming irresistibility, kept where it can't be touched. Perhaps she is her father's girl, but she looks exactly like her mother. And carries herself the same.

She looked around hesitantly, like she wasn't supposed to be there and was afraid someone would catch her. Her eyes passed over me. Well, why wouldn't they? She went up to the counter and said to the woman behind it, "I'm looking for someone. I wonder if you might know her." Exactly like a detective! But without the confidence, or the photograph to show, or the bribe of a folded bill.

"What's her name, sweetie?" the woman asked, and the girl—Zoe—said, "Jennifer Young."

"I—" I tried to say, but it came out a croak, as my voice sometimes does. As I worked to clear my throat, the woman kept repeating the name: Jennifer Young, Jennifer Young. "It does sound familiar," was her conclusion.

"I know her," I said.

They both looked at me like a cat had spoken.

"I think this lady can help you," the woman said to Zoe, as if she'd accomplished something in pointing that out. It's the job of the younger person to move, so I stood there with my hand on my cane and waited. She came up to me. Really, the resemblance is uncanny. I wanted to touch her cheek to see if she was real.

"You know where I can find her?" she asked.

"Of course I do," I said. "I'm Margaret Riley." And when her face remained confused: "We spoke on the telephone."

"Oh," she said. "Okay." She said it in a stunned uncomprehending way. She had the woozy air of someone who's just come out from under an enchantment. "I drove all night, I haven't slept," she said. She seemed to wobble a little, and instinctively I reached out to steady her, and then we both wobbled.

"Let's sit down," I said. "You need breakfast. Let's get you some breakfast."

I took charge of the situation. It's not like I've lost the knack. We got a table, and when she seemed stupefied by the menu, I made some suggestions and then waved Danielle the waitress over and ordered for her. I took the menu from her hands and gave it to Danielle. "Do you drink coffee?" I asked Zoe. She nodded, and I said, "Two coffees, please."

"And a pitcher of milk?"

I said yes, though milk isn't what I want. It's cream. "Now, dear," I said to Zoe, "are you all right?"

"I'm just tired," she said.

"Where did you come from?"

"Ann Arbor. I go to school there."

"And what made you drive down? Did your mother call again?" Once you tell a lie, the only choice is to keep pretending.

She shook her head. "No," she said.

"So. It was an impulse."

"Yes."

"What are you hoping will happen?" The question had more harshness than I intended.

She looked at me with her mother's somber eyes and blinked. "I don't know."

Danielle appeared to set down the coffee and the pitcher. Zoe grimaced when the coffee hit her mouth. It wasn't hot, so I waited for her to say she didn't like it. But she didn't. She took another sip and winced. Her face when she turned it toward me had a blind look, like I'd caught it in a flashlight beam.

"You seem like you need help," I said.

"I don't." She looked down at the table, shaking her head, but I saw that she was tearful.

Sometimes the best course is a detour. "Have you ever been here before?"

She shook her head.

"Well, welcome to the Mountain," I said. "I'm going to tell you about it, all right?" I saw Danielle approaching with a plate. "While you eat, I'll play tour guide."

"Okay," she said.

So I told her about the elevation and the population. I described Natural Bridge, nattered on about caves and waterfalls. I said *sandstone* and *overlooks*. She ate her eggs and toast, nodding as I talked. When she was finished she sat back and looked at me. She seemed awake for the first time since I'd laid eyes on her. "Better?" I asked.

"Yes," she said. And then, "Thank you," with more gratitude than I deserved, but still I liked it. "So it's pronounced swan-ee."

"What? Yes."

"I thought it was sue-wan-nee."

"A lot of people make that mistake."

"It's a funny name."

"You should visit it while you're here. It's a beautiful place."

"I'd like to," she said. "I saw pictures online." She hesitated. "Is that where my mother lives? In Sewanee?"

"No, your mother lives where I do, between here and Sewanee. We're neighbors of a kind."

She nodded.

"Do you want me to show you your mother's house?"

"Now?"

"Or whenever you want."

"Maybe in a little while." But she didn't say this with any confidence.

"Do you have a place to stay?"

She shook her head. Her solemn eyes. She was like an orphan in a basket at my door.

"Well, why don't you come back to my house then. I have a nice guest room. You can take a nap. After you're rested we can make a plan."

"That's very nice of you, but . . ."

"It would be no trouble. I'd be happy to have you."

"Oh, thank you, but it's not that. I just . . . you said . . . how close is your house to my mom's?"

"Oh! Don't worry," I said. "There's a big pond between us."

After that she agreed to come. I asked for the check, waving off her attempt to pay. As we went down the stairs leaving the restaurant, she offered me her arm and I took it. A considerate girl. I was impressed. I can manage on my own, of course, but it's easier not to. She drives a pickup truck. She followed me back to my house. I drove slowly, checking the rearview mirror to make sure she was still there.

All she had with her was a backpack. She carried it by a strap instead of on her back. I said, "Backpacks used to be just for soldiers," and she said, "How did students carry their books?" I couldn't think of the answer.

I led her into the guest room and waved at the two beds. The beds seemed to perk up at our presence, coming to attention. I'd been using this room for massage, of course, but when was the last time someone slept here? "You can have whichever one you like," I said, and I had the fanciful notion that both beds said, *Choose me!*

She came over and touched each one, then picked the one nearest the door. We made the bed together. "Now, why don't you nap?" I said. I made to leave so she could get undressed, but she just climbed into bed and pulled the covers over her. I had a silly urge to tuck them closer, to kiss her on the forehead. I contented myself with turning out the light and telling her to sleep well.

She slept and slept and slept. I thought she might sleep a hundred years. I hoped I was the fairy godmother and not the witch. It was nearly five o'clock when she emerged yawning with a pillow-creased face and said, "I slept a long time."

"You were tired," I said. "You needed it."

She rubbed her face. "Is there a toy store around here? I missed Milo's birthday. And Christmas."

"Well, what are you looking for?"

"A toy? A book?"

I didn't know what to tell her. In Sewanee there's an overstuffed home-décor shop a Victorian might enjoy. It has a heavy smell of potpourri. There are places where you can buy pottery mugs. I don't know where you shop for a child. The Walmart in Winchester is half an hour away, down the steep side of the Mountain. I don't like to drive that road. "It's late in the day, sweetheart. I don't know if anything will still be open."

She absorbed this news, looking worried. "I really think I should get something."

"You don't have to go to your mother's today. You can wait until tomorrow. You can stay as long as you want."

I was surprised how quickly she agreed to this. "Tomorrow, then. Is that okay? Maybe the campus bookstore will have something? And then I can go over there."

"That's a good plan," I said.

She looked around, like she was only now coming awake to her surroundings, and said, "I like your house." I thanked her. She walked around asking me questions about this and that. She studied the portraits of my ancestors while I told her all about them, the general with his beard and the wife with the white cap and the severe expression. She sat down on my couch and put her hand on the scrapbook, still on the coffee table. "What's this?"

"Oh, don't look at that," I said. "It's my scrapbook from the war. It's full of sad stories."

"Which war?" she asked, and I told her, and then I told her about my service, a mild and cheering version, with all the horror ignored. She listened, turning the pages slowly. She stopped before we reached Germany, for which I was glad.

"Margaret," she said, and I waited for a question about the war. "Do you know about my father?"

I answered honestly. I told her what I'd read on the Internet. But I could so easily have lied! *Yes, my dear, I know he's passed*, I could've said, and then pat-pat-patted her hand. Did I tell the truth because I didn't want to deceive her? Or because I thought my honesty would inspire her own? It must be quite a struggle for a good detective to understand herself.

"I guess you think she's innocent," she said.

"Why do you say that?"

"Otherwise you wouldn't have her in your house."

"I don't know," I said. "She'd pose no threat to me."

"Why are you being so nice to me? If you're friends with her, and you know what happened? Don't you think I'm bad? I'm the one that went to the police."

"I don't think you're bad. No."

"Well, I'm here to apologize," she said. "When I woke up I realized it. That's what I'm hoping will happen."

In her voice there was a combination of defiance and tears, an alarming intensity of emotion. I should've been able to offer more comfort. Instead I waited a few minutes, then asked what she wanted for dinner. I took her to Pearl's. I ate plain poached salmon and a little white rice. She had chicken in a sauce. I insisted she eat dessert.

She came for forgiveness, the poor, poor child. That is not what I expected. Forgiveness is a terrible thing to want, because of all things on earth it is the hardest to get. We've gone to great lengths in search of it. We've invented whole religions. And yet no god truly forgives. Otherwise why would there be hell? *Ask and ye shall be*, we say. But we cannot believe it.

Step One

Zoe could easily be mistaken for a student here, and so there's no reason for her to feel like a conspicuous interloper as she walks into the campus bookstore. She lingers near the entrance, touching the books on display. She keeps her head down, hoping the girl behind the cash register won't ask if she needs help. She's avoided all nonessential interactions with other people for so many months now that she's grown terrified of them. Interactions. People. She feels an immense gratitude toward Margaret, for seeming to understand that. For knowing what to do.

Step one: buy a toy for Milo, if she can find the toys without asking where they are.

Two older women come in, talking loudly, then hushing their voices as soon as they're inside. Professor types in cardigans. She's noticed that female professors really seem to favor cardigans, even when the weather's a little too warm for them. She's listening to their talk only because they're too near to avoid it, but it's kind of interesting to hear one of them telling the other how much she hates one of her students, which she does in a normal voice, except at first she whispers his name, after that saying only *he*. Suddenly she breaks off her complaining and says, "Oh my God! I finally saw Jennifer!"

Zoe goes still.

"You did? Pretty great, right?"

"So great. She's amazing. She really did get that knot out of my shoulder."

The other woman sighs. "I have to book her again."

"I already made another appointment. I wanted to do it, like, tomorrow, but I made myself wait two weeks, because it does cost money."

"Did she have any mystical visions?"

The first woman laughs. She says, "No, not really," but it's obvious this is a lie.

The second woman says, "She's really intuitive. She knew immediately about . . ." The women are walking as they're talking, and Zoe doesn't catch the rest. Did the second woman know the first woman was lying? Or could she really not tell? Maybe it would be better to go through life not being able to tell.

Zoe is angry. Maybe that's strange. She's grown used to feeling what she's probably not supposed to feel. She's out of step with what's normal. It's not for these women to talk about her mother, with Zoe standing there a stranger. Her supposedly amazing mother. She and her mother fled the same history, and how did her mother arrive at amazing? She could follow these women and tell them exactly where her mother came from, if she were the sort of person her mother thinks she is. Instead she picks up a guide to Sewanee hiking, because it's right in front of her, and pages through it, dimly registering its pretty pictures until the urge to unmask her mother dissipates. That is not what she came here to do.

She skirts the edges of the store until she finds something she thinks Milo would like: a little tiger in a sweatshirt that says SE-WANEE. A four-year-old has not yet outgrown stuffed animals, right? She starts to walk toward the registers with her purchase, but it comes to her that step one leads directly to step two, and her pace slows. Now that she has the gift for her brother, it will be time to go. "Let's go, Margaret," she'll say heartily, and then she'll help the old woman out to her car, and they'll drive a little ways down the road. She asked this morning if they could walk there, and Margaret said, "Well, you could, but I'm afraid I can't."

That's all that was said about the plan to see her mother. Another thing for which Zoe is grateful. Margaret isn't pressuring her toward action, urging her on her way. Far from it. Margaret seems content to fuss over her, to treat her like an invited guest. She said she would make Zoe hot chocolate when she got back, which breaks Zoe's heart a little, because it reminds her she's not a child. Still, Margaret knows her intentions. Margaret knows who she is, and why she's here, and so in her presence Zoe can't help but know these things, too.

The girl at the cash register has lifted her head and spotted Zoe approaching, and so now she has to proceed, like a normal person would. She buys the tiger. But she isn't ready for step two, which is delivery. She goes back to buy the hiking guide.

She chooses a hike almost at random and drives to the overlook where it starts. Green's View, it's called. There's a car parked on the other side of the circle, engine running, some guy gazing out at the vista. Zoe wishes he weren't there, but she can park right by the trail access, and though the guy might look at her, she doesn't have to see him do it. Because of him she doesn't pause to contemplate the view, lovely as it is, but goes ahead and starts picking her way down the steep and narrow trail. It takes her into a hollow of early wildflowers and enormous boulders, the boulders like castoffs from another planet. At the bottom she tilts her head back to gaze up at where she started; it seems impossibly far away. The trail winds on, and she follows it. Down here she has a blessed sense of being completely unobserved.

Up ahead, just off the trail, she notices a large piece of rusted metal. She's puzzling over its nature and origin—there's no access to this place except by trail—when she happens to look beyond it, back toward the bluff, and sees an entire car. Or the ruins of one. She's not even surprised, the car so incongruous she can barely register belief in its existence. It's upright on its wheels, its roof more or less intact, but the front is smashed so that it yawns like an unhinged jaw. The steering column stands to the side, stuck into the earth, a circle on a pole. It looks like a flower. She clambers up rocks toward the car, and then sees beyond it a second one. This one landed upside-down, rests there in pitiful permanent exposure of its rusty undercarriage. Next to it a strip of red metal. Bright red. Why do some things keep their color, while others get worn away? The car on its wheels has the low-slung look of a seventies hot rod. Inside it the front seat is visible, retaining its pale upholstery.

There is no way for these cars to have come here except in a plunge off the cliff. Glorious or horrifying, depending on the director and the score. Or maybe comical, if the cars were empty. She sees no bloodstains on the seats. Surely even if a body had been extracted long ago, there would still be stains. She looks up again at the top of the cliff. It must be several hundred feet up. Maybe some drunk college kids pushed the cars off the edge, then scrambled carelessly down the trail, slipping and sliding and laughing at their flirtation with peril, to see what they had done. Maybe this is even the most likely scenario. Or the cars might have nothing to do with each other, the second leaping years after the first. Still she imagines one fleeing, the other in pursuit, faster and faster toward the edge of the world, until both of them flew off.

The Ordinary

Milo and Ben play with cars on the floor—smashing them together, saying ow, ow, ow—while Jennifer and Megan sit at Jennifer's
table over tea, syrup-coated plates pushed to the side. Jennifer made
French toast. Sebastian is shooting a wedding and will be gone all
day and late into the evening; Megan as usual has ungovernable
stacks of unfinished work. Jennifer offered to take Ben for part of the
day so Megan could catch up, but Megan's guilt wouldn't allow this.
Brunch was the compromise. Jennifer isn't solving Megan's problems
but distracting her from them, which sometimes is enough. And she
thinks in an hour or so, if the boys are still playing well together,
she might persuade Megan to go get some work done, because she
really is overwhelmed, poor thing, and Jennifer would like to help.
She worries about Megan. She feels for her a deep tenderness that
extends often to Ben and, at times, to Sebastian. She would like to
be an agent of good to them. She would like Milo to grow up with a
friend he can't remember not knowing, as close as he'll come to a sib-
ling. And she's happy to have settled, herself, into friendship. With
Megan she doesn't feel like she has to guard against her own tenderness. Megan won't use it against her.

"They're so cute, aren't they?" Megan says, smiling down at the
boys with pleased fondness. Ben at that moment lifts a car high in

the air, as if it's flying backward from a collision, and utters a long low-pitched scream.

Jennifer almost makes a joke about the juxtaposition of Megan's comment and Ben's pantomime of violence, but instead she just agrees. She's leery of accidentally invoking the face-stabbing incident, which has, thankfully, been forgotten, or at least receded far enough into the background that they can all pretend not to see it there.

Jennifer yawns, covers her mouth, says excuse me. Megan laughs at her. "You yawn like a cat," she says.

"How does a cat yawn?"

"Hugely. Like, with its whole face. Its eyes squinched up. You've never seen a cat yawn?"

"I guess I have. I must have."

"Surely everyone on earth has seen a cat yawn."

Milo says, "I haven't," proving once again that children are most likely to be listening to adults when they don't appear to be.

"I haven't, either," Ben says in proud agreement.

"You've seen a cat yawn, Benjy," Megan says. "Think about the lions at the zoo."

"They show their teeth," Ben says.

"That's right."

"They have huuuuuge mouths," Milo adds.

"Do I have a huge mouth?" Jennifer asks, feeling an absurd spasm of adolescent self-consciousness.

"Mommy has a huge mouth!" Milo says.

"No, it's not huge," Megan says in mock-scolding. "It's totally normal sized." She takes a sip of her tea and shoots a teasing sidelong grin at Jennifer. "For a giant."

Jennifer is about to retort, but then she hears a sound that surprises her: tires on her gravel drive. What she was about to say she'll never afterward be able to remember. Megan raises her eyebrows, listening. "Who could that be?" Jennifer says.

"You're not expecting anyone?" Megan says.

She shakes her head.

"Maybe it's a package," Megan says. "Maybe you need to sign."

"I didn't order anything."

The boys are at the front window. "It's a car," Milo reports. From outside comes the sound of doors shutting. Jennifer could get up to go look, but she doesn't want to. She has a bad feeling about this, which she struggles to ignore. In an ordinary life, people sometimes drop by. Except they don't anymore, not since cell phones. "It's a girl," Milo says.

"What girl?" Jennifer asks.

Milo shrugs, turning away from the window. "I don't know," he says. "Some girl."

"What girl?" Jennifer pushes up from the table.

"I don't know, Mommy," Milo says, in a cheerful singsong, losing interest now that Jennifer's is engaged.

There's a knock on the door. A loud, insistent knock, *one two three*. Jennifer and Megan look at each other like the police have arrived. "Why am I freaked out?" Megan asks.

Jennifer moves toward the door, but Milo is right there, and quicker, and he opens it. "Who are *you*?" he says.

And Zoe says, "I'm Zoe, silly," and then she drops to her knees and pulls Milo into a hug.

Milo yanks out of the hug, looks at Jennifer for help. "Mommy," he says.

Zoe crouches there, looking at him entreatingly, empty armed. "Milo," she says, "don't you know who I am?"

Zoe. Her beautiful daughter, her angry girl. She rises now and looks at Jennifer. Jennifer flinches, then tries to disguise the flinch by holding her whole self absolutely still. Her daughter's gaze is a spotlight, blinding and insistent. Accusatory. It has always hurt to look at her, and now it aches. She looks past her daughter, expecting to see her mother-in-law waving custody papers, a lawyer, the police. But

Zoe is the only one here. Does that mean she's the only one coming? Or is she the advance guard?

"Who *are* you?" Milo asks.

Behind Jennifer, Megan has risen, clearly aware that something strange and fraught is happening. "Ben," she says quietly, "come here," and Ben just does it, no demand she justify her order, not a word of protest.

"He doesn't know who I am?" Zoe looks at Jennifer in puzzlement.

"Mommy!" Milo demands. "Who *is* she?" He steps closer to Jennifer, tugging on her hand.

"I'm your sister," Zoe says. "You're my brother."

"I don't have a brother," Milo says.

"No, you don't. You have a sister."

"I don't have a sister."

"Of course you do, silly," Zoe says. "I brought you this." She holds out a little stuffed tiger.

But Milo won't take it, pressing his body into his mother's side, his brow intensely furrowed, his lower jaw stuck out. "Mommy!" he says.

Jennifer would like to embrace Zoe, then carry her out the door. But that is not possible. What is possible? What should Jennifer do? She feels a sharp longing for five minutes ago. "She's just pretending, sweetie," Jennifer says. "You've never had a sister. You're an only child."

At this, Zoe takes a stumbling step back, her face wiped of all its passionate certitude. Not since she was a small child, not even after Tommy died, has Jennifer seen her this vulnerable, seen her express a sadness that wasn't three parts rage. But she has to save the child it's possible to save. She crouches to look at Milo. "I need to talk to this girl," she says. "Can you go play in your room?"

Milo shoots a nervous glance at Zoe. "Can I watch TV?"

"Yes, you go watch TV," Jennifer says, and Milo clatters up the stairs.

"Can I go, too?" Ben asks, and Megan says, "No, sweetie, we should leave." He protests, and she opens her mouth to speak again, but at the same time Zoe says to her, "Did she not tell you about me?"

"No," Megan says.

"Because I'm not pretending."

"No," Megan says. "I can see that."

"I'm her daughter."

Jennifer looks at Megan, who is looking back at her. "I don't understand," Megan says. From upstairs, to Jennifer's relief, comes the loud blare of a raucous TV show.

"Her name isn't Jennifer Young," Zoe says. "It's Jennifer Carrasco."

"Really?" Megan asks Jennifer.

"Really," Zoe says. "She must have changed it so no one could look her up." Suddenly she turns to Jennifer. "Say something," she demands. She waits, then turns back to Megan. "People think she killed my father."

Megan's face. Megan's sweet face, transformed by horrified astonishment. That fevered blush she gets, which Jennifer has only ever seen caused by embarrassment, but this time is evidence of something else, some new emotion, whatever it is that Megan now feels.

Jennifer looks at her daughter. Her twin, Tommy used to say. "And why do people think that, Zoe?" she asks coolly. "Because you got rid of the bottles he used to kill himself?"

Zoe doesn't look at her. "The police took it seriously," she says to Megan.

"Yes," Jennifer says. "Thanks for that."

"We have to go," Megan says. She has Ben tightly by the hand, and as she leads him past Jennifer, Jennifer can see the tension in Megan's arm, the way she maneuvers so that Ben won't accidentally brush against Jennifer, so that Jennifer, the monster, won't come into contact with her precious son. One minute you are one thing, and the next you are something else. The first thing is lost to you. You can never be the first thing again.

Zoe steps aside to let them leave. Jennifer hears Megan's car door open, hears Megan urging Ben into his car seat, and knows that next she'll lean in to check the buckles, adjust the straps, make sure her child is safe. Then she'll go to the driver's seat, and then she'll be gone, gone, gone.

Jennifer darts outside, past Zoe, as if she doesn't even see her there. She slows a few feet from Megan, who stands grasping the handle of her car door, watching her like a startled deer. "Megan, please," Jennifer says.

Megan waits. She shakes her head. "Is all this true?"

"She's my daughter, yes," Jennifer says. "The rest is complicated."

"I'm sorry." Megan opens the door. "I think it's too complicated for me."

"Megan, please," Jennifer says again. She hears the pleading in her voice. "Everybody has secrets. Your marriage isn't perfect, right? You drink too much."

Megan rears back. That was the wrong thing to say. Though Jennifer knows with a doomed certainty there was no right thing.

"I'm so sorry," Megan says, crying now. "I'm so sorry for you." She gets in her car hastily and shuts the door.

Jennifer doesn't stand there to watch her back away. She tried, and she ruined it, this life in Sewanee, and now it is over. She turns to go back to the house. Inside Zoe is waiting, pacing up and down in front of the glass doors. She stops when her mother comes in. "I'm sorry," she says.

This is not what Jennifer expected to hear, and maybe that's why she proceeds as if she didn't hear it. "Happy?" she asks. She goes far enough up the stairs to see Milo, engrossed in a violent cartoon. Then she heads for the kitchen to pour herself a bourbon from a bottle Erica brought over. Just last week, that was. When it was still possible for Jennifer to call Megan and Megan's friends and invite them over for a drink. After a second's thought she pours a bourbon for Zoe, too. Back in the living room, Zoe's where she left her. Jennifer hands her the drink, then slides open the glass door. She goes outside and sits in one of the wooden chairs. She braces her feet against the railing. She stares at the woods. She stares at the pond. The deck across the way is empty. The bourbon burns her throat.

Zoe will never understand. There is no point in trying to make her. There's no point in telling her any of the stories. Even if she did, who knows what Zoe would think they proved? That's why she never tried. To fight with her would be like fighting with Tommy again, the endless tussle over who was to blame. "You're never kind to me," Tommy would say. "You never laugh at my jokes."

"I don't feel kind," Jennifer would say. "I don't feel like laughing."

"How can I live like that?" Tommy would ask, and the look on his face would be so desolate that sometimes kind was exactly what she'd feel. Her poor baby. He didn't want to hurt her. His sorrow and his guilt.

Zoe comes outside, but she doesn't sit in the other chair. She leans on the railing and looks at Jennifer. Jennifer can feel her gaze. She keeps her own trained on the trees. "How did you find me?" she asks.

"You called me."

"No, I didn't."

"Yes you did, Mom! You called from Margaret's house, and hung up, like I wouldn't see a strange area code and immediately assume it was you. Like I haven't been *wondering*."

"Margaret's house? Margaret?"

"Yes, Margaret."

"I don't know what you're talking about."

"Jesus," Zoe says. "You can't even admit you called me. Tell the truth for once in your life."

Jennifer can feel a tingling in her palm, as though she's already slapped the girl. She takes a breath. "If I wanted to have conversations like this," she says, "I would've been in touch."

"You *were* in touch!"

"I wasn't!" She'd like to take a swig but her hand is shaking. "If someone called you from Margaret's house, then it was Margaret. Of course. Of course it was Margaret."

"Why would she do that?"

Jennifer shakes her head.

"It doesn't matter," Zoe says. "You called, you didn't call. Now I'm here."

"Because of Margaret," Jennifer says bitterly, as if that were the worst of it.

"She wants to help me. She's letting me stay with her."

"You're staying with her? You're staying in her house?"

"I came here looking for you, and I ran into her at the Smoke House."

"She just took you in, a total stranger?"

"She overheard me asking about you. She knew I was your daughter, as soon as she saw me," Zoe says. "She says I look exactly like you."

Above the tree line a tiny plane, a prop, climbs into the sky. "There's something wrong with that woman."

"She said you'd want to see me," Zoe says in a small voice.

"Did she?" Jennifer watches the plane. She imagines that wherever it's going is the next place she and Milo will live.

"But obviously you don't. I didn't know you changed your name. You didn't even tell me where you lived."

Now Jennifer looks at her daughter again. "You called the cops on me, Zoe. For murdering my husband. You don't trust a person after that. You can't trust a person after that. I can't trust you not to fuck up my life. You're proving that right now. Do you not understand why I moved away? Why I changed my name? Did it never cross your mind I'm trying to make a good life for your brother? What do you think it would have been like for him—" She shakes her head. "Now thanks to you we'll have to move again."

"But what about me?" Zoe says. "Don't you care about me?"

"Zoe," Jennifer says. She presses her mouth together against tears. "It never seemed to matter if I cared."

The woods are at first just silent, and then that silence resolves itself into its component parts: the sound of air, the sound of water.

"All right," Zoe says finally. She pushes herself off the railing, carefully sets her glass on it. "I don't actually drink," she says, conversationally, and then she moves past Jennifer. Into the house, then through it and out the other side. Jennifer can hear her. She moves slowly, as if to give Jennifer time to come after her, to tell her not to go. Jennifer listens until she's sure the car is gone. Then she waits, watching the house across the pond, but minutes tick by in empty silence. Where are you, Margaret? Don't you want to see what you've done?

Back inside, the house has an air of aftermath, though little is disarranged. The cars the boys were playing with are still out on the floor. The dishes are still on the table. The tiger Zoe brought sits propped against the teapot. Jennifer picks it up. Squeezing its little tummy, she swallows and swallows again. Then she throws it in the bin with the rest of the toys.

Soon she'll have to pack up. Before the story spreads. Before the clients cancel. Before the looks in the grocery store. She surveys the house with an eye that's already grown nostalgic. Upstairs Milo is curled up in a tight ball, watching a toy commercial. Jennifer sits beside him, puts her arm around him, and pulls him close.

"Is everybody gone?" he asks, and she says yes. She can sense his agitation. He knows something has happened that hasn't been fully explained. But he also seems to know better than to want the explanation. He starts telling her about the TV show. Many hours later, when it's bedtime, she lets him fall asleep in her bed.

But then she is the one who can't sleep. Around two in the morning she gets out of bed and puts her clothes back on. She scoops up Milo, gently, gently, and carries him stirring and murmuring out to the car. He doesn't wake as she buckles him in. She drives to Margaret's house, pulls slowly, slowly up the drive. There's no way to be totally silent but the lights are all out and everyone seems to be asleep. Everyone—by which she means Margaret and Zoe. She knows Zoe is still here because of the truck in the driveway. Tommy's truck.

She eases out of the car, closes the door so it doesn't latch. Then in the dark she walks over to the truck. She puts her hands on it. It feels like metal feels. She looks into the cab. All she can make out in the dark is a new tear in the fabric of the ceiling. It doesn't have a sense of Tommy about it. It doesn't speak for him.

Lights come on, and she jumps back from the truck. Too late for a clean getaway—Margaret has those little streetlamps with which people line their walkways, and when Jennifer crosses to her car she'll be clearly lit by them.

The creak of the screen door, and then the sound of a cane on knobbly pavement. It's Margaret, then. Trust Margaret to come outside when she hears an intruder, instead of calling the police.

Jennifer steps into the light. "It's me, Margaret. It's Jennifer."

Margaret stops where her face is still in shadow. "So it is," she says.

"I don't know why I'm here," Jennifer says.

"She's asleep."

"I thought she would be."

"You thought right."

There's a long silence. "Well," Jennifer says.

"Did you kill him?" Margaret asks. Matter-of-fact, as if it's an everyday question.

"Ask Zoe."

Margaret waves a dismissive hand. "Zoe's been acting out of hurt, can't you see that? Hurt and grief and loneliness. Zoe doesn't know what she thinks. I want to know if you killed him."

"Why?"

"Why?" Margaret repeats.

"Why do you care? What does it matter?"

"It matters," Margaret says.

"I loved him," Jennifer says. She felt fierce before she spoke, but now there are tears in her eyes. She shouldn't have said that out loud. "I couldn't help it." Her voice is shaky. Stop it, stop it! Just stop talking. Just run away.

"I know," Margaret says.

"What do you mean *you know*? What could you possibly know?"

"Oh, Jennifer." Margaret sounds so weary. "Please answer my question."

"So you can tell Zoe?"

"No. I'd never do that."

"Why then? I don't understand."

"You'd understand if you'd listened to me. Don't you see what's happening here? I'm letting you tell."

"You're *letting* me tell?"

"I think you might want to."

Jennifer blinks. In the dark she can't make out Margaret's expression. She sees the gleam of her white hair, her white cane, her two pale hands. "Yes," she says. "I killed him. Yes. I killed him. I did."

Margaret says nothing. How dare she say nothing?

"I killed him," Jennifer says.

"I know," Margaret says. "I heard you."

What was her tone? What is she thinking? Jennifer can't tell, won't ask, won't wait around for more. "Goodbye," she says, or thinks she says. She gets into her car, where her son is still sleeping, and leaves Margaret and all that Margaret knows behind.

Where should they go now? she asks herself, hands on the wheel. Somewhere beautiful. Somewhere far away. She went to Hawaii, once, with Tommy. They went to the island of Kauai, on a honeymoon funded by his mother. They rented a one-room cottage with a huge bed enclosed by a mosquito net whose purpose seemed romantic rather than protective. They woke with the sun to the sound of roosters crowing. They ate pineapples and lychee fruit. They hiked an eleven-mile trail along a breathtaking coastline and spent the night on a beach, with other hikers and an outpost of hippies who shared the milk from their goats. Jennifer was purely, truly happy on that island, and so was Tommy, and she could go back there now to live with her son and tell him stories about his father, whom she loved. His father, who slept beside her on a starry beach and was a wonderful man.

The Unsolvable

Zoe is gone. When she got back from Jennifer's, she said, "I don't think my mother loves me."

"Oh, Zoe," I said. "I'm sorry."

"She hates me."

"Can a parent hate a child?"

"Clearly," she said.

I didn't know what to say to that. Did my father hate me, those times when he looked at me like he did? The time he looked at me, a plump and clumsy child in my heavy shoes, and said, "Every father hopes his daughter will be a butterfly"?

I offered what I could in the way of consolation: food, company, a bed. She wanted to hear more about my family history. I told her about my mother's older sister, who held court in her big house for years and years, and how my mother always felt in her shadow. Then about my grandmother's sister, who was addicted to laudanum. I told her every story I could think of. I didn't mean for them all to be sad, but that is so much of what there is.

After she was settled, I still couldn't sleep. And so I was awake when I heard Jennifer outside. I didn't tell Zoe about her mother's late-night visit. I think it's best if she forgets she has a mother now.

This morning I fixed her eggs. I poured her orange juice. I walked her outside. "Call when you get home," I said. "I want to know you got back safe."

"I will. I promise." She hugged me. "Thank you for trying to help me," she said.

I said she was welcome and patted her on the back.

At the door of her car she paused. Her eyes were glistening. "Did my mother really call me?" she asked. "Because she said she didn't. She said it was you."

I didn't have time to think about what was kinder, the lie or the truth. Even with time to think I still don't know. "It wasn't me," I said.

Zoe nodded. She swallowed. "I really don't know why I came here," she said. "I don't know what I want from her." She looked at me like I might have answers, but I don't. I have none.

He came in like all of them, on a stretcher. I saw right away that he had a chance to live—he wasn't gut shot, he had all of his head. His hand was bandaged—it looked like a finger or two was missing—but the real trouble was his legs. He was a tall man, and I would have bet that after the surgeons got done he would be much shorter. He could wait, though. He could wait. He was moaning. He opened his eyes and saw me and in his gaze was the desperate pleading pain I'd grown used to. He said, "Please, nurse," and automatically I soothed him. "Don't worry, don't worry," I said. "We'll take good care of you."

But then I took in his face. You see, he was the man. He was the one. I hadn't realized it, so focused on his injuries, on whether he would live or die. He was the one who did that to my friend. To Kay. I'd known all along what he looked like, though I'd never known his name. Because I followed her, the night she went out with him. I followed her out of the tent a few minutes after she left, and though my intent had been to call her name, to stop her, to attempt reconciliation, just as I spotted her—no, no, I was about to lie. Why? Why always lie, until we are dead? I was about to say her date appeared and stopped me speaking. But the truth is once Kay was in earshot I had minutes to catch her—three, four, maybe five—and instead I followed without speaking, without her knowing I was there. I obeyed an impulse to go unnoticed. Maybe I wanted to get a look at her date. Maybe I wanted to see the life she lived without me. Because I was jealous, or because I was curious, or afraid, or, or, or. I don't know *why*. I just know that's what I did.

I saw him waiting for her. He had a pitiful bouquet clearly snatched from a roadside garden, and while I couldn't hear him, I could see by his face that he'd made a joke about it but was also proud to have it on offer. I could see his face but not hers, so I've never known what she was thinking. That he was sweet? That his bouquet was charming? That she was happy to go on this date, after all? Or that he was too eager, too insistent, too *something*, something she already sensed. That she didn't want to go with him, wanted to plead a headache and go back to the tent. But back in the tent there was me.

He held her down. I don't know exactly what happened. She didn't tell me. I didn't ask. That was all she said: *He held me down*.

I killed him.

If he had been gut shot he might have bled out and died screaming, and that is what should have happened, that is what should have been. But it was only the legs! In all the chaos I had no trouble injecting the extra morphine unnoticed. It wasn't even hard. I could have considered it sufficient punishment for him to live without his legs. But that would still have been living.

Learning to say, to *mean*, "only the legs"—how could you imagine that wouldn't do something to a person?

I keep thinking of Jennifer's face in the light from my little streetlamp. How, at last, the rock rolled away from the cave. I looked at her and I *saw* her. Nothing was hidden, nothing stashed away. It was astonishing to see, miraculous as starlight—a human face without a trace of the mask. At the sight of it my heart thrilled and broke. And I kept my own face in the dark, so that she would not know it.

It wasn't when she said *I killed him* that this happened. It was when she said *I loved him*.

I've started rereading another Agatha Christie, in hopes that its tidy structures will help me contain my own life. Detectives are after certainty. That's why people like them—they paper over the unsolvable with deductions and photographs.

I sit here with my book, waiting for Zoe to call.

What Jennifer Did

He was propped up in bed with his foot in that boot. Surgery had fixed the break, but three weeks later it still hurt. He'd been augmenting his prescription meds with other painkillers. One of his drinking buddies had a hookup, Jennifer assumed. She hadn't asked. Tommy had taught her to be uncurious. She'd found his stash, three fat bottles in a little brown paper bag like you use for school lunches, or drinking liquor in the street. She was standing near the bed with the bag in her hand, and they were fighting. "So now the drinking's not enough?" she said. "Why not start gambling? Why don't you go fuck a prostitute? Or maybe you have already." She was suddenly struck. She asked, in a small, quiet voice, "Have you?"

He had the nerve to look affronted. "No," he said. "How could you ask that?"

She shook her head. "I don't know what you won't do," she said.

"How could you say that? How could you think that? I'm in pain, Jennifer. My ankle fucking kills me all the time. The pills are for the pain. I don't know where the rest of this is coming from."

"You do know where," she said flatly. And looking at his face, she could see that he did. He knew he'd failed in all the ways she said he had, and he knew he'd fail her again in the future, just as she said he would. He looked at her—raw and naked and *sorry*, so sorry—and then his expression hardened.

"Just give me the pills," he said.

"Fine," she said. She took all three bottles out of the bag and opened them and shook them over the bed, a rain of pills, saying, "Fine, fine, fine," while Tommy said, "Jesus, stop it, stop it." A furious duet. When the bottles were empty, she was panting, and she threw them at him, so that he had to duck. "Here are the pills," she said. "Why don't you take them. Take them all."

She grabbed his glass from the bedside table and took it into the bathroom, where she filled it so full it spilled when she set it back down next to him. "Thought you might need this," she said.

He was looking at her with what she thought was a dull hatred, but would seem to her later to have been blank despair. "You wish I was dead," he said, and his voice was flat and cold with conviction.

"Wow, Tommy," she said. "You catch on fast."

Did she think he'd do it, when she left him there with the water and the sea of pills? Did she believe *you catch on fast* would be the last thing he'd ever hear her say? These are the questions she asks and cannot answer. With time she's arrived at what she thinks was in his mind when he swallowed every pill she gave him. She believes he loved her, and that for him that love had always transcended everything, his transgressions and hers, and finally he'd understood that for her it no longer did, hadn't for a long, long time. He'd thought they had a great love. She convinced him at last that it was an ordinary one. Believing that, he despaired. If his story wasn't an epic romance, then it was a squalid little tragedy.

But it *was* a great love, Tommy. It was. And she is so, so sorry.

The Lives I've Saved

Jennifer is gone. Jennifer and her little boy. I don't know where they went. I hope they're happy there. I sit out on my back deck and see nothing at the house across the pond. No lights. No people. A few weeks ago I drove over there and looked in the windows. The house is empty, neat as a pin. No stray toys on the floor, no lost crayons. No clues. No evidence.

I did not mean to do them harm. I've never meant that. I've had many friends. I've saved many lives. I should have kept a record of all the lives I've saved.

Lately I go beyond standing beside the pond and imagining Virginia Woolf. Lately I fill my pockets with stones. Then I walk slowly back toward the house, tossing them out as I go. I won't do it. There is Lucy, who may yet come visit, and now there is Zoe, who says she wants to visit, too. She has a friend she might bring down, someone who likes to hike. I think perhaps, if Zoe needs one, I might offer her a job for the summer. Her duties would be minimal. She could stay in the guest room, be there just in case. It would make Sue the librarian happy. We all get older by the day. Each breath, and we are older.

I stand at the edge of the water but I don't ever wade in.

I will live until the last possible minute. I will have every second.

I am not sorry.

Acknowledgments

For more than fifteen years I tried and failed to write a novel based on the experience of my late grandmother, born Nina Jean Riley, in the Army Nurse Corps during World War II. Though Margaret's story bears only minimal resemblance to my grandmother's, much of my information about what it was like to be a field-hospital nurse in the ETO came from conversations we had, as well as her scrapbook and her letters home to her parents. Kate Moore was also indispensable, in describing to me her time as a nurse with the Army Reserve in Iraq and helping me imagine what it's like when casualties arrive. I read widely in WWII histories and found the following books particularly useful: *Women Were Not Expected* by Marjorie Peto; *G.I. Nightingale* by Theresa Archard; *Bedpan Commando* by June Wandrey; *And If I Perish: Frontline U.S. Army Nurses in World War II* by Evelyn Monahan and Rosemary Neidel-Greenlee; and *No Time for Fear: Voices of American Military Nurses in World War II* by Diane B. Fessler.

My thanks to Susan Autran for lessons on dancing and Suzanne Smith for lessons on massage; to Detective Jennifer Mitsch for invaluable advice; to Leigh Anne Couch for prompting my memory of Sewanee landmarks (I took some liberties); to Carmen Toussaint Thompson and the Rivendell Writers' Colony for allowing me to stay there while I revised this book; and to Cheri Peters, Wyatt Prunty, and John and Elizabeth Grammer for bringing me there in the first place. I'm grateful for the support of UC's Taft Research Center and my colleagues Jay Twomey, Michael Griffith, and Chris Bachelder.

My editor, Sally Kim, is all a writer could hope for: she always guides me toward a better version of the novel I'm trying to write. I'm so lucky to be working with her on a fourth book, and I'm grateful to her and to the other people at Touchstone, particularly Etinosa Agbonlahor. I'm equally lucky to have the fabulous Gail Hochman as my agent; she is a marvel of energy and insight. For early reads, my thanks to Holly Goddard Jones and Amanda Eyre Ward. My husband, Matt O'Keefe, line edited the manuscript, giving thoughtful consideration to every sentence, and the book is much better for his time and attention.

To my children, Eliza and Simon, thank you for letting me steal your funniest lines.

About the Author

Leah Stewart is the critically acclaimed author of *The History of Us*, *Husband and Wife*, *The Myth of You and Me*, and *Body of a Girl*. She received her BA from Vanderbilt University and her MFA from the University of Michigan. The recipient of a Sachs Fund Prize and an NEA Literature Fellowship, she teaches in the creative writing program at the University of Cincinnati and lives in Cincinnati with her husband and two children.

leahstewart.com

THE
NEW
NEIGHBOR

Ninety-year-old Margaret Riley is mostly content hiding from the world. Antisocial and fiercely independent, she rarely leaves her Tennessee mountaintop home, preferring weekly trips to the local library to replenish her collection of mystery novels to visits from extended family. But all this changes when she spots a young woman who has rented the long-empty house across the pond.

Jennifer Young is also looking to hide. On the run from her old life, she and her four-year-old son, Milo, have moved to a quiet town where no one from their past can find them. In spite of her fears of discovery, Jennifer can't ignore Milo's eagerness to attend school and make new friends, and she finds herself drawn into a larger circle of acquaintances.

In her new neighbor, Margaret sees both a potential companion and a mystery to be solved. But Jennifer refuses to talk about herself, her son, his absent father, or her past. Frustrated, Margaret crosses more and more boundaries in pursuit of the truth, threatening to unravel the new life Jennifer has so painstakingly created—and reveals some deeply guarded secrets of her own.

For Discussion

1. "I am always alone. Sometimes days go by in which the only other people I see are on TV." (7) How does Margaret Riley feel about living on her own in her remote house in the Tennessee woods? In what ways does being alone equate with loneliness for Margaret? How do the effects of solitude reveal themselves in her character?

2. Why does Margaret feel compelled to snoop on her new neighbor across the pond? What draws her attention to Jennifer? What role does Margaret's love of mystery fiction play in her treating her new neighbor like a puzzle to be solved?

3. How would you characterize Tommy Carrasco, Jennifer's former husband, from the details of her recollections? What role does the intensity of their early romantic relationship seem to play in their marriage's dramatic unraveling and Jennifer's life choices? Do you think Jennifer is a reliable narrator of Tommy's life and motivations? How does her version of Tommy compare to Zoe's?

4. "In what room of my house was I willing to take off my clothes and have a stranger touch me? In no room at all." (43) Why

does Margaret elect, under the pretense of wanting a massage, to make contact with Jennifer? What is the significance for Margaret of meeting Jennifer? Compare both women's experiences during their initial therapeutic session.

5. How does Jennifer's relationship with Megan Summerfield, the mother of one of Milo's preschool classmates, develop over the course of the novel? What roles do Megan's husband, Sebastian, and her young son, Ben, play in that evolution? To what extent does Jennifer's relationship with Margaret undergo a similar arc? Compare what Jennifer chooses to conceal and reveal in these relationships.

6. "Still, I think it is Kay she reminds me of." (62) Given their lack of physical resemblance, why does Margaret repeatedly conflate Jennifer with Marilyn Kay, her beloved wartime friend? How does Margaret's attachment to Kay factor into her conflicted feelings about exploring her memories with Jennifer? Why does Margaret choose Jennifer to be the chronicler of her memories?

7. In the aftermath of Tommy's death, Jennifer finds herself incapable of escaping people's curiosity about the nature of her involvement. To what extent is Jennifer is justified in keeping the facts of Tommy's death and the true story of what happened from Milo?

8. "It wasn't just Jennifer's opinion that Zoe had loved Tommy more. Zoe herself had frequently said that. Even before Tommy died Zoe had treated her like an evil stepmother whose only purpose in the story was to cause misery." (85) What does Jennifer's characterization of Zoe reveal about her own feelings toward her older child? How does Zoe's discovery of Jennifer's involvement with another man affect their mother-daughter relationship? Discuss Zoe's agency in the disintegration of her family.

9. How does Milo's fleeting memory of his real last name—Carrasco—alter the course of Jennifer's existence on the Mountain? How does Milo's revelation play in to Margaret's obsession with digging into the details of her new neighbor's life? To what extent is Jennifer wise to feel anxious about her true identity coming to light?

10. "When I looked up *Jennifer Carrasco* on the Internet and found those articles, I felt a hard-boiled unsurprise. It turns out I am a detective after all." (221) Why does Margaret succumb to the impulse to search Jennifer's home? To call Zoe? Where do those impulses come from? How does Margaret feel about having succumbed?

11. Why does Zoe's unexpected arrival at her house lead Jennifer to make her confession to Margaret? To what extent is Jennifer's confession true or false? To what extent is Margaret's claim: "I did not mean to do them harm," completely credible? Margaret says, "I am not sorry." What do you think she means? Do you believe her?

12. Kay and Tommy are ghosts that flit in and out of Margaret's and Jennifer's anguished memories and hearts. What else do these ghosts have in common, and why might this coincidence play a part in Margaret's attachment to Jennifer?

A Conversation with Leah Stewart

What drew you to rural Tennessee for the setting of *The New Neighbor*? Please discuss your experience and association with this region.

I have family associations with the area: my father's mother was from Murfreesboro, Tennessee, about an hour from Sewanee, and she and my grandfather lived after retirement in Clifftops, a community between Monteagle and Sewanee. Also, after I graduated from Vanderbilt, I started working for the Sewanee Writers' Conference, which I did for two weeks every summer for ten years. Some of those summers I worked for the Sewanee Young Writers' Conference as well, and one school year I lived there as a visiting writer. Now I go back to see friends and to work at Rivendell, the writers' colony there. All this to say I've spent a fair amount of time in the place.

But more significantly, it's the kind of place to which it's easy to become profoundly attached. It's beautiful—rushing water, huge boulders covered with deep green moss—and it has a very particular appeal that's related to its isolation. It feels like a secret place, a feeling that's augmented by the solitude of walking alone in the woods. When you leave the towns at the bottom of the Mountain, even when you leave Monteagle for Sewanee, many of the markers of contemporary civilization recede and you feel like you've crossed into an enchanted land. And because it looks so much the same, year to year, it has an out-of-time feeling. If I were a different kind of writer, I would have set a fantasy novel there. It's easy to imagine fairies hiding in the trees.

The mystery genre crops up throughout *The New Neighbor,* **and the novel itself unfolds like a double mystery. What attractions does this genre hold for you as both an author and a reader?**

In *Aspects of the Novel*, E. M. Forster says that mystery demands intelligence and memory on the part of the reader—"part of the mind must be left behind, brooding, while the other part goes marching on." I've thought about this a great deal in teaching, and then applied some of those thoughts to my writing, and part of what I take from Forster is that a story always engages the mind more thoroughly when it contains mystery, no matter what its genre. When I taught a class on writing with mystery, I included Raymond Chandler, but also, for instance, a short story by Danielle Evans called "Robert E. Lee Is Dead." No one would call that a mystery, but what I wanted the students to see was how it was driven by the mystery of character—what makes people who they are, what makes them do what they do.

When you're compelled by a work of fiction, it's activated your curiosity, and mystery does that: it makes you wonder, it makes you want to know, it makes you try to solve the problem yourself. I enjoy a well-plotted whodunit, but I'm much more likely to be moved by it, to continue to turn it over in my mind long after I've read (or watched) it, if the mystery at the heart of it can't actually be solved by identification of the murderer. The pleasure I take in Sherlock Holmes stories is real, but not as intense as the pleasure I take in the British TV show, which highlights the mystery of personality as much as—really, more than—the puzzle to be solved.

I like immersive fiction that engages both emotionally and intellectually and that asks profound, unanswerable questions about human nature and causality. So, in the mystery genre, I love Tana French. And I love Margaret Atwood, who isn't classified as a mystery writer but uses mystery brilliantly. Her *Alias, Grace* is a big influence on this book. My favorite literary writers often make great use of mystery—Kazuo Ishiguro, for instance, who makes you wonder about his characters' worlds and histories as a way of investigating questions of memory and self-delusion and human connection or the lack thereof. Mystery is a way of making the reader interested in whatever it is you want to explore, so that Dennis Lehane talks about the mystery as a social novel, and you can see that in his work, and Chandler's famous essay "The Simple Art of Murder" describes his kind of mystery as demonstrating that a noble man (read Marlowe) can resist temptation and uncover "hidden truth" in a corrupt world.

Margaret's character defies many stereotypes of elderly southern women. How much of a challenge was it for you to narrate parts of this novel from the perspective of an unconventional nonagenarian?

There were many challenges to this novel, but that wasn't one of them. In my adult life I've spent a great deal of time in the company of elderly female relatives—my husband's grandmothers, my grandmothers, and my great-aunt. Several of them were and are tough-minded and blunt. My maternal grandmother, who was a WWII nurse who went back to school and earned her PhD at Vanderbilt, and my great-aunt, who is a retired professor of medieval literature at UCLA, are models of accomplishment over the obstacle of gender expectations. Also it's been my experience (which I think research backs up) that people speak their minds even more as they age. In other words I think that stereotype of the sweet old southern lady is almost entirely a fiction. The "steel magnolia" stereotype perhaps comes closer to the truth, at least among the people I know.

So Margaret came very easily. Margaret was actually a great deal of fun, because she says what she thinks, which is a luxury in which most of us don't indulge. I had far more trouble with Jennifer, who has more in common with me superficially—age, time spent living in Clovis, New Mexico, a young son. But Jennifer is a guarded and careful person, and I'm not, so sometimes I struggled to know what she would and wouldn't say. When my husband line-edited the book for me, part of what he did was cut places where I'd had Jennifer say too much.

Jennifer's close bond with Milo and her deeply fractured relationship with her daughter, Zoe, are compelling on many levels. What major and minor themes of motherhood do you feel this book interrogates or explores?

I didn't really think about this book being about motherhood, though of course you're right that it's very much a part of the Jennifer sections. I wrote a previous novel, *Husband and Wife*, in which I was very aware of exploring the joys and frustrations of motherhood. In writing this one I was more focused on the question of how we cope with our own histories—in particular those moments we can hardly stand to remember, when the worst happened or we were at our worst—and also on the ways in which love shapes us, for good and ill. When I started the Jennifer sections, I was thinking in part about those heartbreaking, irresistible, messed-up boys of TV and film (say, Tim Riggins from *Friday Night Lights*) and what it might be like to be married to one of them twenty years after high school. So Jennifer's relationships with her children developed from my exploration of her relationship with Tommy. The questions about motherhood that emerged have to do with how the child becomes a player in the marital relationship, and at what point, in a problematic relationship, the need to protect your children overcomes your love for your husband or perhaps your belief that it's better for the children to stay with him. Here I was thinking about how, over and over again in narratives, the mother stays with a husband or boyfriend who is terrible for the kids. The book explores, through Zoe and Jennifer, how the actual personalities of child and parent might affect their relationship, beyond any idealized notions of what that relationship should be. And through Milo and Jennifer, I'm looking at the profound, joyful simplicity of the love that can exist between a parent and a small child, and the melancholy of knowing that it will grow complicated, and also, of course, the desire to forestall that. Via Margaret, I'm looking at how norms and expectations of the parent-child bond have changed through the years. Margaret, like many older people I know, is baffled by contemporary parenting.

At any point in your depiction of the connection between Margaret and Jennifer were you tempted to turn the tables, so to speak, and have Jennifer trespass into Margaret's life?

I don't remember considering that. In fact, in an earlier draft, Margaret kept trying and failing to attract Jennifer's interest, and the WWII stories were narrated by Margaret in her journal, as she imagined she'd tell them to Jennifer, rather than out loud to Jennifer. My editor, Sally Kim, made the excellent suggestion that I have Margaret actually tell Jennifer the stories. Once I rewrote toward that, I found it natural to make Jennifer more curious about Margaret, and more affected by the stories she tells, than she had been in an earlier draft, which I think is a significant improvement to the book (and an example of what good editing can do for your work). And here's a place where you can see the influence of *Alias, Grace,* in which someone listening to someone else's oral history is changed and marked by the stories he hears. Sometimes I want to make a certain move in my fiction, but I lack confidence about it, and seeing another writer successfully execute that move convinces me that I might be able to as well.

Examples of substance abuse in this book crop up in the life stories of Tommy Carrasco, Megan Summerfield, and Marilyn Kay. In all three instances, you blur the lines between individual dependency and external motivation. Are these sorts of ambiguities and morally ambiguous situations the ones you find yourself drawn to as a writer?

Absolutely. I'm endlessly interested in complication, specifically the complications of psychology, and this interest leads inevitably to the ambiguous. I'd probably never write about a character who was purely good or bad or made purely good or bad choices. So, for sustaining my own investment in my work, I don't worry about whether a character is likable but about whether they're interesting—often what makes them interesting to me is the way they're in conflict with themselves. My work asserts over and over that multiple, contradictory things about a person can be simultaneously true.

Jennifer has a tormented love for Tommy and feels uniquely responsible for his death, but Tommy committed suicide. When Jennifer confesses to Margaret that she killed Tommy, do you think she means it?

Yes. This is, to her, the unbearable truth, the thing she works hardest not to acknowledge—her own deep conviction that what happened to Tommy was her fault. She certainly knows that she didn't *actually* kill him. One reason she tries to harden herself against memories of Tommy and against Zoe, who is a walking accusation, is because that helps her focus on the literal fact: Tommy was an alcoholic who cheated on her and couldn't be trusted with their small child; Zoe was wrong and Zoe betrayed her; and Tommy committed suicide. She needs to focus on that knowledge in order to function and so make a good life for Milo. But what it's concealing is overwhelming guilt and grief and loneliness.

Both Margaret and Jennifer are haunted by their pasts, by what could have been, and by the people who impacted them most profoundly. Which of these characters did you find yourself most drawn to, and why?

I'm fascinated by the mix of charisma and danger in Tommy, and by the joyful life force and determined toughness of Kay, and the sorrow of their diminishment. I suppose the character besides Margaret and Jennifer who came to interest me most was Zoe. Originally, though she herself still showed up in Tennessee, her point of view didn't enter the book. Adding her point of view was another excellent idea my editor had. Because I'd already written multiple drafts looking at Zoe from only Jennifer's perspective, I really enjoyed complicating her character, as well as Tommy's and Jennifer's, by entering her mind. Once I wrote Zoe's point of view, I understood that Tommy actually was a wonderful father as well as a terrible one. (Contradictory things can be simultaneously true!) Writing the scene when Zoe finds Tommy dead, I understood the emotions that led her to accuse Jennifer of his murder in a visceral rather than intellectual way, and that was enormously satisfying, getting to know my own creation better.

Enhance Your Book Club

1. In *The New Neighbor,* Jennifer asks herself of her former hus-
    band, Tommy, "Who would she have been without him? She
    has wondered this, now, for ten years or more, and she thought
    when she came up here she'd finally find out." (68) Have the
    members of your book group think about the people who have
    made them who they are. They may want to write down the
    names of those who have influenced them most. Members of
    your group may want to share and examine the identities and
    roles of these formational figures in one another's lives.

2. Over the course of their relationship, Jennifer gives her neigh-
    bor, Margaret, weekly therapeutic massages and helps her by
    transcribing her experiences as a field-hospital nurse in World
    War II. Have members of your group talk about the importance
    of neighbors in their lives. They may want to consider the types
    of neighborly (and not-so-neighborly) behavior that Margaret
    and Jennifer exhibit toward one another by way of comparison.
    Which of their own neighbors are they curious about?

3. Both Jennifer and Margaret seek out the Mountain as a refuge
    from the outside world. In Jennifer's case, the seclusion enables
    her to escape from her tragic past. Why has Margaret chosen

isolation? How do they each feel about that choice? Ask members of your group to reflect on the places where they feel most truly themselves. How do they experience their lives in places of isolation compared to their time in the company of others? If members of your group had to imagine going "off the grid" like Jennifer, and assuming a false identity, where would they go, and how would they transform themselves?